Time and Time Again

For Holly –
thanks for your encouragement.

Best wishes,

Rick Taylor xx

by

Rick Taylor

Grosvenor House
Publishing Limited

This book is published by
Grosvenor House Publishing Ltd
28-30 High Street, Guildford, Surrey, GU1 3HY.
www.grosvenorhousepublishing.co.uk

A CIP record for this book
is available from the British Library

ISBN 978-1-906645-04-5

I should like to dedicate this book to my wife Ann and daughters Sarah and Rachel, who, in a small but significant way, provided inspiration for the storyline. I should also like to thank my colleagues Holly and Susie for actively encouraging me to continue and complete the project I had started.

…when 'past' is not always 'gone'

Time present and time past
Are both perhaps present in time future
And time future contained in time past

T.S. Eliot, Burnt Norton

CHAPTER 1

Setting the scene

I suppose I've always fancied myself as a bit of an author. I guess that's why I've always written my diaries in the style of a novel. Well, it makes it a bit more interesting, doesn't it? Not that I really expect them to be read by anyone else. Mind, you, if ever this journal *were* to fall into the hands of some curious reader, I hope they would indeed treat it as a work of fiction. In fact, this account is really for my own benefit, because I can scarcely believe for myself the reality of recent events—if indeed they *can* be considered recent. I want to get them down in writing while they're still fairly fresh in my mind, otherwise they'll fade into obscuritylike some kind of half-forgotten dream (or maybe I mean nightmare).

But to set the scene, as it were, it was a little over forty years ago that William Draper came to reside in Roxbury, one of England's smaller cities. With a population of some 100 thousand or so, it supports a few light industries, has a university consisting of several colleges, and boasts a medical teaching centre comprising a half-dozen hospitals and clinics dotted around the city. That's where I come in: you see, most of my working life has been spent in hospitals, or medical facilities attached to the University. My first appointment was as a technician in the Dunkirk Memorial Hospital in the pleasant suburb of Hardington Mountford. This was originally an army hospital during the Second World War, but had since become part of the NHS, specializing in neurology, dermatology and respiratory medicine, plus a few other lesser specialities. I was very happy there at first—the work was quite fascinating, and I enjoyed the interaction with patients, as well as the research side of the work. As time went on, however, I began to get a bit restless, and it was rather frustrating that I seemed to be making no progress at all, career-wise.

After about 12 years there, though, I managed to get promotion to the Parklands Clinic, a small but prestigious paediatric assessment centre just up the road from the Dunkirk. It was quite a different scene there—very informal and unstructured, with plenty of scope for innovation and using one's own initiative. My colleagues—and to some extent even the boss—were a friendly bunch, and we all gelled together very well. I had a certain amount of authority, with responsibility for training the junior staff, which I really enjoyed. But once again I found myself up against a promotional ceiling, and after eight years there I felt I just had to get moving again. Luckily, a vacancy for a chief technician came up at the Roxbury Royal Infirmary (known locally as the RRI), the city's main general hospital. I applied for the job, although it was a hard decision, as I particularly liked working with children, plus the generally laid-back atmosphere of Parklands. Furthermore, I'd be going back to my former boss, Dr Emlyn Pritchard, who was, to put it mildly, a hard man to please. Dr P was a native of Wrexham; he had read medicine at Manchester, then gone to work in some of the world's major medical establishments, such as the Mayo Clinic in America. He was certainly not lacking in intelligence (although there were many who disagreed with a lot of his ideas), but unfortunately he did lack some of the gracious attributes a good boss needs to make his staff feel at ease and work smoothly and efficiently. (During my time at Parklands, Dr P's department at the Dunkirk had been relocated to the RRI.) Anyway, I decided I really needed the promotion, so I applied for the post, and somewhat to my surprise, was offered it. It was a useful stepping-stone, and although I moved departments within the RRI a couple of times since then, I've worked there ever since.

But of course, alongside my professional life I had a fairly active personal and social life. I enjoyed the facilities that Roxbury had to offer: I frequented its cinemas, theatres and concert venues, and joined a local church that had been recommended to me by my pastor back home in Devon. It was, in fact, at Hardington Free Church that I met a certain young lady by the name of Katherine, and, to cut a long story short, the path of true love led us eventually to marriage and setting up home together. Our first home was a rented flat on a moderately large housing estate. 29 Valley Crescent was our humble abode for almost a year before we managed—with a bit of financial help from friends and family—to get a mortgage and a new home, a mid-terrace but quite respectable three-bedroomed house at 35 Rockall Avenue, near to the centre of Hardington. The ten years we spent there were by no means always easy, but we have a lot of happy memories of that phase of our family life, not least the arrival of our first daughter, Sally. She was a bonny, cheerful baby, and brought us a great deal of joy.

A year or so later there were a number of big changes. That was the time I began my new job at Parklands; we also moved house again, and daughter No 2 arrived. Our new home, at 26 Upper Meadow Close, was more spacious, a semi with a lovely long garden in a secluded street quite close to my place of work. But a few years later we were on the move again—this time a little way out of the city. We had liked living in Hardington: it was one of Roxbury's nicer suburbs, and there were all the facilities we'd needed within easy reach, but we'd really wanted to live in a village, and have our daughters Sally and Hazel grow up in a more rural setting. So, shortly before my career move to the RRI, we moved to the village of Clunmore, just west of the city, and about half an hour's cycle ride to and from my workplace.

I can't help thinking sometimes how different it was in those early years of setting up home together than it is for the youngsters of today. Our first home was sparsely furnished with whatever furniture we could get together—nearly all of it second-hand, and little more than the bare necessities. We had a radio and a record player but no television; we didn't even possess a fridge—until one weekend when the joint of pork we'd bought one day was ready to walk out the door of its own accord the next! Nowadays newlyweds expect to start their life together with a good range of new furniture, kitchen equipment, household appliances and everything required for all-round entertainment, supplied, of course, by parents, relatives and friends responding to ever more expensive wedding gift lists. Bit by bit we gathered and acquired a few more items here and there, and we didn't feel unduly deprived.

Katherine, or Kath, as I used to call her in the early years, was reasonably happy with her job as a teacher in the local primary school. Some of the kids came from rough homes, but they were, to use a familiar cliché, rough diamonds, and she enjoyed opening their wondering eyes to some of the mysteries of the world about which they knew nothing from their home environments. Similarly, I enjoyed my work at the Dunkirk, making fascinating discoveries about the workings of the human body, and in particular, the nervous system. When later, I began working with children, it became even more fascinating, as by that time we had started to produce some of these delightful, often mysterious creatures of our own, and I was intrigued to follow their physical and intellectual development in the light of what I was learning at work. Often at the end of a day's work I'd be deep in a world of my own as I pedalled home, pondering some newly acquired facet of infant behaviour, and whether the ride home was just a couple of minutes, as when we lived in Upper Meadow Close, or half an hour, after we'd moved to Clunmore, I scarcely noticed the passing of time at all, and would usually find myself back home almost before I'd realized it. And that, I suppose, is how this whole mysterious business came about.

CHAPTER 2

How it all began

It was when I was in just one of those moods of almost oblivious reverie (my better half had a much less complimentary term for this phenomenon!), totally lost in thought and cycling home in a kind of autopilot mode, that I first made the astonishing discovery. This was when we'd been enjoying village life for some twenty years or so. Although now working at the RRI, I occasionally had cause to spend some time at the Parklands Clinic, to do some data processing for which we hadn't the facilities in our own department. We had a reciprocal agreement with our sister department there, and sometimes one of their technicians would spend some time with us, using equipment that we had but they didn't. I'd been at Parklands that afternoon, and as I left, I couldn't help reflecting on the days, nearly twenty years before, when I used to work there full-time. My mind then wandered to my home situation at that time, when Sally was a three-year-old toddler and Hazel barely a year old. Turning left out of the clinic drive, I would pass the end of Upper Meadow Close (and. Incidentally, Rockall Avenue) on my way into the city centre and thence out into the country.

So wrapped up was I in this mental re-enactment of former days that, as I rounded the slight bend just before the end of Upper Meadow Close, I turned—instinctively or absent-mindedly (call it what you will)—into that road, and continued to No 26, our former home. Entirely without thinking of the illogical action I was carrying out, I opened the front door of the car port (we called it a garage, but it was open at the back and not really very substantial), wheeled my bike past our red Triumph Toledo and walked through into the garden to be greeted warmly by my wife.

'Hello, Billy,' she called, brightly, 'It's nice to see you home so early.' It was only then that I was jerked into reality. 'Billy'—she hadn't called me that for over twenty years!

[Perhaps I should explain—we were each blessed with names capable of mutating into several nicknames or pet forms, and over the years as our relationship matured and our circumstances changed, we somehow—almost involuntarily—called each other by different ones in turn. During our engagement and the first year of married life, Katherine used to call me Will; I in turn called her Kath. As we acquired our 'own' real home (not a rented one, that is), we somehow adopted the seemingly more intimate forms of Willie and Kathy. Several years later, for no particular reason I can recall, I experimented by calling my beloved Katie; she said she liked that, and for a while it stuck. At the same time, for perhaps understandable reasons, I expressed my dissatisfaction with Willie, and for a couple of years at least I became Billy. Finally the slightly more dignified form of Bill emerged, while for her part, Katie became Kate, and thus we've remained to the present. Perhaps one day, when I am a retired gentleman, I shall consider it proper to be addressed by my full name of William again, as I used to be by my parents.]

I was astonished! What on earth had happened? This was no longer my home. We had sold our Triumph Toledo long ago, and got through a couple more cars since. What's more, my wife, who, while not yet quite eligible for the description of 'growing old gracefully', had certainly begun to acquire a few care lines and the odd grey hair, thanks to the stresses of having two teenage daughters, was looking a good twenty-odd years younger than when I had left her that morning! 'Oh, er, yes,' I muttered, desperately trying to cover my confusion, 'the boss let us off.' I put on as cheerful and unconcerned an exterior as I could, but inside I was in total turmoil. How could this be? One moment I'd been idly thinking myself back into my former life, and now here I was, actually in it! Surely this had to be some sort of a dream—this sort of thing just doesn't happen…does it? And why was it that Kate looked so much younger to me, yet apparently I didn't seem that much older to her? At least, she didn't comment on it, and I couldn't pretend to myself that I still possessed the relatively youthful looks I had when I was known as Billy. I even peered at myself in a mirror later, and my face seemed no different from the one I'd shaved that morning, in 36 The Willows, Clunmore. This really was too freaky for words, and I began to wonder if I were hallucinating. Could I even be losing my sanity or something?

Obviously my troubled thoughts were beginning to show themselves outwardly. 'What's the matter, dear?' I heard, somewhere in the distance, 'Aren't you feeling well?'

'Uh…oh, no, it's all right,' I responded, hesitantly. 'Um, Kate, I mean, Katie,' I continued, just remembering that this young lady was not yet ready for the name by which I now knew her, 'have you got the newspaper? There's something I wanted to see in it.'

'It's on the table in the breakfast room, love,' she replied, 'But don't be long—I need you to collect Sally from the Robertsons'. She's playing with her friend Ella from toddler group. Brenda said Ella's been keeping on at her to let Sally come to her house, so I said she might as well. Hazel's asleep in her pram—you can take her round there with you.'

'OK,' I replied, unthinkingly, as I stepped inside and grabbed the paper. My only aim was to look at the date. Yes, there it was—I couldn't escape the fact—I was back in April of 1982! I quickly scanned the headlines, amazed at the 'news' stories that to me were history.

'Come on, love,' I heard Katie gently chivvying, 'I said I'd collect Sally in an hour when I left her, but now that you're home, I'd like you to go, so I can get on with our dinner.'

But then an awful thought struck me. Who on earth was Brenda Robertson? Presumably I must have known her once—or known *of* her—but any memory I might have had of her was now well and truly lost in the mists of time. Furthermore, I hadn't a ghost of a clue as to where she lived! There was no way I could go off to collect our infant child, but if I'd asked Katie where to go, it would probably have seemed extremely odd—for all I knew, we'd had dinner there the night before.

'Er…w-why don't we both walk round?' I stammered. 'It's a nice evening, and I'd like us both to go together for a change' I ventured. 'I'm not that hungry, and dinner can wait a bit.' I waited with my heart in my mouth to see if the bait would be taken.

To my immense relief, Katie replied, 'Well, why not? It *is* nice when we do things as a family, and I enjoy these little excursions together,'

As we set out, I just couldn't comprehend what was happening—here I was, with my considerably younger wife, and our daughter, our *baby* daughter, asleep in her pram—the pram we'd sold many years ago to a young couple expecting their first baby. I'd got up that morning to overcast skies and the threat of showers all day, yet now it was a bright, warm, sunny day in spring, 1982! Somehow I'd been jerked back in time over two decades. I could see distinct differences in the makes and models of cars—and their registration numbers—from the ones I was used to seeing early in the 21st century. Surely this had to be a dream—and yet it all seemed completely real, but how could it be? My mind was working overtime, struggling for plausible answers to this weird paradox. Maybe I had had an accident—come off my bike, most likely—I'd hit my head and got concussion: this was my battered brain reliving old scenes as though they were real today.

Katie looked at me with a frown. 'You're very quiet, dear. Is something wrong?'

'Er...no, just thinking,' I replied, trying hard to sound normal, as well as attempting to think of a way out of this amazing predicament I'd somehow got myself into. I could think of no more practical solution for the moment than just to go along with the situation, and hope some solution would eventually present itself. I recalled watching films such as '12:01'[1] and 'Groundhog Day'[2], in which the main character had been trapped in an ever-

---

1. New Line Cinema/Chanticleer Films, 1993.
2. Columbia Pictures, 1993

repeating prison of time until some decisive incident had jerked him out of the time-loop. Pure fantasy, of course, or so I'd thought...but maybe there *was* a grain of truth in those stories. Perhaps, even, this was the after-life, and like our hero in Groundhog Day, I was doomed to go on repeating the day—or a couple of decades—until I'd become a much better person. Perhaps the Catholics had got it right about Purgatory, and here I was in it.

These and many other thoughts came flooding into my troubled mind, but I couldn't make much sense of any of them. I don't know what Katie thought of the rather trivial babbling that passed for conversation from me as, deep down, I was turning over much heavier matters. Anyway, we walked on together, and in a strange way, I began to enjoy this odd re-enactment of past times, just as if I were watching a family video, long forgotten but recently unearthed from under a pile of cassettes in a cupboard. Every now and again I'd spot a house, minus the extension I'd seen added in later years, or a tree which, that morning I'd seen as a semi-mature maple, now shrunk to a mere sapling. As we passed a field that had been one of our favourite strolling-places, I remarked, almost without thinking, 'What a pity—that field'll be covered in houses in a few years' time.'

'Surely not,' replied Katie, 'I thought it was supposed to be left for—what was the expression—informal public recreation? Isn't it in some deeds or something? There was an article in the Roxbury Times a couple of months ago—the owners aren't allowed to sell it for property development.'

'Oh, they'll find some way of getting round that— they always do,' I asserted. 'You mark my words.' I nearly added, 'I'd be willing to put money on it,' but decided I'd better not sound *too* definite about it.

After ten or fifteen minutes we were at the door of 13 Yorkshire Terrace (I made a note of the address in case I should be required to go there again), and Brenda Robertson let us in. there was our little Sally (gosh! I'd forgotten what a cute toddler she was!), engrossed in some game with her young playmate. I looked around at the furnishings, the ornaments, the various other arte-facts that were distinctly early 80s, and when Katie accepted Brenda's offer of a cup of tea, I was quite happy to agree, and I listened to the ladies' conversation with a degree of attentiveness that was quite unnatural for a potentially bored husband, as I was eager to pick up clues as to who lived where, what sort of work their menfolk did, and in particular, where the toddler group was held. I felt rather like an infiltrator in some alien society, gathering as much information as I could, to enable me to pass myself off as one of them.

Eventually, little Sally realized Mummy and Daddy were around, and she came and gave me a loving hug and kiss. I felt both thrilled and slightly guilty—almost as if I had no right to be accepting affection from this child. Hazel had woken up by this time, too, and it was agreed we should be on our way back home. It was just then that an awful thought struck me—from what Katie had said about my getting home early from work, it was reason-able to suppose that my other, younger self—the *real* Billy—would appear soon, and how was I to deal with that? Indeed, what effect would it have on the other family members? An odd feeling of dread began to come over me, and I started to glance around furtively to see if I were approaching (it's a very strange feeling, looking for one's own self), and I made up my mind that as soon as I saw myself appear, I (the older me) would suddenly pretend to play hide-and-seek, dash off and conceal myself somewhere and let the younger me deal with the family's confusion as I somehow appeared from the other direction on a bike! He—or rather, I—would have some difficult questions to answer, such as how I'd managed to spend half an hour over at the Robertsons' while apparently I'd still been at work, why there was another bike at our house, and so on. But as I considered this, something instinctively told me that would not happen—I somehow just *knew* that I wouldn't meet myself. That was a basic tenet of all those sci-fi yarns: no-one can occupy the same space-time frame more than once, and I convinced myself this would hold true for me now. And, it appeared, I was right—we continued right to our door, went inside, and carried on all our usual family activities: I played with the kids while Katie cooked the dinner; I fed the baby, read a bedtime story to Sally, then sat and watched telly with Katie when the little ones were asleep. My 'other self' never showed up, but I did wonder where he was. Could he perhaps have swopped time and place with me? Was there now (now?) a much younger looking Billy somehow catapulted forwards in time, bewilderingly faced with a new home, a somewhat older-looking wife, children who had grown up and left home, and trying to get to grips with unfamiliar technology such as DVD players, DAB radio and so on?

Once or twice without thinking I let slip a remark that had my wife puzzled. For example, when one of the famous episodes of 'Open All Hours'[3] came on,

---

3. BBC TV, Series 3, March-April 1982

I blurted out, 'Oh, this is my favourite one—it's hilarious!'

'What do you mean?' asked Katie, 'How can it be? This isn't a repeat.'

'Oh no, er...' I fumbled for an explanation. 'I, um, I mean, the *show* is my favourite—Ronny Barker—he's brilliant!'

'Oh,' she replied, looking a trifle puzzled.

Fortunately some of our 'traditions' hadn't changed over the years: milky coffee at nine o'clock, a brief prayer together to thank the Good Lord for the blessings of the day (my contribution was a bit vague, and majored on the events of the evening), and then off to bed.

As I pulled the bedclothes up over me, I tried hard to relax, and put to bed all the myriad thoughts and impressions that were racing through my puzzled brain. And as I did so, I convinced myself that when I awoke, I would be back in my 'own' bed, in my 'own' century, and in my 'own' home, 36 The Willows, Clunmore. Thus, eventually, I sank into a kind of grateful oblivion. I must have slept very soundly, for it seemed almost instantly that I was waking up again, with bright sunshine streaming through the gap where the curtains had been left slightly apart. As I opened my eyes, I was initially startled, as one sometimes is when, say, on holiday, and an unfamiliar room greets the eyes on waking. Then I remembered— and then my heart sank a little, as I realized it had *not* all been a dream; and I had not returned to my proper time and place; and I was probably doomed to re-live a second time all the events of the last twenty or so years.

I had sometimes caught myself thinking how nice it would be to go back and experience again those high points in my life—the elation of passing an important exam, that bewilderingly sweet sensation of falling in love, the wonder of sightseeing in some exotic location and so on. But then I realized that, along with life's highs there were also many lows, and I felt that it is not given to us to pick and choose which of all these diverse experiences we can seize and which discard. All in all, I was content to have made it thus far, and I should not wish to go back over all that ground again.

Anyway, for the moment I just had to get on with things, and play the cards fate had dealt me. I got up, washed, dressed, made Katie the cup of tea she always enjoyed in bed, and I played with the children a little before it was time to head off to work. Work—ah, that was a thought! *Which* work? Was I destined to resume my job as a mere senior technician at Parklands, with the unenviable prospect of having to work my way up again to the level I had achieved since long ago leaving that establishment? Right then I made a vital decision. No— I was not going to allow myself just to be swept along by this bizarre tide of events, this inexplicable quirk of time. I was going to take control of the matter and get myself back on track. As I kissed my wife and little ones good- bye, I sped off on my bike, and at the end of the road turned decisively right, towards the RRI, instead of left for Parklands. (I'd made some excuse for leaving home much earlier than usual, as my hours of work were different for the two places.)

I cast my mind back to how I'd entered this peculiar time-warp. I'd been thinking about the old life, back in the 80s—picturing it so vividly in my mind that I'd ac- tually ended up there (or then, if you like). So now, I reasoned, what I had to do was reverse the process—as

I cycled through town I actively thought about the tasks I'd been doing at the RRI a couple of days ago, and the things I'd been doing with Kate. We'd just been to see the latest Harry Potter film, for example, and I fixed my mind on that, flushing out, as it were, any thoughts of the 80s. It wasn't an easy task, for I kept finding myself entertaining those niggling 'What if...?' thoughts: What if it doesn't work? What if I get to the RRI and find all the old departments that have moved to the new hospital, and the old consultant who ran the department where I now worked? When is 'Now' anyway? I firmly thrust these thoughts away as I approached the familiar edifice of 'my' hospital. Just then something happened that gave me great encouragement. What was that car I'd glimpsed, going the other way? Had it really been a Fiat Punto? I really didn't like that model at all, but just now the sight of it filled my heart with unspeakable joy, for it meant I could not possibly still be stuck in the eighties.

I hastily locked up my bike and bounded gleefully up the stairs to my workplace. I didn't even wait for the lift to come down from the fourth floor (where it invariably was whenever I arrived). My colleagues all seemed a trifle mystified when I greeted them with such enthusiasm, as though they were long lost pals I hadn't seen for many years. In a way they were right, I suppose. I breezed through my work that day, sending up frequent prayers of thanks that I'd made it safely back from the past. I couldn't wait to get home after work, but one thought troubled me: how was I to account for my absence the previous night? I'd had no anxious phone calls at work, asking where I was, and more to the point, where the heck I'd been since yesterday morning, but

I was somewhat afraid of the reception I'd get on arriving home.

When I got there, however, the greeting could not have been more nonchalant. 'Oh, hello, love,' remarked Kate, not even looking up from the report she was typing, 'There's a letter from your cousin on the living room table—he's sent some photos.' I was greatly relieved, and yet more puzzled than ever. She hadn't even noticed I'd been away, I thought—or perhaps I hadn't. Maybe I'd been like the children in the 'Narnia' books[4], who'd passed through the back of the wardrobe, spent days or even weeks in a strange land, and then re-entered their own world at exactly the same time they'd left it. But no—there was the newspaper lying on a chair, and the date showed that a day had definitely passed. At the time I couldn't explain this mystery, though I've since concluded it was because I was *expecting* a day to have passed. I went to the desk where I keep my trusty diary: that would surely tell me, as I usually wrote up the day's events every evening. But no—the previous day's page was blank. As I felt it would seem a bit silly asking Kate what we'd done the evening before, I just left it, thankful that, unlike the man in '12:01', I was not stuck in some weird time frame over which I had no control.

---

4. CS Lewis, The Lion, the Witch and the Wardrobe, etc.

CHAPTER 3

Too hard to resist

I'd found my bizarre excursion into the past so scary that
I decided not to repeat the experiment. It's all very well
reading stories or watching films about time travel—Back
to the Future[1] and suchlike—but actually doing it yourself is quite a different matter. Although I'd always
enjoyed such stories, I really never honestly believed it
was possible, and even now I just about managed to
convince myself that it had all been a dream or something—my overactive mind playing funny tricks on me.
But inevitably my resolve eventually melted—rather as, I
imagine, someone who has ventured into the dodgy world
of drug-taking simply cannot resist having 'just one more
fix', and before they know it, they're inextricably hooked.

I managed to resist the urge to go back into my past
for a good six weeks, but the situation just got to me. The
situation being Kate's mood—I'd come home from a
pretty demanding day at work (I'd had to stay late, dealing with a particularly complicated medical case) and
found her slumped in a chair in front of the TV set—
again. Not that I'd been expecting my dinner to be ready

---

1. Universal Films

for me on the table, all nice and hot, and the little wifey greeting me sweetly, her apron tied neatly around her waist: we shared the household chores, and I often did the cooking, which I quite enjoyed. But I had hoped to find my beloved a little more cheerful, maybe even greeting me with one of the lovely smiles I knew she was capable of. But no—ever since her last full-time job had come to an end a year ago, she seemed to have little to exercise her potentially active brain and creative hands. She did a bit of voluntary work at the nearby old people's day centre, and occasionally managed a little private after-school tuition, but much of her days were spent in becoming increasingly bored, and then in the evenings she seemed to have little will or energy to go out, or do anything much, in fact.

I rustled up a quick meal for us both and we sat in front of the telly together. It was one of those programmes where people turfed out long-forgotten items from their attics and managed to sell them for a tidy sum. This particular family had a small selection of old dolls stashed away in their loft—costume dolls from different countries: a typically Dutch-looking one with a white apron and a funny hat with pointy bits curling up at the sides, a Bolivian lady in a brightly-coloured poncho, and things like that. At this Kate brightened somewhat.

'Do you remember that book you once bought me?' she asked.

'Of course I do, dear' I replied. How could I forget? I'd been racking my brains trying to think of something nice to give her for her birthday. Like most men with their womenfolk, I suppose, I'd always had great difficulty finding suitable gifts for Kate. And it certainly didn't help matters that her birthday came in mid-January, so soon after Christmas when I'd already used up all my bright ideas. In the end, while browsing through a local bookshop, I'd taken the plunge and spent rather more money than I could afford on a big, glossy reference book about costume dolls. It was beautifully illustrated with dozens of coloured photos, with full details of how to make your own collection of dolls—how to buy, swop, make and display dolls of all shapes, sizes and nationalities. Apparently some enthusiasts manage to make a reasonable living either making their own dolls or buying and restoring old ones, and then selling them. Anyway, at the time I had the notion that Katie (as she was known then, of course) might like to adopt a new hobby, and get some enjoyment out of it. But sadly, it seemed I'd missed the target badly on this occasion.

'I did *try* to look grateful at the time, love,' she said, 'only I was just a bit too preoccupied with looking after two very lively and demanding toddlers to care about starting something like that. I enjoyed looking at the pictures, of course, but after a while I just left it on the shelf, and then...' Her voice tailed off into an awkward silence and a sheepish expression came to her face.

'Yes, I remember—you gave it away—to a *charity shop*!' it had been a week or so after this dreadful deed that I'd noticed the book's absence from the bookshelves in our living room, and when I'd enquired about it, all I'd received was a half-mumbled 'explanation' that it had been 'lent to a friend'. At the time I'd pretty well believed her, but a certain caginess in her voice told me there was more to this than met the eye. Then I recalled that, several days before, Katie had got down some old boxes of books and things from the loft and said she was going to 'recycle' them. Putting two and two together, and donning my Sherlock Holmes deerstalker, as it were, I'd visited the half dozen charity shops in Hardington: Red Cross, Mind, Oxfam and so on. At each one I examined the second-hand books on display (and in fact, I couldn't resist buying a few, like the one on Ancient Persian Scripts, and another about Steam Railways in India and Pakistan). Finding no trace of the volume I was seeking, I addressed the volunteer ladies in each shop with an enquiry as to whether they had any books on collecting dolls. Each time I was given an apologetic shake of the head and a suggestion that I try such-and-such a book-shop in town. I almost didn't bother with the last shop on my list, the 'Help The Aged' one in Brewer Street. But when I made the usual enquiry, the lady there replied, 'Oh, I'm very sorry—we *did* have one, but I sold it only yesterday. It was a really nice one, actually' and then she went on to describe perfectly the gift I had presented to my beloved (and at no little cost, I might add!).

There had been some cross words at home that evening. I'm afraid I was rather harsh with my loved one, and I later regretted some of the things I'd said to her. She'd apologised abjectly for her actions, but had explained that she really wasn't interested in that partic-ular activity: she hadn't the time, the resources or the energy for such a hobby. As I was thinking over those events, my mind drifting back into the past, a voice from the present cut in on my thoughts.

'Do you know, love?' murmured Kate, 'I really wish now that I hadn't got rid of that book. I've heard quite a bit about collecting dolls recently (there was an article in Sunday's paper about it too), and I wouldn't have minded having a hobby like that to ward off the boredom.'

'That *is* rather a shame,' I replied, 'that's what I was hoping for when I got you the book. I guess my timing just wasn't right.'

I almost let the matter drop at that point, but later that evening I began to wonder if by some chance I could still get hold of a copy of the book. After all, you could argue that it's never too late to start a new hobby or interest, and it could well bring a little more colour and enjoyment into my beloved's life. Now that the girls had grown up and left the nest, and without a regular job, Kate would do well to devote a fair amount of her enforced leisure time to an absorbing and possibly lucrative pursuit. I spent a while surfing the net, trying to see if the book were still available. Unfortunately, it had long been out of print, and none of the usual book suppliers could obtain copies. I tried eBay too, but alas without success.

Just as I was pulling the bedclothes up around me and about to consign myself to the land of nod, I was still lazily turning these thoughts over in my mind prior to putting them to bed as well, when suddenly a crazy idea occurred to me. I'd done it once, so I could try it again—revisit our former home, indeed, our former life. I'd go back in time and just jolly well get that book! If I could somehow think my way back to the period between Katie's birthday and the book's disposal (about four months, as far as I could remember) I'd point my bike decisively in the direction of UMC (as we used to call our former street), and hopefully find myself back in the right place and time to rescue my valuable trophy. I lay there, thinking out my strategy, and eventually fell asleep determined to put my plan into action the next day.

It was fortunate (or perhaps I should say fate) that I was due to spend the whole of that next day catching up on a backlog of processing at Parklands. My initial thought was to make the detour to UMC at the end of the working day, as I had done before. Then it occurred to me that I could just as easily 'pop home' in my lunch hour, find the book and smuggle it back to work and take it home (our present home) in the evening. I wasn't quite sure how I would explain to Kate how it had mysteriously turned up after so many years. I suppose I could say I 'happened' to come across a copy in a second-hand shop (very convenient, after last night's discussion!). Anyway, as the morning dragged by (funny how the passage of time isn't uniform: it drags when you can't wait for some special event, then positively flies when you're enjoying yourself), I found myself becoming at once both highly excited and intensely nervous. All sorts of doubts and questions kept bubbling up in my mind, and I had severe difficulty concentrating on my work. What if it doesn't work this time? I wondered. Then it doesn't matter, my other self replied—I won't have lost anything. But what if I can't get back to the present this time? I was lucky last time, but maybe I'd be tempting Providence too far. Supposing… I forced myself to cease this idle speculation.

At last midday arrived and I hastily threw on my jacket and headed for the door.

'Aren't you joining us for lunch?' asked Clare, one of my colleagues.

'No thanks,' I replied, adding carelessly, 'I'm popping home.'

'Did you say home?' asked Clare, a puzzled look on her face.

I realized my mistake. 'Home' in the present century was half an hour's cycle ride away. There was no way I could 'pop' there and back in my lunch break. Thinking furiously, I blurted out a lame correction: 'Oh, sorry—I meant to…er, Paul's home—one of my friends from our old church. He lives just up the road.'

Clare didn't seem entirely convinced, but knowing I couldn't possibly have meant my actual home, she accepted my reply and said, 'OK, then—see you later.'

I told myself firmly I'd have to be more careful what I said in future (or in the past), and make sure my brain was firmly in gear before engaging my mouth!

I sped out of the clinic drive, but then pedalled more slowly on approaching Upper Meadow Close, as I endeavoured to focus my thoughts on how things used to be back in the year I was aiming for. I'd managed to narrow the time down in my mind to a month in which, I thought, the aforesaid book was still in our possession, and I hoped I'd got it right. I hadn't got round to climbing up into the loft the previous evening to dig out my old diaries and check for sure. Arriving at No 26, I had managed so successfully to think myself back into the situation of those days, that, completely without thinking, I leant my bike against the fence, pulled the bunch of keys out of my pocket and inserted one into the front door lock. It was only much later that day that I realized that *today's* key had opened *yesterday's* lock! How had that happened? Had my mind-over-matter facility transformed my keys as well as the time-space situation? Or maybe this really *was* all a dream—after all, the whole scenario was just the sort of thing that happens in dreams, wasn't it? And yet…this was the second time I'd managed to send myself back into the past—the first time involuntarily, but on this occasion quite by my own volition: not the sort of thing you can usually do with dreams. I decided it was probably best not to think too hard about all these enigmas, or I'd end up tying my brain in knots. Just let nature (if this *was* nature!) take its course: I'd been given some strange sort of gift, it seemed, so maybe I should just use it in the best way I could and not enquire too deeply into the whys and wherefores of it all.

As I entered the hall, a voice came from upstairs: 'Oh hi, love. Hazel's just dropped off to sleep. She's been a bit crotchety after the disturbed night she had, and she wanted me to play with her. Sorry—I haven't had a chance to make any lunch. Put the kettle on—I'll be down in a minute.'

Through the breakfast room window I could see little Sally playing in the garden. She'd got her teddies and other soft toys seated round in a circle, all with tiny plastic cups from her toy tea set in front of them, and she was chatting happily to them as she poured each a drink from a little red teapot. She looked so sweet and innocent, and I counted myself really fortunate to be granted the opportunity to relive this wonderful sensation of being the father of young children. It's a kind of magic you just can't describe, and which, all too easily, alas, you tend to forget as the kids grow older. Even the experience of having grandchildren is something quite different (although that is brilliant too). For a moment I was lost in wonder and admiration, but then I recalled the real reason for this voyage back into the past. Flicking the switch on the kettle, I slipped into the living room, and once again a surge of old memories and impressions came over me as I looked around at all the items of furniture and kiddie toys we used to have. Of course, it had been only a few weeks ago, in effect, that I'd had this experience before, and yet it seemed so fresh and new again. Walking over to the bookshelves, I scanned the wide range of titles there. I thought I would have no difficulty finding the book, as it had been quite large and conspicuous. But there was no sign of it. I noticed there were a few gaps on the shelves, but I took no notice of that—we probably hadn't yet filled the space to capacity, or maybe Katie had lent some to her friends at the young mums' group.

'What are you looking for, love?' Katie's voice behind me startled me and I jumped.

'Oh, er…a book, dear, just a book.'

'Which one was it you wanted?'

I decided to be bold. 'The one about dolls, you know—making and collecting them and stuff.'

At this her face reddened visibly. 'Oh, um…' she was verbally fumbling.

'It's just that I wanted to lend it to someone at work— you know, Jenny the secretary' (I'd managed to recall the name of the young lady I'd worked with at that time). However, I could see that Katie was experiencing some kind of inner turmoil.

'I, er… oh, I think Lena's got it,' she mumbled, unconvincingly, 'Yes—I'm sure that's the book I lent her last month. Oh well, if she gives it back…I mean, *when* she gives it back you can let Jenny have it. She can keep it as long as she likes.'

But at this I inwardly cringed. Katie's tone of voice told me that this Lena (whoever *she* was) would never return the precious book. My worst fears had been realized—I was too late: the book had already gone. My heart sank.

Katie busied herself in the kitchen with what I felt was a forced cheerfulness. She knew I'd put a lot of effort (and cash!) into getting her that book, and OK, so I'd misjudged it, but I think she was feeling more than a little guilty at disposing of it so quickly, and so cheaply. Sally was called in from the garden and the three of us sat and ate our ham sandwiches. At least I was able to enjoy chatting to my little daughter, which was a real delight. Then Katie glanced at the clock and said, 'Oh come on, you two—it's nearly time for Sally to go to nursery school.'

I recalled vividly our trips to nursery. Sally went to Hardington Nursery School every weekday afternoon, and depending on the timing of my lunch hour, I would take her there in the child seat on the back of my bike. It was, as the Americans would say, several blocks away, and I would contrive to make the journey there by as many different routes as I could; there were about 13 or 14 different ways to get there (including the short footpath between Yorkshire Terrace and Cheshire Drive). Later, while I was still at work, Katie would take the pram and collect Sally. We had a special seat mounted on top of the pram, so that baby Hazel could lie inside, while toddler Sally sat on top. Later, when they'd both grown too big for this arrangement, we'd managed to acquire a double pushchair (the tandem-type, not those really wide ones that are such an obstruction in supermarkets and on pavements).

As toddler and I said a cheery goodbye to Mummy, we left together by the front door and I lifted the youngster up into her child seat. It wasn't until we were on our way down the road that I realized that there *was* a child seat on the bike! I'd come to the house on my 'now' bike, and left on my 'then' model! Deliberately trying to ignore yet another paradox, I continued to the nursery school by what was, in fact, the most direct and straightforward route, little Sally chatting away merrily behind me the whole time, giving a running commentary on all she could see. 'There's an old man with a doggie', she'd say, or 'There's no pavement here' and things like that.

I delivered the little one to her beloved nursery (she thoroughly enjoyed it there), helped her hang her coat up on the peg with a bluebell above it and left. My thoughts inevitably turned back to the book. How disappointed I felt, to have missed the opportunity to get it back. I began thinking of alternative strategies. Perhaps I should come back in time again—a week or so earlier—and rescue it from its fate. Or I could go down town and buy another copy, as it would no doubt still be in print. Then I had a bright idea: the Help The Aged shop was just around the corner. If Katie had only recently taken the book in, it might still be there, and I could retrieve it. It was worth a try, so I pedalled round as fast as I could and went in. I went instantly over to the shelves where the second-hand books were displayed and searched. It was not there. My heart sank (again).

'Can I help you, dear?' asked one of the ladies on duty, a pleasant-sounding pensioner with wavy grey hair and a smart tweed suit.

'I hope so,' I replied, 'Um... I think my wife brought in some books and things recently, but there was one book that got put in by mistake. You see, it was my birthday present to her, and she's upset that it's been accidentally discarded.' I decided a little white lie was justified here. 'In fact,' I added, rather unnecessarily, it may have been my fault that it was put in with the others.' I described the book to the lady, and her face lit up with a smile.

'Well, fancy that!' she chuckled, 'I was just saying to Edith here (wasn't I, Edith?) that it seemed far too nice a book to give away. You're in luck, young man—it was only brought in last week, and we haven't finished sorting all the books out yet.'

I was rather pleased to be addressed as 'young man', something that hadn't happened to me for many a year, but I was even more delighted that my quest had been successful. 'Uh, I'd be willing to pay you something for it,' I ventured.

'Don't be so silly,' replied the tweedy lady, 'I wouldn't hear of it! It's your wife's by rights and she shall have it back.'

I left the shop ecstatic. Carefully placing my prize (wrapped in a WH Smith carrier bag) in the child seat, which served its secondary purpose of parcel carrier, I set off down to road back towards Parklands. As I did so, I began to think myself back into the twenty-first century. As I got back to the clinic, I was greeted rather excitedly by Clare.

'Oh, Billy, you're just in time. I've got Louisa from the RRI on the phone. She's got a problem with one of the analysers, and needs your advice.'

I rushed in, picked up the phone and managed to sort out the problem, although it took a good fifteen minutes or so. Then I went back to the processing I had been doing before lunch, and, for the time being, forgot all about the book, still sitting outside in the child seat on the back of my bike. I finished my work a little earlier than expected, so I grabbed my briefcase, called out my goodbyes and went out to my bike. Then I got a big shock. The bike was there alright—my 'today' bike, not the 'yesterday' model with the child seat I'd left there earlier. The child seat had gone—and with it the book I'd gone out of my way to rescue!

I was stunned; I hadn't anticipated this. I peered down behind the bike to see if the book had fallen down there when the child seat had disappeared. But no—there was no sign of it. What was I to do? Somewhat disconsolately, I mounted my trusty steed and set off slowly in the direction of Clunmore. It must have taken rather longer than the usual half-hour, as I was travelling more ponderously and deliberately than usual. In fact, I was doing just that—pondering and deliberating. But so wrapped up was I in my thoughts, considering what would be my best plan of action, that before I'd realized it, I was coasting down the home straight into the quiet cul-de-sac that was The Willows. By this time I'd decided my best plan of action was to go back to my old life again tomorrow, perhaps to an earlier date, before the book had left our home, and rescue it again. I wheeled my bike round to the back door and entered.

'Oh, is that you, dear?' came a surprisingly cheery voice from within, 'You're early, aren't you?'

'Yes, I suppose I am, a bit,' I answered, 'How are you?' (I'd been more than a little concerned for Kate's welfare since last night—indeed, I had been for some months, really. With no special interests, and little or no work to get her out of the house, she had retreated into herself more and more, and this was definitely not healthy.)

'Oh, you know me,' came the reply, 'always busy, dashing here, rushing there: never a spare moment, never a dull moment!'

This really took me by surprise. No, I *didn't* know her: this was a very different woman from the dull, listless one I'd left in bed that morning, but I liked what I saw. She came out into the hall to greet me with an affectionate peck on the cheek, and I couldn't help noticing how energetic, slim and bright she looked. What had brought about this transformation? Had I somehow strayed unwittingly into yet another time frame? Had I come back to my present home but not *quite* in the present? I glanced at the adjustable calendar on the hall shelf: it still said the same date I'd set it to before leaving for work.

Then I noticed them. Several dozen of them: costume dolls, of all different sizes, colours and nationalities, lined up under the stairs. All the shelves that I had last seen stacked with books—mostly old paperbacks, dusty with age and neglect—had been made into display cases, and were now filled with these dolls. I couldn't believe it. How had this come about? Realizing that Kate was eying me rather quizzically, I quickly turned and walked into the living room. There were more dolls there—on shelves, some in plastic presentation packs just standing on items of furniture, and others in various stages of manufacture or restoration, lying on the table. Then I saw IT! There was THE BOOK! Open on the table, well thumbed and somewhat tatty, with evidence of various ad hoc repairs to its pages, and it looked as if the cover was loose as well. I'd just rescued it and then immediately lost it, but somehow it had been preserved in our family's possession. I tossed a few theories around in my now rather benumbed mind. The best I could come up with was that after the 'now' me had left the 'then' bike (with its precious cargo) outside the clinic, the 'then' me had somehow taken over from where I'd left off and conveyed bike plus book back home, and somehow preserved it for posterity—and what a posterity indeed!

It was all a bit mind-boggling, so I purposely tried to switch off my puzzled thoughts and concentrate on the present—this new present I had somehow created. Nevertheless I couldn't help thinking how, through a simple act I had changed the whole of the future for myself and my family. It reminded me of the lads in Thomas Hardy's short story 'Our Exploits in West Poley'[2], who, in exploring a cave in the Mendips, diverted an underground stream by blocking its path with a boulder. A simple act indeed, yet it deprived their village of the millstream—the lifeblood of the community, as it were, and gave a neighbouring village the precious gift of running water.

Kate's words cut in on my thoughts: 'Sorry, love, do you mind getting yourself something to eat tonight? Arlene's coming for me in ten minutes.'

'Arlene?' I queried, 'Who…' I checked myself. This was evidently someone I was supposed to know.

'You know, dear, Arlene Wilkins, the chairman of Dollybirds. It's a business meeting tonight.'

'Oh,' I replied, faking enlightenment, 'I thought you said *Eileen*.'

It didn't take much power of deduction to figure out that Dollybirds was a local group of women with a passion for collecting dolls. In fact—now here's a strange thing indeed—as I set my mind to it, I was aware of a 'memory', albeit a somewhat sketchy, hazy one, which was forming, or rising out of my subconscious. Although I had never actually experienced it, I could begin to 'remember' accompanying my wife to exhibitions in various town halls and exhibition centres, watching her skilful fingers sewing together some intricate ethnic costume, and helping her to find, and bid for, various items on

2. Various publications, e.g. 'Old Mrs Chundle and other stories', edited by F. B. Pinion, MacMillan.

internet auction sites. It was as if my mind was somehow catching up (admittedly somewhat imperfectly) with the new reality I had created, and which had given me a new history.

I was actually glad to be on my own that evening, because it gave me a chance to think things over—to assess the events of 'today', and how I'd been given the opportunity to intervene in some way, to make life more fulfilling and enjoyable for another person—the most important other person in my life, actually—and, as a sort of by-product, I'd also improved life for myself. I realized that this was a very wonderful and special 'gift' I'd some-how been given, but that it was one that gave me immense power, and that along with it came a great responsibility to use it wisely and with great care. With my Christian upbringing and convictions, I resolved to put this amaz-ing tool to use wherever possible for the good of others (although I could see no harm in using it also for my own enjoyment, to dip into my past and sample afresh those special moments, just as one does when flicking through an old photo album, or watching a family video). And with thoughts of doing good to others, my mind wandered back to the conversation Katie had had over lunch, before I had taken Sally to nursery.

CHAPTER 4

Local hero

Something Katie had said in conversation on my most recent foray into the past had left me rather troubled, yet strangely excited. While we'd been munching our ham sandwiches prior to my taking Sally to nursery, she'd remarked, 'It's poor little Damien's funeral on Friday. I saw Carole this morning—she's ever so cut up about it. I said I'd go with her to give her support. It's awful, losing a child in any circumstances, but such a lovely, lively little toddler like that—he was always so full of health and energy. It's so tragic.'

As it happened, I knew exactly who she was talking about—how could I forget? Had events turned out slightly differently I could possibly have saved him. Damien Winterton was a bonny, bright little two-year-old whose mother had been expecting him at the same time as Katie had been carrying Hazel. Damien and Hazel had attended the same toddler group, held in one of the local church halls on Monday, Tuesday and Thursday afternoons. It was about ten minutes' walk from our house, although sometimes she would take the car, and on other occasions when my hours would permit, I would do the job. Depending on the timing of my patients, and hence my lunch hour, I could nip home, walk the pushchair and Hazel briskly to St Anselm's Church hall, deposit the child (she was always eager to get stuck into playing with the toys and her little friends, so I didn't have to linger), walk equally briskly home to find lunch ready for me, eat it at a moderate pace and still have time to sit and chat to Katie for a while before taking Sally to nursery and returning to work. (I'd tried taking Hazel to toddlers in the child seat on my bike, but for some reason it upset her at that age. Later she got to enjoy it, as had her big sister.)

I would have taken Hazel myself on that fateful occasion, except for the conference that was taking place at Parklands that day. It had been arranged in conjunction with a similar institution in Birmingham, and the boss had persuaded me to present a paper on the subject of 'Benign centro-temporal epilepsy of childhood'. I had been very interested in this particular condition, and had built up a collection of around a dozen cases that fitted the criteria. I'd presented them at an interdisciplinary meeting within Parklands itself, but the boss felt that it was worth sharing with a wider audience. As I recalled, it had actually gone rather well, and I'd felt quite pleased with my performance. I had even managed to field successfully a number of questions from the floor. But, due to the timing of my contribution, it had meant I hadn't been able to take Hazel to toddler group that lunch time, and when I'd got home after work it was to hear some very bad news.

Katie had taken Hazel in the car, since she was feeling too tired and weary to walk, having just got over a cold. As they turned into the road that led to the church hall, they were passing a line of parked cars when a bright red balloon floated out from between two of them and across the road just in front of the car. (I presume it was a helium balloon that had lost most of its lift, as it was apparently only about a metre off the ground.) Anyway, Katie made some appropriate remark to Hazel (who, being in the child seat in the back, hadn't seen it) and continued along the road. But seconds later, as she glanced into the rear-view mirror, she realized that something awful had happened. A child had rushed out into the road after the errant balloon, and had been knocked down by the car behind ours. Katie had stopped immediately, got out and looked back, and viewed with horror and disbelief the sight that presented itself. There was her friend Carole, screaming frantically, beside herself with anguish—it was little Damien who had been knocked down, and was now lying, apparently lifeless, in the road. The distraught driver was Mrs Fraser, who worked at the local library; she had screeched to a halt and leapt out of her car, but was now standing motionless with shock, unable to believe the sight of a toddler lying in a pool of blood. Katie had done what she could—she'd driven swiftly along to the phone box further down the street, dialled 999 and summoned an ambulance. Alas, although help had arrived within a few minutes, poor little Damien had been pronounced dead on arrival at the RRI's A&E department. The funeral was an extremely emotional and harrowing occasion, and sadly, Carole, who was expecting her second child, subsequently suffered a miscarriage. Unfortunately, the disaster didn't end there. Carole's husband Jim began to spend more and more time with his mates at the social club, while Carole herself hit the bottle in a big way. A year or so later, divorce followed, Carole went back to live with her mother, a widow living in Stevenage or somewhere like that. Katie had tried hard to comfort her and encourage her, but all to no avail, and eventually she lost touch with her.

Mulling all this over, back in the comfort of my 21st century home, I determined to do something positive. If, I reasoned, I had been granted this strange 'gift' for a purpose, then what could possibly be a more deserving cause than this? I made up my mind that I would deal with this tragedy and divert the course of history. A plan was already forming in my mind, but little did I realize how true were to prove those words of the Bard of Ayrshire[1], 'The best-laid schemes of mice and men gang aft agley'. Well, that's what he *said*—I think what he was getting at was that, despite making apparently foolproof plans, we usually end up scuppered by Murphy's Law.

Next morning I called out a cheery "'Bye" to Kate as I let myself out of the back door and pedalled off on my trusty steed. I was actually due at the RRI that morning, but instead I made my way to Parklands. Since my usual starting time there was later than at the RRI, I had time to linger a little en route, and work out my plan. The main obstacle was that conference, which had kept me from taking Hazel to toddler group, and at first I made plans how to absent myself from it at the requisite time. But that wouldn't do—the boss had put a great deal of trust in me, and was relying on me to make a good show of it (as in fact, I *had* done, I reminded myself). No, I had to find some other way. Maybe I could just call in sick that day, I mused, but again, I felt I'd be letting the side down badly. Then it struck me—I could get Maria to do

---

1. Scots poet Robert Burns, 1759-1796

it. Maria was one of the junior technicians, but she was bright, capable and ambitious. I recalled that I'd been intending to groom her to make case presentations herself, and I knew that she had it in her. In fact, with the benefit of hindsight, I knew that she *had* presented papers at subsequent meetings—and an extremely good job she had made of it too. She'd carried it off with all the poise and aplomb of a seasoned professional (no doubt having been a regular star in her school's drama productions had given her the boldness and self-confidence she needed).

The plan I evolved, then, was to go back in time a couple of weeks before the sad day of Damien's accident, and start to prepare Maria for the role she was, unknowingly, to play in the little lad's salvation. As I was approaching Parklands (about five minutes' ride away), it occurred to me that I was about to enter into new territory, as it were. Prior to this my forays into the past had always been on *leaving* work and going to the 'wrong' house, as it were. This time I was going to attempt the converse—leaving home as usual but going to the 'wrong' workplace in the 'wrong' time...or, I suppose, the right place in the wrong time...or...oh well, I'm sure you know what I mean. Then I remembered how, after my first 'temporal adventure', I'd woken up in the past, but cycled purposefully to my present workplace, and it had worked. So all I had to do was to *think* myself back into the past at the right time, just as I'd done, in fact, over the matter of the dolls' costume book.

Pushing all fear of failure to the back of my mind, I pressed firmly on the pedals and turned decisively in through the gates of the Parklands Clinic. Striding firmly up to the door of the department, I opened the door and entered. To my great satisfaction, there was Jilly the secretary, just taking the dustcover off her electronic typewriter, not Elaine, booting up her PC. I'd done it— I'd arrived back at the time I'd intended. Furthermore, Maria arrived soon after, dispelling the fears I'd had that I might have chosen a day when she was on leave. Unfortunately, however, our respective duties kept us apart for most of the day, and I was dying to get her aside for just ten minutes, to introduce her to the idea of preparing to present a case or a paper at a meeting. Finally, just half an hour before going home time, I managed to call the young lass into my room and discuss the possibility with her. Her reaction could not have been more positive (as I knew it would be, having already witnessed it before, but a month or two later than this, if you catch my drift). I decided to go straight in for the big one, and showed her all the material I'd prepared for the talk on 'Benign centro-temporal epilepsy of childhood'. She eagerly agreed to study it, making copies as necessary, and have a try at 'presenting' it in a week's time 'in camera', as it were, her 'audience' being myself alone.

I sped home very satisfied with my achievements, making some mild excuse to Kate for my later than usual arrival. She had hardly noticed, in fact, being engrossed in the latest dolly project. (Later I discovered I could target not only the date of my arrival but also the time.) Next day I set off for Parklands again, this time aiming for a week later than my previous visit, and to my immense delight I discovered I'd been able to time my appearance on exactly the day I'd intended. I found time for Maria to try out her presentation skills and she did it beautifully. She had obviously taken the project seriously, and had been practising. I gave her a couple of tips on her delivery, and made the odd correction here and there, but in all honesty I couldn't have done a better job myself. We were all set, then, for the big one, and little did my protégée realize that she would be thrust into the limelight rather sooner than she'd expected! At least, that had been my plan....

But alas, something *did* 'gang agley'. I successfully arrived at Parklands on the morning of the conference, making it clear to my colleagues on my arrival that I felt somewhat below par. It had been my intention to 'take a turn for the worse' as the morning went on, and hand over to Maria before the time at which my presentation was scheduled. But something was wrong, and it wasn't long before the truth began to dawn on me—Maria wasn't there! Usually she was conspicuous by her lively, cheerful presence, sharing a joke with the other girls as she tossed her blonde ringlets back and giggled in her infectious manner. With her cute, dimpled face and sunny disposition, she was a popular member of staff, and her confident yet unassuming personality endeared herself to all. (But, make no mistake—she was as bright mentally as she was in every other way—by no means 'just a pretty face'.) When she was not around, it was as if the sun had gone behind a cloud, and on this occasion, I detected a distinct air of the overcast about the place.

'Where's Maria?' I asked, trying to sound nonchalant.

'Oh—she called in sick,' someone replied, 'Or at least, her mum did. Tummy bug or something.'

My heart sank. To think of all the trouble I'd gone to in preparing for this moment, and it had all been in vain. What a cruel blow fate had dealt me—or rather, to poor little Damien, who would be beyond my power to save. It was with a heavy heart, and with little enthusiasm, that

I settled down to participate in the conference, and the first talk, 'Towards a more meaningful paradigm of psychoanalytic practice in paediatrics', given by Dr Hugh Rathbone of the Hayward Institute of Child Medicine, was to me (and, I suspect, to most of the others present) about as engrossing as listening to a live commentary on ivy growing up the wall of a Roxbury college.

But then a miracle happened. After the aforesaid learned discourse (which drew not a single question from the floor, despite desperate attempts by the chairman to evoke some semblance of interest), a message was hastily conveyed to me that the presenter of the next item, Professor Edgar Threlgood, an expert on cognitive function in premature neonates, had been delayed en route, and would I mind presenting my paper now rather than at the end of the morning session? I didn't need to consider the matter: I jumped at the chance—literally, as it happened, sending my chair flying in my haste to get to the speaker's podium. The chairman made some weak joke about a contributor's unwonted eagerness to say his piece, and it was with a fair measure of inner restraint that I gathered my composure and set off on my talk. If I say so myself, I think I did a pretty good job of it, and as if to confirm my assessment, there was a veritable bevy of questions afterwards, to the extent that the chairman eventually had to step in and move the meeting on to the next item. I think it was about the interrelation of thalamic dysfunction and adolescent personality deficit, but to be honest, I wasn't particularly interested: I was simply plotting my early getaway. Rather than cause a stir by elbowing my way out during one of the pre-prandial submissions, I quietly absented myself during the mid-morning coffee break (having extricated myself from the clutches of a Mrs Muriel Hathaway, a retired but eager member of the teaching profession, Special Needs being her particular passion). I called in at the department to let Jilly know that the non-specific ailment I had declared earlier had reached a sufficient pitch to merit my exit homeward, and then left.

Not wishing to make Katie suspicious (or anxious) by arriving home mid-morning, I cycled off in the other direction and stopped to stroll through a wood. It had been one of my favourite haunts—somewhere that I could wander quietly, alone with my thoughts and prayers, just turning matters over in my mind, ruminating on the good things of life, fretting perhaps a little over the unpleasant things, but generally emerging satisfied that I'd sorted out a few matters in my (I felt) pretty logical brain; and those that I couldn't get my logic round, I'd turned over to my Maker, whose wisdom I knew was far greater than mine. In the immediate situation, I mused, what I should do was, so far as possible, replicate the journey Katie had made to toddler group on that day, but with myself, rather than her, in the driving seat (quite literally, in fact). But I had to be alert and ready to stop at once when the balloon emerged, and prevent the child from rushing out to his death.

Having devised my plan, I timed my arrival at No 26 for my usual (old) lunch break. Rather than set off straight away with Hazel in her pushchair, I made some excuse to dawdle a little. In fact, the perfect opportunity presented itself, because I noticed that the morning's post had brought my latest copy of Linguistics Monthly. (Yes, I know—it's pretty sad, but *I* enjoy that sort of thing.) Finding an article I feigned immense interest in, I deliberately ignored Katie's reminders to 'mind the time, love.'

When I judged the moment was right, I abruptly put down the magazine, exclaimed, 'Goodness! Is that the time?' and added, 'I'd better take the car.' Bundling our toddler into her child seat, I started the engine and drove away, trying to adjust my driving to the (very slightly) more modest style of my beloved. As we approached the fateful spot, I caught a glimpse, up ahead, of Carole pushing Damien in his pushchair, and—sure enough—he was clutching a bright red balloon. My heart began to race, both with excitement and trepidation. It seemed I'd timed things perfectly—I was at the right spot at the right time. I actually noticed the wind getting up a little, as a paper bag blew across the forecourt of the garage to my right. I knew what was about to happen, but when it did, it took me unawares. True enough, the balloon blew out into the road, but to my horror it happened, not just in front of *our* car, but in front of the one two cars ahead of me! At that moment it also dawned on me that the one immediately in front was that of Mrs Fraser—she who had, through no fault of her own, and to her everlasting anguish—run into the little lad as he'd darted out between parked cars, ignoring his mother's urgent cries and eluding her despairing lunge to try and grab him.

All I could think of was to lean heavily on the horn to try and warn the poor lady. Several heads turned to see what the commotion was about, and unfortunately, it had the very opposite effect of that intended, for Mrs Fraser looked away from the road ahead in order to peer into her rear-view mirror. And that of course, was when it happened. The sound of the impact was sickening—all the more for me because I knew exactly what was happening, indeed, had anticipated it, willing it all the while *not* to happen. I was distraught. How could my carefully worked-out plan have gone so badly wrong? I did what I could, and rushed to the nearest phone box just as Katie had done (this was, of course, before the mobile phone era), but I knew in my heart that it was in vain. What made it worse was that I had to go back and tell Katie about the awful event, and I think it had a more distressing effect on her than that of seeing it first-hand.

I was glad to get back to my own time and home that evening, but I was determined not to let the matter rest. There was no way I was going to let myself be defeated, and I planned to get it right next time. So, next morning, I set off for work exactly as I had done the previous day, and I again 'aimed' for the day of the conference. I walked confidently through the door of the department, and to my surprise was met by the cheerful face and chirpy greeting of Maria. How odd, I thought—why was she here, and not laid up sick at home? 'Hi, Billy,' she chirruped, 'Sorry I couldn't make it yesterday—I had this really bad tummy bug, but thankfully, I'm much better today.'

What had she said—Yesterday? What could she have meant? The conference had been on a Monday, and that was the day I'd just come back to, wasn't it? It had been Monday Maria'd been unwell, not Sunday, which would, in any case, have been irrelevant. Surely this wasn't Tuesday? But it was, as I soon discovered when I looked at the secretary's tear-off calendar, and was congratulated by my colleagues for my performance at yesterday's conference and asked if I was feeling better. Somehow—I knew not how—I'd miscalculated, and come back to the wrong day. I didn't bother to go home to lunch that day; in fact, I didn't bother to stay at Parklands for the afternoon. I made my escape at lunchtime and cycled straight to the RRI, where, to my relief, I was able to carry on in the present—the 21st Century present—as though nothing had happened.

Next day I took up the challenge once again, and set off for Parklands ever more determined to arrive back there on *Monday*, the day of the conference. But imagine my puzzlement and frustration when I discovered I'd come back, not on Monday, nor Tuesday, nor even on Wednesday—but *Thursday* of that fateful week! How on earth could this have happened? I asked myself over and over again. As I cycled home later (somewhat languidly and with no great enthusiasm), I was turning the matter over in my mind when all of a sudden it dawned on me, and a basic principle of time travel (at least, in *my* experience) became clear to me. I realized that, although I was able to return to any day in my past once (through one of the 'time portals'), I could not revisit that day a second time. Hence, when I aimed for a day I'd already revisited, I was propelled into the next day *after* that! I'd returned to the day of the conference—Monday of that week—and then the Tuesday. I'd already gone back to the Wednesday (that was when, over our lunchtime sandwiches, Katie had said about Damien's funeral coming up in two days' time), which explains why the next jump forward had been to the Thursday. As I began to pick up speed on my ride home, so my mind changed up a gear and I began to formulate Plan C (or was it D? I'd lost count).

Once again I set off for Parklands in the morning. (This is getting to be something of a habit, I found myself thinking.) But this time I was aiming for the *Thursday* of the week before the conference. It worked, of course, but it was nevertheless to my profound relief. We were all in the throes of preparing for the coming conference—

moving items of furniture into and out of the small lecture theatre, so as to optimise the space available; checking the slide projectors were all working (this was, of course, long before the welcome advent of Power-Point), and for me, getting my notes and slides together in a logical fashion. The following day, Friday, we were to have a practice run, so that those of us taking an active part in the proceedings would be able to do so without any unforeseen mishaps.

Towards lunchtime I was getting both excited and jittery with the anticipation of what I hoped to do. When, to my horror, the boss asked me to carry out some task that I reckoned would involve me in going to lunch rather too late, I politely but firmly made some excuse based on family commitments, and suggested (success-fully, to my relief), that he get one of the junior techni-cians to do it. The time came; I slipped swiftly out of the department and sped on my bike the short distance to 26 UMC. Katie had fed Hazel, and was having a well-earned rest on the living room sofa while Sally was play-ing contentedly with her toys. (At this point Katie was still getting over her cold.) I quickly got the pushchair ready, put Hazel into it, grabbed her drink bottle and bade Katie Bye-bye. 'My word,' she remarked, you're eager today!'

I sped off down the road at an unwonted pace, but slowed dramatically when we'd reached the point where our route to toddler group joined Carole's. From there I could see some way ahead, and Carole was not in sight. So far, so good; now I just had to make sure to meet her at some point. Playing for time, I initiated a game with Hazel whereby we dodged into gateways and alleyways, pretending to hide from some dreadful enemy, and when we'd both tired of that, I dawdled at the shops, pointing out to the toddler things that I thought she might find interesting. Just as she began to complain, 'Come on, Daddy—I'm missing some playtime!' I was glad to see Carole approaching, as it happened, from one of the side streets. This slightly took me by surprise, but what mattered most was that I was able to meet her 'accidentally', and we walked along together. (She had, by the way, been to her cousin's for coffee and a chat.)

At first we exchanged pleasantries—about her pregnancy, mainly, comparing it with Katie's second one. I then (skilfully, I thought) steered the conversation round to prams, pushchairs, buggies and the like, expressing some alarm that she had not strapped Damien into *his* buggy. 'No,' replied Carole, 'I suppose I ought to, but to be honest, it's too much trouble—the clasp is a bit fiddly. Anyway, he doesn't like to feel hemmed in.'

'But that's not the point,' I countered, 'at their age, safety is vital. Why,' I continued, embarking on an impressive but entirely fictitious anecdote, 'at Parklands only last week, we heard of not one but *two* cases of unrestrained children jumping out of their buggies and coming to grief before their mothers could grab them. One poor little lad—as a matter of fact, he reminded me very much of your Damien—the same cheeky grin, and lots of fair curls—was holding a nice red balloon when it blew out of his hand. He leapt out of his pushchair and darted into the road to get it, and was immediately knocked down by a car. Apparently it so upset the poor driver that she vowed never to drive again. And the poor little lad was rushed off to hospital with a severe head injury. He survived, apparently, but he's so severely disabled that he's got no quality of life at all. Such a shame—he was such a bright, lively little chap. I knew him because his elder sister had come in for tests because she'd had a couple of faints and they weren't sure whether they were seizures or not.'

'Oh dear,' replied Carole, 'that's dreadful.'

'Yes, 'I added, 'and the worst thing is, it was so easily preventable. That poor mum must have gone through terrible mental turmoil, blaming herself for not fastening the lad's safety strap.

Hoping I hadn't laid it on too thick, I changed the subject swiftly. 'Anyway,' I ventured, 'how's little Damien getting on these days? He seems a very cheerful, friendly lad.'

'Yes,' replied Carole, 'he's got lots of friends—it seems to be the party season at the moment: he's been to two birthday parties already this week, and he's been invited to another one on Sunday! It gets a bit expensive buying presents!'

That'll be where he gets his balloon from, no doubt, I thought. We reached the hall, I deposited Hazel, and hurried home, hoping my words of wisdom would sink in. I determined to come back in a couple of weeks' time to see the outcome of my labours.

I needn't have bothered, because a very odd thing happened when I got home (back in my own time) that evening. Kate and I had sat down to our evening meal after all the usual greetings and comparing our days' work (I'd grown quite adept at describing occupational activities that weren't actually untrue, but which concealed the fact that they had in fact taken place many years before). Just as she was dishing out the boiled pota-toes, Kate suddenly announced, 'Oh, darling, I heard some wonderful news today—Sally's old college friend

Helen's getting married next month—to Damien Winterton. I had to go over to Hardington on a small errand this morning, and who should I bump into but Carole! It was really nice to see her after so long, and we had coffee together in La Cantina. She looked *really* well, and of course, she was absolutely full of it about the wedding. She said Jim's done ever so well in his work—he's landed several really big contracts, so they're helping Helen's parents pay for the wedding. It's going to be a no-expense-spared event, and guess what? We're invited! Carole was *so* pleased to have met me—she'd been trying to contact us, but she'd somehow lost our address. She said she's never forgotten how you undoubtedly saved Damien's life when he was a toddler—she couldn't get over how you'd given her such timely advice about making sure he was properly strapped into his buggy. The way his balloon had blown out of his hand was exactly the way you'd said it had happened with that other poor little boy—it was so uncanny. Had she not fastened his strap, he'd have been out of the buggy like a shot!'

Nothing could have prepared me for this astonishing situation—as Kate chattered excitedly on about what a sweet girl Helen was, and what a smashing couple they made, my mind was in a daze. How could such an incredible coincidence have occurred? How was it that, on the very day (in the present) that I'd gone back in time to try and save that little lad's life, I should just 'happen' to return to learn what was later—many years later—to become the boy's destiny? Why, for instance, could not the news of Damien's imminent marriage have come to light the following week, or several months after my return from my mission? It seemed to me that it was 'meant' to come about in this way—that some higher

Power (well, it must have been God, I guess) had ordained it that I would see the fruit of my labours without delay.

And once again, that strange, eerie experience came over me—I began to perceive a memory forming, coming into my consciousness from somewhere, nowhere—wherever. I began to 'remember'—rather vaguely, I'll admit, but the memory was definitely there—how, after the turn of events that had prevented Damien dashing heedlessly into the path of the fatal car, Jim and Carole had treated us to a superb meal at a posh restaurant and showered me with gifts. Carole had even written a letter to the Roxbury Times, commending me for my vital advice, and urging all parents to ensure their little ones were properly secured in their pushchairs, car seats, etc. I even 'recalled' how embarrassing I'd found the whole business: I'd never intended to become a local hero, and I found all the undue attention somewhat unnerving. Still, I was pleased that I'd been able to transform a family's fortunes so dramatically. Oh, and I also experienced a 'memory adjustment' as regards Helen. Kate and I had met her several times when Sally had been doing her foundation course. She was certainly a nice-looking girl—she was petite, with wavy, auburn hair and green eyes: quite striking, really. But she always seemed lacking in self-confidence, and never seemed able to maintain a serious relationship. She'd had a few boyfriends, but for some reason didn't seem able to keep them. Sally had kept in touch initially when the two girls had gone off to their respective universities, but Helen had apparently dropped out in her second year after suffering some sort of breakdown, and after that the contact had ceased. Now, however, I 'remembered' an alternative version of events (strange how I was able to recall both versions, like one of those books or films where you can decide on different turns of the plot). The new memory was of Sally continuing to keep in touch with Helen, who, encouraged by 'this fantastic bloke' she had met (though a name was never mentioned), had really come out of her shell. She had developed a very active social life (the two of them had joined various music, drama and other societies, were often seen together in clubs, and had also gone to Ibiza together). Furthermore, her academic progress had improved massively too, and she had achieved a first in Sports science.

I was amazed at the way these new memories had come into my consciousness, almost as if they had been ideas for a novel, originating from my own imagination (but, through casual conversation with Kate and Sally, every detail was subsequently shown to be correct). However, what amazed me most was how so much good had come out of my simple desire (though it had proved far from simple to carry out) to reverse a tragic accident. I couldn't help feeling a tad like some kind of superman with awesome powers for good, and I wondered what other beneficial deeds I might be able to perform. But alas, I was to discover—almost to my supreme cost—that things could turn distinctly bad!

CHAPTER 5

In the dog house

As I wrestled with a particularly recalcitrant length of aluminium tubing on my workbench in the garage, I began to turn the air about me a delicate shade of pale blue. You know the kind of thing: 'Oh bother! Drat! Flippin' 'eck!'—stuff like that. I was working on my yet-to-be patented compact hi-gain UHF antenna with which I expected to be able to pull in digital TV from a very distant transmitter to the southwest. All right, so maybe I am a bit sad, and for a reasonable monthly subscription I could get any channel I wanted on Sky, but I enjoy a challenge, and I was keen to achieve my goal free of charge. The only trouble was, I just didn't have the tools and equipment I really needed to perform the delicate manipulations (cutting, drilling, screwing, soldering and so on) with any degree of perfection. As I messed up yet another piece of carefully cut and shaped metal when it slipped in the inadequate jaws of the workbench, I cursed my lack of forethought in leaving behind so many useful tools and things when we moved to Clunmore. Back in UMC I'd had a proper workshop (it was originally the garage, but a glorified car port had since become the repository of the family vehicle), and a sturdy, fixed bench, with a proper vice and everything. But No 36 The Willows had no such luxury. The integral garage had a rather flimsy bench at one end, and not a lot else. I'd decided to cut down on the DIY when we moved, but inevitably my intentions were thwarted by lack of funds to hire workmen to carry out all the jobs that naturally cropped up, and necessity dictated my agenda as household handyman. I managed pretty well on the whole, but there were always the tricky jobs—like this one—that really required more specialized facilities.

As I continued wrestling, and stringing together a whole series of 'If onlys' in my mind and under-the-breath mutterings, the obvious thought eventually came to me. Of course I still had access to the equipment I needed—all I had to do was to simply step back in time (simply!—the mere thought made me chuckle) and there it was. With a frisson of excitement, I hastily gathered together all the components of the antenna I'd so laboriously fashioned, put the finishing touches to a couple more, and stuffed them all into a carrier bag and put it in my bike basket. Next morning I kissed Kate goodbye with the usual cheerful pleasantry, and off I pedalled. I was due to be working all day at the RRI, but mid-afternoon I invented some urgent pretext to go to Parklands. There was in fact a finished report I'd wanted to get to the consultant there—it wasn't that urgent, but it suited me to maintain that it was. I delivered the missive, chatted to my colleagues there for a while, then made my way to my old home.

It amazed me with what ease I slipped into my past life. I chose no particular date, but just 'aimed' for some vague timeframe and there I was. It was a Friday evening as it turned out (ideal, I thought, as it was likely to be more relaxed than most other weeknights). Katie had already started to get some tea ready, albeit more of a light snack than our normal more filling repast.

'I'm just popping out to the workshop, love,' I chirruped, 'there's a small job I need to finish.'

Katie rightly interpreted my 'small job' as something likely to take more than just a minute or two. 'Don't be long, dear—don't forget we're going to the opera with Mum tonight.'

'Well,' I replied, 'we've got plenty of time, haven't we?' (I had mistakenly thought my mother-in-law was coming down on the coach and that our evening out was to be here in Roxbury.)

'No, we haven't,' she countered, a hint of irritation in her voice; 'We've got to *get* there first!'

'Okay,' I breezed, 'don't worry—let me just finish this.' I was of course far more concerned to carry out the job that had been my sole aim in coming back to this place and time, but I had stepped unwittingly into a situation where tinkering with bits of metal in the workshop was about as far down the list of family priorities as it was possible to imagine.

I pressed on with my task, ignoring the increasingly exasperated cries emanating from the kitchen just across the way. 'Come *on*, love—*please* don't leave all the work to me. The children need feeding and getting ready, and I *must* change my clothes.'

Quite irrationally, I was getting annoyed myself—I had come with a purpose to fulfil, and now here were these people trying their best to thwart my attempts.

I was unable to step back from the situation and put it into its true perspective.

Eventually I completed my construction, and was, to be honest, very pleased with the finished product. But in so doing, I had thoughtlessly sacrificed the good will of my nearest and dearest. My wife, worn to a frazzle and driven to distraction, was now shouting at me and being needlessly but perhaps understandably short-tempered with the children, who in turn were playing up: crying, being disobedient, fighting each other—doing everything imaginable to get what should have been a pleasant evening off to a very bad start.

The drive to Coventry was, to say the least, an ordeal. There was always a certain amount of slow-moving traffic getting out of Roxbury at the rush-hour, but if you caught it relatively early it was never too bad. But early we were not, and to make matters worse, roadworks on our nearest exit route had caused a ridiculously long tailback, and it seemed ages before we were out on the open road. Unfortunately it wasn't very open. As it was a Friday evening, traffic was heavier than usual, and it was just our luck to be preceded onto the motorway—just—by an 'abnormal load', complete with police escort, flashing lights, the lot! I think it was a massive transformer bound for some power station in the Midlands, and it completely blocked two lanes. That should have left Lane 3, but for some reason the cops were blocking that off to would-be overtakers as well. The result was a rapidly lengthening queue of vehicles crawling along at about 15 mph, their drivers fuming with frustration and their passengers getting more and more fractious by the minute—and we were no exception.

There was I muttering, 'Why on earth did they choose to move this thing right now, anyway? For goodness' sake, it's the start of the weekend rush—couldn't they have done it at night or something?'

Meanwhile Katie was getting in sharp digs at me: 'If you hadn't been so intent on fiddling around with your wretched contraptions rather than looking forward to taking Mum and me out for a treat, we wouldn't have been in this hopeless mess!'

The girls didn't help much either—there were sibling squabbles (quite unusual, as they normally got on very well together), cries of: 'I'm hungry!' and the inevitable 'Are we nearly there yet?'

Fortunately, just as I'd worked out an alternative route from the next exit point, the abnormal load left the motorway where I had intended to, so we were able to get back to a decent speed again—in fact, I rather over-did it, and the engine temperature began to creep alarmingly towards the red danger mark.

'You were going to book the car in to get that fixed!' Katie fairly screamed at me, 'You *know* that radiator's got a leak!'

'It's OK, love,' I replied, trying to effect a calming tone. 'It's booked in for Tuesday morning,' I lied. 'Anyway, there's a service station in a mile—we can top it up there.'

I did top up the radiator, but it added another half hour to our journey, because the children naturally wanted to go to the toilet, and then their mother felt bound to buy them some sort of edible substance to keep them from starving to death—or driving her to distraction by their constant whining. At last we reached Katie's parents' house in Wyken. It was an unpretentious two-up, two-down terraced brick house. I parked untidily outside the gate and the children spilled noisily out of the car and rushed to the front door. They didn't have to ring the bell, for their grandad was already standing in the open doorway, where he had been, apparently, for at least half an hour, anxiously scanning the street for our belated arrival. 'You'd better come in quick,' he said, 'Mother's getting in a bit of a state!'

If there's one thing my mother-in-law cannot stand it's being late for anything—be it a WI meeting, a church service or (especially) a visit to the theatre or opera. She likes to arrive in plenty of time, so that she can 'imbibe the ambience', as she puts it. She prefers to take her seat in plenty of time so that she can approach the performance in a relaxed manner—and eye up all the other operagoers and their suits, dresses and accessories. But this evening she was to be deprived of this, as we arrived, hot and bothered, not merely after all the aforementioned preliminaries, but actually a few minutes late for the start of the performance.

At the house we'd just dumped the kids on Granddad, ignored the beautiful spread of food Mother-in-law had so lovingly prepared and carefully arranged on the dining table (it was a veritable work of art), bundled her and ourselves into the car and sped off towards the theatre. Poor Katie had not had time to freshen herself up, we were tired, hungry and thirsty, and Mother-in-law was quite crotchety, to say the least. Fortunately, we found a parking space within easy reach of the theatre, and we hurried up the road to the entrance doors. Picking up the tickets we'd booked beforehand, we marched towards the door to the stalls, but we got no further.

'I'm sorry,' said the man at the door (without a trace of sorrow in his voice), 'you can't go in now—the performance has started. You'll have to wait till the interval.'

I need hardly spell out the ladies' reaction; indeed, the very recollection of that dreadful moment even now fills me with anguish and horror too painful to describe. Our protestations fell on very unsympathetic ears, and we trudged disconsolately away, the ladies' stony faces seeming quite out of place above their beautiful dresses, and I feeling most uncomfortable in my best suit. We walked to a café down the road, but none of us felt like consuming anything more than a cup of tea. Conversation was minimal and strained. I was not included in it. I was well and truly in the doghouse.

We walked back to the theatre after 45 minutes and were admitted after the first of the three acts, but we couldn't really enjoy the rest of the performance. Katie's favourite part of the opera—and, as it happened, also her mother's—had been in Act 1, so we'd missed the best part. As for me, I couldn't pick up the plot, and even if I had been able to, I was too preoccupied with my own misery—which, I had to admit, I'd brought entirely on myself. I need not dwell on the rest of that evening.

We returned to the house, picked at the food our hostess had prepared, and turned in. The girls had long since gone to bed in the little annex Katie's parents had had added to the back of the house. It had large patio doors and a sizeable window in the roof, so in the summer it was rather like a conservatory, but its stout brick walls and double glazing made it nice and warm in the colder months, and the girls enjoyed sleeping there on the camp beds that were erected for them when they came to stay.

Katie and I shared a none-too-large double bed in the modest second bedroom, and judging by the cold shoulder (literally!) she gave me, I've no doubt that, had there been room for a couch there as well, she'd have made me sleep on it!

We had intended to stay the weekend with my in-laws, but next morning, Katie's mood (matched closely by her mother's) was so black that she made some feeble excuse (which was all too readily accepted) that we should return to Roxbury without delay. To the children's disappointment at missing out on the usual treats provided on a weekend visit to Granny and Grandad, we threw our things back into the car and set off south again. We had to put up with the girls' whines of 'But *why* can't we stay longer?' and I had to put up with an extremely irritable wife, who seemed intent on finding any and every little thing to pick fault with. She criticized my driving (even the route I was taking), my lack of forethought as regards the car repairs, my scruffy clothes, my hair that needed cutting, and the way I had (apparently) left the kitchen such a mess before going to work the previous morning.

Then the bombshell dropped: 'It's no good,' she exploded, 'I've had enough of you—you've been driving me mad with all your stupid preoccupations. You don't care anything at all for me and the children.' (This was by anyone's reckoning a gross exaggeration, but at times Katie was prone to making such extravagant remarks. I'll admit, I had my fair share of annoying habits—probably rather more than my fair share, if the truth be told, but we all have our faults, don't we? And marriage is about bearing with each other's little quirks and foibles, and learning to make compromises and bear with one another's faults gracefully.) 'I want a divorce!' came the final hammer blow.

'What?' I countered, incredulous and shocked, thinking, 'Surely you can't be serious?' But she gave every indication that she was. I tried to make light of it, and bade her be quiet in front of the children (happily, however, they were by now fast asleep).

The rest of the journey was made in stony silence. I turned on the car radio and tuned to Radio 2. Some jaunty light music began to cheer the frosty air inside the uncomfortable prison I felt I was in, but before long Katie turned it off, muttering, 'You'll wake the children.' On arriving home our actions were purely mechanical. Katie went straight to bed, leaving me to tuck the girls up in their beds. When I tried to get in beside Katie, she told me: 'You can go and sleep in the spare room!' I didn't argue; I knew it was best in circumstances like these to retire gracefully and let the matter blow over. She'll probably still be a bit sore in the morning, but it won't last, I thought.

I slept badly, of course, the disasters of the preceding day preying on my mind throughout a fitful night. So I woke tired and irritable—a mood matched exactly by that of my other half. I tried my best to appease her with offers of help in the kitchen and with the children, but her frosty response was always, '*I can do it, thank you!*'

Seeing that my presence was doing more harm than good, I made some excuse about needing to pop into work (although it was a Saturday), to attend to some vital, unfinished piece of work that was needed for a case conference on the Monday. 'Don't bother coming back!' were the needlessly harsh words I heard being hurled after me as I went out the door to my bike. I pedalled disconsolately off, reflecting on the events of the last few hours, and wishing I had been a good bit more thoughtful towards my nearest and dearest ones. Sure, I'd got the job done that I'd come to do, the evidence being the multi-rodded aluminium assembly strapped to the back of my bike. But any sense of satisfaction I might have had at having completed what had previously seemed an impossible task had been more than offset by the gloom I felt over the severe *faux pas* I had committed in the process. If there was one thing guaranteed to annoy my beloved, it was insulting her mother—of whom, naturally, she was justifiably fond and proud. And I had committed the Unforgivable Sin.

As I pedalled, somewhat wearily, back to Clunmore, I did my best to assume a cheerful disposition, feeling, surely, that Katie would soon have got over her offended and somewhat belligerent mood. It would all blow over, I convinced myself, as so many other little tiffs had done before. Katie was a wonderful, loving wife and mother, but was prone to taking offence a little too easily, and more than able to summon up that fiery temper of her Irish grandmother.

And so it was a much more cheerful Bill Draper whose bike glided gracefully round into Warwick Avenue in Clunmore, and then off into The Willows. Down at the end of the close was No 36, with its bright blue garage doors—although, I thought, they seemed distinctly turquoise now. Dismissing it as an effect of the darkening evening light, I decelerated into the drive and past the car parked in the driveway—the car...but then I noticed that it wasn't *our* car. This was a brand, sparkling new Mercedes, and very posh it looked, too.

'Funny,' I thought, 'We must be having visitors, although I can't think who.' I assumed Kate had parked our car out on the road, and that I hadn't noticed it. Manoeuvring round into the side passage, I tried to push open the wrought iron gate (which, inexplicably, looked as if it had fairly recently had a fresh coat of paint). It was locked—which it sometimes was if we were both out together, but this was unusual. I fished my keys out of my pocket and found the one for the padlock. But it didn't fit! And furthermore, it was a completely different type of lock.

'Whatever is she up to?' I thought, as I walked round to the front door and rang the bell. To my surprise, the door was opened by a stout, red-faced gentleman in his seventies who sported a magnificent handlebar moustache. He looked like the archetypal retired senior officer from the Army or the Air Force. 'Yes?' he enquired, abruptly.

I stammered in my confusion, 'I – I – er, is…is…'

'Well, man,' exploded the Major General, who was obviously rather short on the virtue of patience, 'Don't just stand there spluttering—spit it out!'

I composed myself as best I could and continued, 'Is Kate there?'

'Kate? Kate who? Who the blazes are you talking about?' The face was changing rapidly from red to purple.

'Who is it, dear?' came a faint, unsteady voice from within, as a short, frail little old lady came into view from behind the Admiral of the Fleet.

'How the hell should I know?' he raged, 'Just go back inside, Muriel—*I'll* deal with it. Just some blithering idiot wanting someone called Kate. Never heard of the woman (this was addressed to me now)—never been anyone of that name here. Just clear orff and leave us alone. Get enough of you bounders trying to trick your way into our homes and steal our belongings.'

Gingerly I made one more attempt. 'Is there a couple named Draper in this neighbourhood?'

'For God's sake, NO!' he roared, 'Now leave us in peace. On yer bike!'

I obeyed his last command to the letter, and pedalled off up the road as fast as I could. I had visions of him sending a bulldog—or maybe a pack of Rottweilers—after me, and decided not to chance my luck.

But what on earth was going on? And more to the point, what was I to do? Clearly my mishandling of the opera business had set in train a series of events that had changed our future drastically. Whether Katie had indeed carried out her threat to divorce me, I could only conjecture. Or perhaps although we'd managed to patch things up between us, her parents on the other hand had been so incensed at my disrespect and thoughtlessness that they had deprived us of our inheritance, or enough of it to necessitate our having to settle for a more down-market residence following our move from UMC. Either way, I had no home to go to, and I needed to get some sleep and a clear head to work out how to reverse this tragedy. I went back into town and let myself into the department at work (I was privileged to have my own key, as I would sometimes do some private research after hours). Although I had left the Eighties on a Saturday, this was now a Friday evening 'back' in the 21st century. That was fortunate, as I was able to sleep—albeit rather fitfully—on one of the departmental beds, without fear of being disturbed the next morning.

As Saturday dawned, I rose, washed, dressed and set about trying to formulate a plan. I made myself a good strong cup of coffee, and helped myself to a handful of biscuits from a packet that one of my colleagues had brought back from a holiday in Portugal. Various conflicting thoughts and scenarios raced through my head, but gradually a plausible one came to the fore. I knew I could not return to that fateful day itself—I had already proved the impossibility of reliving a day more than once. I therefore determined to go back to the previous week, and try to head off the debacle another way. Having formulated my scheme in detail, I set off, heading once again for No. 26. This time, as I approached, I concentrated my thoughts on the Wednesday of the week before my previous visit. I can't explain why I chose Wednesday—something in the back of my mind made the suggestion, and, as it happened, it was the right choice.

As I wheeled my bike through the carport to the back of the house, there was Katie, hanging out some washing on the line. I'd been trying to formulate an excuse for my appearance at that unusual time of the morning, shortly after I'd have left for work, but fortunately the rather lame, unconvincing one I'd had in mind was not needed.

'You *are* a chump!' was the unexpected greeting, followed by: 'I was wondering how long it would take you to realize you'd asked for the day off, to get those jobs done! You were obviously so keen to get to work that you were out of the door before I could stop you!'

Although she said this with a chuckle, I detected a hint of irritation in her voice, and I remembered how, on that dreadful drive back from Coventry, Katie had berated me for, among other things, my 'stupid preoccupations' of late. I bore this in mind as I asked, 'Where's the list of jobs you wanted me to do?' (I *knew* there'd be a meticulously itemized list somewhere—Katie *loved* making lists—she fairly lived by them, but I hadn't seen one pinned up in the usual place, on the notice board in the breakfast room.)

'Oh, it's here, love,' she chirruped, 'I just had to add another item to it.'

'That's my girl,' I thought, 'there's always *just* one more thing to add to every list, especially when it concerns jobs for me!'

'You can be getting on with them this morning while I take the girls to this holiday play scheme thing at the church.'

I had no idea what this play scheme was, but fortunately, there was a leaflet about it pinned up on our notice board, from which I subsequently learned that it was from 9 till 12:30. Katie would be gone for about four hours, including the time it would take to push our tandem-style double buggy each way—probably more, as she would doubtless chat to some of the other mums on the way back, so wouldn't be in a great hurry. I scanned the list and gave a silent prayer of thanks that all the jobs—odds and ends in the garden and around the house—could easily be accomplished in a couple of hours.

'Had you anything planned for this afternoon, dear?' I asked, nonchalantly.

'Not particularly,' came the reply, 'if you're not still busy we could take the children to the park, I suppose.'

'OK, we'll see,' I breezed, as she got the girls' coats on and started to bundle them, and the buggy, out of the door, 'see you later, then.'

I waited till they had disappeared out of sight down the road, then made three phone calls, the first being to

our friendly local garage. Fortunately Dick, the proprietor and chief mechanic, confirmed that he could see to
the car's leaking radiator there and then. Business was
always slack on a Wednesday morning, he said. So, fifteen
minutes later I drove the car round there, and Dick, as
usual clad in his filthy overalls with his face and hands
covered in oil, greeted me cordially. He always looked a
terrible sight, and his workshop looked completely disorganized, but he was an excellent mechanic, and never
overcharged. After a quick perusal of the offending radiator, he said he'd have it fixed in half an hour—it just
needed draining, a touch of welding, and refilling.

This gave me time to do a little shopping while the job
was being done, and I hastened to the florist and got a
lovely spray of flowers for my beloved—a good mixture
of colourful and sweet smelling varieties, such as freesias
and those orange ones (the name escapes me for the
moment). Having picked up a chequebook from the
bureau before leaving the house, I called into the bank
and cashed a cheque to give myself some cash for the day.
Back to the garage, to find the welding had been done.
As usual, when I asked for the bill, Dick made a dismissive hand gesture and said, 'Oh, call in and pay me some
other day—I haven't made the bill up yet.' Just to avoid
any difficulties, I gave him a couple of notes, the value of
which I knew would far exceed the cost of the job, and I
told Dick to treat himself and the missus to a drink. He
thanked me profusely, and stood watching me drive off,
no doubt wondering at my unwonted generosity.

Back home, I raced through Katie's list of jobs at
record speed, and then got out a road atlas to study
alternative routes to avoid the roadworks and other
hazards we had encountered in the week to come (if you

follow my meaning!). I had to bear in mind that one or two roads I'd choose in the next century had not yet been built. Working out a suitable route, I wrote myself a note and tucked it behind the tax disk in the car, ready for the trip we were to make nine days hence. I labelled it clearly, so that, hopefully, neither of us would remove it in the meantime.

When Katie returned with the girls, I greeted her immediately with, 'Don't take your things off—we're going out! Oh, and these are for you' (producing the flowers) 'to say sorry for being a bit off lately!'

'Why, darling, they're lovely,' she replied, her face a mixture of delight and amazement, since, it appeared, I had not been in the habit of making such loving gestures at that particular phase of our marriage. A warm hug and kiss were my welcome reward for this gesture.

'I've got all the jobs done,' I explained, as I ushered my little family out into the car, 'so I thought we could check out that new mini-theme park that's opened recently over in Berrington.' (This was a small town about 15 miles away, and by a quirk of the memory, I'd realized Dwarfland must have opened a few months before, and a quick check in the phone book followed by a call had confirmed my belief.)

To cut a long story short, we had a very nice lunch in the restaurant there, and the kids thoroughly enjoyed exploring the streets of what was, in effect, a glorified model village, with tiny people, vehicles, animals etc. doing all sorts of things in very lifelike ways. There was much excited chatter in the car as we drove home, and Katie congratulated me on my brainwave, saying it had been a wonderful outing, and that I'd been very clever to think of it. I secretly hoped that my other brainwave would be equally successful.

Next morning I kissed my wife and children goodbye and set off for work. At the end of the road I turned right and headed for the city centre and my 'present-day' workplace at the RRI. By now I was getting quite good at 'thinking my way' into a particular timeframe, so I was not surprised to find myself back at work on the Monday following my fitful night's sleep there that weekend. As an added bonus, there was my 'patented' high-gain wide-band TV antenna, on the workbench where I'd left it. To be honest, I'd forgotten all about the article that had set off this whole amazing train of events.

After a routine day's work I set off for home again, but I left the aerial at work and headed back towards UMC, where, to appreciate the outcome of my little plan, I 'thought my way' back to the Monday evening following the trip to Coventry. To my utter joy and re-lief, I was greeted enthusiastically by spouse and daughters alike.

'Come in, sweetie,' chirruped Katie, 'We're just about to eat—I've cooked your favourite meal!'

At that point I'd have cheerfully eaten a plate of pigswill, so relieved I was to have got back into favour. The girls presented me with drawings they'd made of themselves having fun with Grandma and Grandad (Hazel's was just a coloured scrawl, but it was neverthe-less a priceless work of art to me), and Katie told me in glowing terms how wonderful it had been of me to reserve a box for the three of us at the opera, and even to arrange, somehow, for her mother to meet the leading artistes backstage after the performance. I didn't go into detail about the little white lies I'd told the theatre proprietor on the phone about my mother-in-law's recent sad loss, and that it would cheer her immensely if she could meet the stars of the show.

It was on a wave of euphoria that I set off for work next morning. 'Bye, darling,' Katie kissed me as I was going out of the back door to get my bike, then added, 'Oh, be a love and post this as you get to the end of the road.' I stuffed the envelope into my jacket pocket and set off, gliding down the road as if I were on cloud nine. I was ecstatic that my plan had worked so well. My colleagues couldn't understand why I was in such a good mood that day, and at home time I set off with a song in my heart and the aerial on the rear carrier—and also the envelope still in my pocket, as I discovered when I arrived home and fished for my keys. 'Oh bother!' I thought, 'I forgot to post it. Let's hope it wasn't anything important.'

CHAPTER 6

The pendulum swings

As I wheeled my bike round the side passage to the rear of the house, I got a real shock, though quite a pleasant one, as it happened. It was the garden! When we'd first moved to No. 36, I'd been very keen on gardening, and had kept our moderately large plot in quite good nick. The lawn was always mown to a nice short length, the borders neat and tidy, and filled with a profusion of colourful flowers; the hedges were trimmed regularly, and at the far end I grew a balanced variety of vegetables—we were virtually self-sufficient, in fact. Whenever we had friends or relations visiting us, I would proudly show them our wonderful garden, and they would make suitably favourable noises of praise. But sadly, over the years, as the children grew up, and family life made ever-increasing demands on my time (and Kate's, for that matter), the garden became neglected—not very much at first, but gradually I would find I hadn't time to trim the hedges, prune the roses, or mend the fence. Of course, the effect of children playing in the garden also took its toll on the lawn, the three apple trees we possessed, and the flower borders. By the present time our poor garden was but a shadow of its former glory. Much of it had reverted to nature; in fact it reminded me of the tale of the old Westcountry gardener who was complimented by the local vicar on the splendid appearance of his plot. 'It's wonderful,' said the parson, 'what can be achieved when God and man work together in harmony.' 'Arr, vicar,' replied the gardener, 'but 'E didn' make a very good job of it when 'E 'ad it all to 'Ees-self!'

Anyway, what I saw before me now was a complete transformation—the lawn resembled a golf green, the hedges and shrubs were neatly trimmed, paving stones perfectly aligned, flower borders magnificent—and there was a really smart garden shed, not new, but obviously well looked after. To be honest, I quite expected Charlie Dimmock and the rest of the Ground Force team to pop out from somewhere and yell 'Surprise!'

As I let myself in the back door (which was not locked), I was amazed to find myself walking into an attractive, well equipped kitchen, not the rather tired old one I'd had breakfast in that morning. 'Hello, dear!' came Kate's cheerful greeting from the living room, so I made my way gingerly in that direction, wondering what other surprises were awaiting me. Under the stairs in the hallway were the now familiar display cases of costume dolls, but on turning into the living room, I was greeted not only by more dolls (no change there), but also a really smart home cinema system, complete with surround sound, DVD recorder – the lot! Lying on the attractive glass-topped coffee table was the latest satellite TV guide. How this had all come about I simply could not conjecture—what could I have done in the past to make such an improvement to our standard of living in the present? I wracked my brains but just couldn't think.

Kate was watching a programme about making and exhibiting costume dolls (what else?!) on some obscure Sky channel, so rather than disturb her, I rustled up a quick meal for us both in the microwave (it had so many extra features on it that it took me longer to figure out how to use it than it did to cook the food!). As I sat down next to Kate to eat my meal, it suddenly occurred to me how ironic it was that I had had to go through so much trouble and turmoil for the sake of a television aerial that was now well and truly redundant!

As I somewhat distractedly picked at my food with half an eye on the television, still musing over my recent adventures, I suddenly remembered the envelope I had forgotten to post, so I went to the coat rack in the hall and retrieved it from my jacket pocket. It was a brown business-type envelope with an address in Wallasey, and prepaid second-class postage. I opened it (very carefully, in case I should need to reseal it). **CONGRATULA-TIONS!** was the heading on the letter inside. It continued: 'You have been specially selected to attend one of our promotional presentations at a venue near you', and it went on to list the free meal, wine, vouchers etc. we could look forward to if we were to attend the next presentation at the Roxbury Royal Hotel in a month's time. As I further examined this 'sensational offer', it occurred to me that it was one of those ploys to persuade you (against your better judgement, of course), to 'invest' in a timeshare arrangement for an apartment in Corfu. Katie had filled in our details and indicated our intention to attend, and then it gradually began to dawn on me. I recalled how, encouraged by some friends who had entered into a similar arrangement with a different firm, we had taken the plunge ourselves and 'invested' in an 'unbeatable' deal that would 'guarantee' us unlimited holidays for the next 20 years. We'd pored over all the details and examined the small print. It had seemed infallible—nothing could possibly go wrong. But of course, it had. We'd rather rashly sunk all our savings into this venture—and raised a secured loan on our house as well. Everything was going well: we were sent detailed accounts of the progress of the arrangement, invited to a further presentation to display beautiful pictures of the apartments, plus a video showing all the lovely beaches and other attractions in the vicinity. We'd got so excited, and our anticipation had been shared by our two little girls—to the extent that they could take it all in.

Then came the bitter blow. The firm we were dealing with had seriously overstretched themselves financially, and there had also been a rather nasty legal case that had gone against them. Apparently, there'd been a problem with the filtration system at a swimming pool on one of the apartment complexes: dozens of people had gone down with a serious infection which had been traced to some bacteria in the water. As a result of the large amounts of compensation that had had to be paid out, the firm had gone bankrupt. We—and for that matter, scores of other investors—had lost everything: thousands of pounds down the drain. We applied for compensation, of course, but something in the firm's charter (it was based in Mauritius, as we later discovered) allowed us absolutely no comeback. We were shattered. All our dreams had come to naught. We'd picked ourselves up financially in the end (as you have to in such circumstances), and fortunately, due to a moderate legacy from a fairly well-off uncle who'd died, we managed to get our finances back on a relatively even keel. But we struggled, and more or less got over it eventually.

What had happened now, of course, was that the ill-fated envelope had not been posted, and we had not sunk all our cash into the doomed venture. Now this was the result—we'd managed to give ourselves a much better standard of living, ironically through an act of neglect! As I tossed these thoughts around in my stunned brain, I once again experienced that extremely weird sensation of a 'memory', albeit hazy and patchy, forming in my mind, of how we'd been puzzled at the lack of response to our application to join the time-share scheme. We'd put it down to the scheme being oversubscribed, or for some reason our application being considered ineligible. We'd waited a month or two on the off-chance that the delay was due to the complications of processing all the applications, but eventually we'd given it up as a bad job. Sometime later we read, to our astonishment, about the firm's having gone bust, and all its investors losing what turned out to be millions, and we'd thanked the Good Lord that we had not been among them. After that we invested our money in some secure bonds, and were able to draw on the substantial proceeds for many years thereafter.

It took me a long time to get to sleep that night—I lay in bed turning these thoughts over in my mind, amazed at the ability I apparently had to change my own destiny, and that of my family. Indeed, I was able to benefit many others, because I was aware, in that strange memory-forming way, that over the years, Kate and I had used a substantial proportion of our wealth to contribute to various good causes. It was as I was tossing around a number of possible other 'projects' by which I could further enhance our lifestyle that I must have drifted off to sleep.

I didn't do any more time-travelling for a few weeks. Life was busy, I had some important pieces of work at the hospital to wrap up, and family life generally was quite demanding. But one day a couple of months later I was off on my travels. I'd been doing some processing at Parklands, and the case I was working on had been investigated for a cardiac abnormality at the Dunkirk Memorial Hospital, just a little further up the road. There had been a fair amount of correspondence between the cardiac department and my own, and I needed to check out one or two details that hadn't quite been settled. As the Dunkirk was literally just around the corner, I hopped on my bike and was there in a jiffy. I locked up my trusty steed in the bike shed I had used so often during my first 12 years in Roxbury. It was still there, believe it or not—a little more battered and worse for wear, but essentially the same. A wave of nostalgia swept over me as I walked through the doors into the main corridor—I had done this thousands of times before in my twenties and early thirties, and some of the memories came flooding back. Like, for instance, when a water pipe had burst at the top of the corridor, causing a river that ran all the way down, finally flooding Ward 9 at the bottom. Or when, due to an electrical fault, the fire alarms went off simultaneously in all the wards, and there was a massive pile-up in the corridor of all the beds carrying patients too ill to get up. That had been such a farce that it was a darn good job that it *was* a false alarm, otherwise the outcome could have been very serious indeed. However, some good came of it, because the management appointed a task force to investigate emergency evacuation procedures, and they subsequently implemented more logical and workable exit strategies.

Anyway, there I was, strolling down the corridor to the Cardiac Department, which, by chance, was in the very part of the building where my old department had been. I was thus wallowing in nostalgia and mentally reliving scenes and events of well over 30 years ago, when, there before me was my old boss, Dr Emlyn Pritchard! At first I ignored him, thinking that my powers of imagination had been so strong that I'd managed to conjure up in my mind's eye a figure so real that I could almost reach out and touch him. Except that he beat me to it! He extended his right arm, caught me by the collar and literally dragged me into the department.

'Now you jus' look yer', he began in his thick Welsh accent, 'I told you yesterday I won't tolerate lateness, and it's three minutes past nine!'

I checked my watch—a little strange, as I'd left Parklands in the early afternoon, but I was getting used to turning up in the past at whatever time of day I happened to be thinking about, and on this occasion I'd imagined myself arriving at the start of the day.

'Maen ddrwg gen i,' I replied (I felt an apology in his native tongue might smooth things over a bit) 'but there was an accident in Shepherds Way. The road was completely blocked and I had to go round the other way.' This was, of course, a blatant lie, but it sufficed to cool the boss's temper—for now at any rate.

'Well, OK,' he responded, 'but I suggest you set your watch a few minutes fast to allow for the unexpected eventualities that crop up like this.' I cringed inwardly as he went on: 'Now I've got a special job for you today—

it's very important, so you'll need to give it your full attention.'

As he continued, a light began to dawn—although in truth it was more like the most awful darkness and gloom welling up inside me, for I recalled this day almost as if it were yesterday, and the horror of being in the boss's bad books for a very long time. To be marginally at odds with Dr Pritchard was on par with being summoned to the headmaster's office and suffering his severe disapproval; but to be actually in his bad books was like…well, believe me, you just don't want to know! This, I recalled, was the ultimate employee's nightmare: the mother of all horrors.

Emlyn explained: 'We've got the financial auditors coming round this afternoon, see? And we've got to be putting a jolly good case for the extra funding we need to be able to get the extension for the Research Unit.' It had long been the boss's ambition to expand our rather cramped premises to make room for some of his pet projects. He was always full of bright ideas—well, some of them were indeed bright, but the majority were somewhat odd, to say the least. Still, I didn't complain (much)—I had a job that paid moderately well, even though a lot of the work was pretty mundane and repetitive. Sitting at a machine punching holes in tape for hours at a time, for example, was not exactly the epitome of excitement. Still, I'd hoped it would lead to something more rewarding in the not-too-distant future.

Dr P went on to explain (though from my vivid recollection of that fateful day, I could practically have quoted him word for word) that he wanted me to make a count of all the patients we had seen in the five most recent financial years, and also to make a secondary count, calculating the percentage of total patients seen, of those with 'that condition we are investigating'. For some reason, he made it sound like a top secret assignment—whether or not it was a hangover from that wartime slogan 'Walls have ears', I couldn't say, but his innate distrust in any but his closest associates not to divulge the details of his latest 'project' always caused him to play his cards very close to his chest.

I relived in my mind the events of that day: I had spent a good two hours wading through the registers, counting off the patients, and listing those with *that condition*. I then spent a further hour setting out my findings in a neat table, because it was the nature of the boss to make matters infinitely more complicated than necessary, and he had kept interrupting me to get me to add additional details that he thought might further support his case. It was a great pity that these thoughts hadn't all occurred to him at the same time (preferably before I'd started the exercise), as I'd had to keep going back over my work and amending it. And it is my contention that it had been because of all these interruptions that I had failed to notice that one of the registers had been missing. Unfortunately, as it happened, it had in effect been the most important one, because by chance it would have revealed a high concentration of patients with *that condition*, and would have increased the overall percentage significantly.

As usual with all Dr P's assignments, it was completed only just before the deadline, and he had not had time to check my figures before the auditors arrived. They examined my table—and even complimented me on its neatness and clarity—but, after a great deal of deliberation and rumination they came to the reluctant conclusion that the volume of cases passing through the department did not quite fulfil the criteria for awarding the necessary funds. This of course went down like a lead balloon with Dr Emlyn Pritchard, and the atmosphere in the department could be compared pretty closely to that on the day of a severe thunderstorm—the black, overcast mood, the rumblings and grumblings of severe discontent, and the harsh, unpredictable lightning strikes of a vile temper that could be provoked by the slightest matter. But worse was yet to come—the following day it transpired that the funds which could have been ours had been awarded instead to the Radiology Department, considered by Dr Pritchard as our arch enemies. I never fully discovered the reason for the bitter enmity between my boss and Dr Jasper Willoughby, who was the head of Radiology. By rights our two disciplines should have been working hand-in-hand, but some ancient quarrel, long forgotten by all except the two 'duellists', had ruled out any but the most basic, minimal degree of interdepartmental co-operation. Talk about adding insult to injury! This was a severe kick in the teeth to my boss.

But if you thought that was the worst you'd be mistaken, for a week later the missing register had been found—alas, by Dr P himself. He had been reaching for a book off the shelf above a filing cabinet in the secretary's office and had accidentally knocked something (a calendar, I believe) down behind the cabinet. He'd got one of the juniors to help him move it out so that he could retrieve the fallen item…and there it was—the register! It was immediately apparent that it had lain there for some considerable time, for it was covered in dust and cobwebs. I need not record in detail the events of the next minutes, indeed, hours—in fact, I dare not, lest the intense heat of the boss's ire be somehow transmitted to the very pages on which I write this, and something akin to the flames of hell be kindled. In fact, my life was made hell on that account for far longer thereafter than I care to recall. I was soundly berated for not having noticed that a significant chunk of vital information had been missing from my calculations, and of course any attempt to shift the blame (justly, I felt) onto the man himself, on account of his frequent interruptions, was like throwing petrol onto an already fierce conflagration. It is still too painful for me to dwell long on those dreadful events; suffice to say, my name was mud for months, nay, years afterwards, and all hope of the promotion to Senior Technician I'd been counting on were well and truly dashed.

So, here I was—by some cruel twist of fate, pitched back into what was undoubtedly the very worst day of my whole career, or at least, the start of a desperately black phase of it. If there had been one time I should have wished to avoid reliving, this was it! But wait—could it not have been that I had been sent back to this very day for a truly significant purpose? Was not this my golden opportunity to right a terrible wrong, which, after all, had not been my fault? I set about my task with unwonted enthusiasm, and sped through the first two registers with great glee. I even anticipated some of the boss's 'extras', which I knew he would demand as I was in mid-task, and he was in fact quite impressed at my forethought (little did he know it was actually afterthought!). Then came the *coup de grace*—I went to the boss and said, 'Doctor, there seems to be a register missing. See—this one ends in March of one year, but the next starts in December of the next.' He didn't actually compliment me on my powers of observation, but I thought he looked a little impressed. He immediately instigated a search, and of course, I made sure I was the hero who thought to look behind the offending cabinet.

There were smiles all round and, to cut a long story short, I was able to finish my task knowing it was the complete version—and in considerably less time than I'd done originally. This gave the boss the opportunity to peruse the figures—which now presented a much more favourable picture—and prepare his case more persuasively. When the auditors arrived I was able to display my work with great aplomb, and for once it seemed I was totally at one with my usually very demanding, and often rather critical, boss. The exercise was a huge success: the auditors agreed that our investigations constituted a valuable contribution to medical science in general, and to the prestige of the hospital. We would, they assured us, be awarded the grant, and we could expect our research annex to begin being built within the year. So pleased was the boss that he sent two of the girls out to buy cakes, and he produced a bottle of sherry from a cupboard in his room and we had a celebratory party. For once I was Flavour of the Month!

I cycled home on a cloud that evening. Almost imperceptibly making the transition form past to present as I pedalled cheerfully out to Clunmore, I tried to envisage the vast benefits my actions would have brought about. How sweet it had been to rectify a dreadful wrong—both to the department, which had missed out on some much-needed funds, and to myself and my family, who'd had to endure my grief and despondency for months after the event. It had taken a huge toll on my own health, both mentally and physically, and my loved ones too had had to expend a lot of emotional energy in trying to encourage me and help me get back onto an even keel. The amount of despair and hurt that whole affair had caused us was something I would have given big money to erase—and, as it turned out, that was exactly what it had cost me.

Coasting down the short slope to my home, I prepared to greet my darling wife, although as like as not she'd be caught up in a flurry of activity preparing for another Dollybirds convention or something. I didn't mind—I liked it when she was busy, because it meant she was happy, and that made me happy too.

Without paying any attention to the car parked in the driveway, or to any other details, I manoeuvred my bike round to the side gate...but what was this? It was locked, and, with a sickening realization, it dawned on me that the lock was different—and yet horribly familiar! I'd seen it before, of course, after the Coventry fiasco. It was, incidentally, at that brief moment in time that I had one of those bizarre thoughts that sometimes pop up in your mind at the most inappropriate moments. How ironic, I thought, that, after we'd returned *literally* from Coventry, my exasperated wife had chosen to send me there *metaphorically*! I briefly chuckled at the joke. But this was no laughing matter—it was, as a sports commentator had once remarked, *déjà vu* all over again! I backed my bike out of the side entrance, and as I turned, my eyes confirmed the awful suspicion that had welled up within me, for there, in place of our own modest car, was a sparkling Mercedes! Before I had time to beat a hasty retreat the front door was flung open, and out burst the Wing Commander, already purple in the face.

'YOU!' he bellowed, 'What the bloody hell d'you think you're doing here again?' It had been several weeks since our previous explosive meeting, but the Admiral of the Fleet had obviously not forgotten my face.

'I told you before,' he roared, 'Bugger orff! If you're still on my property in five seconds I'll damn well have you horse-whipped!'

All things considered, I felt this was not a suitable time for explanation or negotiation. I leapt on my bike and pedalled frantically away, leaving the Major General still screaming abuse at me and shaking his fists in the air. Some of the neighbours drew aside their curtains to see what the cause of the fracas had been. That there weren't more spectators, I mused, was probably due to their being used to their military neighbour's frequent belli-cose rantings at the poor hapless callers who had made the mistake of darkening his door.

Oh dear, what a catastrophe—seconds earlier I'd been on Cloud Nine, rejoicing at a terrible wrong I'd put right, but somehow it had had an entirely unforeseen effect. As I pedalled disconsolately back into town, once again to doss down on one of the department's beds at the RRI, I tried to reason things out. What could have been the effect of my performance at Dunkirk that day? (It had not really been that actual day, of course, although in my own personal experience it felt like it.) Gradually, and with the aid of a very hazy, half-formed 'memory', I real-ized that, as a result of my new-found favour with the boss, I'd remained in his employ for much longer than had originally been the case. After the funding fiasco, I recalled, Dr P had made my life so miserable that I had looked elsewhere for the promotion I'd been seeking, and my path had eventually led to the position of Senior

Technician at Parklands. Presumably, without this 'negative incentive', I'd changed my destiny in such a way that I'd stayed on at Dunkirk, and thereby missed out on a much better post elsewhere. For all I knew, the 'other me' was still in a dead-end job at Dunkirk, earning far less than I was now.

In fact, that was almost certainly what had happened, because as I looked around the department I could see no evidence that I had ever been there—the technical posters I had designed were missing from the walls, gone were the cheeky cartoons I'd stuck to the cupboard doors in the beverage area, and—my desk! Instead of its usual slightly chaotic covering of papers, books, components of equipment and other debris (I wasn't inherently untidy, I reasoned—it was just that in my exalted position I was far too busy to keep things in order), there was a vast expanse of desktop, on which rested a pile of carefully arranged papers, inscribed in a neat feminine hand. So I had failed to climb the promotional ladder, and as a family we'd had to settle for a far more modest dwelling. I actually tried to home in on my new memory to attempt to discover exactly where it would be, but (probably for the best) it was all too hazy and vague, and the location remained a mystery. So I retired to a hospital bed that night, and began to formulate yet another escape plan. I was still puzzling over it as I drifted off into an uneasy sleep.

I woke with a start next morning, as I heard the sound of a door being unlocked. I glanced at my watch—it was 7:15. Bother, I thought, I'd slept longer than I'd intended: it was a working day and Donald the cleaner had arrived to carry out his daily duties before the staff arrived. He mustn't find me here, I said to myself. Fortunately he had gone into the next room along the corridor, so I gingerly sneaked out and beat a hasty retreat before he had time to catch me. I took a devious route around the hospital's labyrinthine corridors to where I'd left my bike locked up and set off at once towards the Dunkirk Memorial Hospital.

My plan was still only half-formed, and as I drew near to my destination, I was considering at what particular time I ought to make my entry. If I were to march boldly in on a normal working day, the boss would be sure to see me and collar me for some task immediately. Virtually nothing escaped his eagle eye, and I didn't want to be pitched into some other enterprise without any choice in the matter. I knew of course that I couldn't go back to that same fateful day—I would have to pre-empt it by at least one day. Should I go after hours or at a weekend and hope to find some means of entry? (Needless to say, we were not allowed duplicate keys to the department.) No—that would be too risky: I would probably have to break in, and that would set off the alarm, with unimaginable consequences. Then I remembered that Dr Pritchard regularly went over to Berrington on a Wednesday afternoon. There was a small satellite department there, run by a part-timer, Melanie Hodson. I'd often felt sorry for the poor girl, stuck there on her own for three days a week, with no colleagues to keep her company, and only a visit from the boss once a week to do reports. I did meet her once or twice at Regional gatherings, and she seemed a very quiet, diffident little mouse of a girl. I'd tried to engage her in conversation, but she wasn't at all forthcoming. Shame, I'd thought—she was not unattractive in the physical sense, but personality-wise she was about as dynamic as a wet dishrag.

Anyway, as I approached the bike shed, I 'thought my way' back to the Wednesday afternoon of the week preceding the one I'd already visited. However, I was deeply conscious of the fact that I was now faced with a difficult moral dilemma. I naturally wanted to reverse the 'course of history' I had previously set in motion: although I realized it would once again cause my family and myself much mental anguish, it seemed the only way to restore my present situation to what it should have been. But, I reasoned, by doing that I would be depriving my former department of the funds to open up a prestigious new research annex, and I would be depriving Dr Pritchard of a long-held ambition. Should I sacrifice that for my own ends, or should I set aside my own moderately rosy future for the good of medical research? As I wrestled with these worrying thoughts, it dawned on me that Dr P and I were not the only parties involved in the situation: there was also Dr Willoughby, whose plans for the extension of the Radiology Department were also worth considering. It didn't take me long to weigh up the relative merits of the two schemes: although I felt a certain loyalty to my own boss, despite his often cranky and cantankerous ways, I also had a high regard for Dr Willoughby—I had witnessed a number of his learned presentations at interdisciplinary meetings, and I had been quite impressed with the scope and quality of his work. I pressed on with my plan.

As I entered the department I began to wonder how I could retrieve the register from behind the filing cabinet without drawing undue attention to myself. Passing the office, I glanced in and saw Pauline the secretary sitting at her desk. She acknowledged my arrival and carried on typing. (She had been trained to monitor the entry and exit of everyone passing her door.) Fortunately none of the other staff were around—it was still lunchtime, and only Pauline was there to keep an eye on things. She would go to lunch when the others were back. As I was still considering my next move, I was relieved to hear Pauline call out: 'Keep an ear out for the phone, will you? I need to pop into the toilet.'

'OK,' I called back, and listened for the receding tap-tap-tap of her high-heeled shoes and the sound of the toilet door closing. This was now my moment—I shot into the office, heaved out the cabinet and, as I'd expected, found the register there, thick with dust and cobwebs. I picked it up, hastily shoved the cabinet back into place and dropped the register into a plastic carrier bag that lay conveniently behind the door. At this point I was faced with another dilemma, albeit a minor one: now that I'd got the offending article, what should I actually do with the wretched thing? My first instinct was to leg it out of there, along with my prize. But then, I thought, it wouldn't be right to take it away altogether. I needed to find a place where it would eventually be found, but not for a long time. I was frantically looking round the department for suitable hiding places, when suddenly I hit upon the perfect one—of course: the boss's desk! He was such an untidy bloke that his desk was piled high with books, papers, aged and yellowing journals, not forgetting a plethora of bizarre nicknacks he'd brought back from his travels around the world. If he were look-ing for, say, a pen, he'd spread both his hands out and press them repeatedly down on the current layer of papers on the desk and feel around for an object under-neath. However, there were layers and layers, not unlike the strata of a sedimentary rock formation. I knew that if

I lifted the whole lot up from the bottom and slid the book underneath, there would be no chance of finding it within the next decade. So that's what I did: after brushing the dust and grot off the book into a bin with some paper towels. I buried it under all the boss's junk and nipped out of the 'hallowed room' before anyone could come onto the scene and catch me red-handed.

I waited till the secretary had returned to her post, then made some excuse to leave the department. 'Uh, there's a patient I have to check on over in the ward,' I told her, as I hastened past the office. As I made my escape, it did occur to me that, presumably, my 'old' self (or rather, I suppose, my 'young' self) would be coming in from lunch at any moment, and might well be asked by Pauline how this mythical patient had been. I decided I'd just have to leave the matter to fate—I felt sure my other persona would manage to come up with some suitable explanation.

It was not without some feelings of regret and indeed a hint of gloom that I pedalled my way wearily back to my present-day home. After all, I'd effectively just let myself in for two or three years of misery in a job I wouldn't enjoy, and this was to have a detrimental effect on my family life. Still, I reasoned, it had to be done—as I recalled those dark years in my career, I knew that I would come through them all right, and that my family would stand by me, and indeed, we would all become the stronger for it. And that, as it turned out, is what happened—to my intense relief, as I glided round the bend and down into our little close, there was *our* car—not some posh Mercedes (nice as it would have been to have one), but a welcome sign that all was back to normal.

As I let myself in, there was the comforting smell of something tasty cooking in the oven, and I found Kate sitting in the living room poring over some papers relating to Dollybirds (an agenda for the next meeting, or minutes of the last, perhaps). She scarcely noticed my presence at first, then, without so much as a glance in my direction, she muttered, somewhat distractedly, 'Had a nice day, dear?'

For her it had been a mere eight or nine hours since she had last seen me, but for me it had seemed half a lifetime, filled with despair and anguish, opportunity and disappointment, surprise, shock, scheming, satisfaction, relief and elation, plus a few other emotions thrown in for good measure! By way of reply, I managed, 'Oh, you know, love—pretty much as usual!'

After our meal and a while relaxing in front of some rather banal film on the telly, I said to Kate (who was now perusing a mail order catalogue), I think I'll turn in, love—I'm feeling a bit tired.'

'OK,' she said, I'll be up in a bit.'

I knew it would be quite a long 'bit'—she looked pretty settled in her own little world. So I lay in bed for a fair while, pondering over yet another weird adventure. My thoughts turned to the words of our pastor in last Sunday's sermon. He'd quoted those words in Romans chapter 8, verse 28: 'For we know that in all things God works for the good of those who love him, who are called according to his purpose.' He'd gone on to illustrate it with the story of Joseph (you know—the one with the Amazing Technicolor Dreamcoat[1]). His brothers had

---

1. Andrew Lloyd Webber and Tim Rice. (www.reallyuseful. com)

spitefully sold him as a slave to some traders going to Egypt, but he ended up as Pharaoh's right-hand man, and proved to be the salvation of millions of people— including his own brothers. 'You meant it for evil,' he later told them, 'but God meant it for good.'[2]

How right our pastor was—he'd said that we can't always expect life to be a bed of roses: in an imperfect world we have to expect troubles at times, but often, if tackled in the right spirit, they can prove the gateway to greater blessing. I suppose it's like that RAF motto: 'Per ardua ad astra'—through hardships to the stars.

So, as I drifted into a satisfied sleep, I told myself firmly that I had nothing to fear from the storms of life that inevitably come upon us. They're certainly not fun, but to use that old cliché, 'they're all part of life's rich tapestry'. On the whole they're unavoidable—except when, through our own silly mistakes we bring them on ourselves, as I was soon to find out. Oh, and incidentally, the next time I went back to work at the RRI, there was much consternation about some vagrant who had somehow got into the department and spent the night on one of the beds. Oddly, though, there'd been no dirty marks or lingering smell, and no sign of a break-in! We were all admonished to make absolutely certain that we locked every door and shut every window at the end of each day's work!

---

2. Genesis 50:20

CHAPTER 7

Getting in on the act

Not long after that, curiosity got the better of me again—at least, that's what I told myself, because more than likely I had succumbed to a 'senior moment' on leaving Parklands after another processing session and turned into Upper Meadow Close while on 'autopilot' as it were, my mind being elsewhere, trying to solve some logistical problem, or quite possibly trying to remember a bizarre tongue-twister in Amharic or some other outlandish language.

As I pedalled along the tree-lined road the luscious green leaves of the plane trees, the glint of the sun on brass and silver door fittings, and the once-familiar sounds and smells of that street evoked strong memories that took me back—in more ways than one—to the time when I had lived there, and once again I was acting out my daily after-work routine of that era. Little did I realize that I would shortly be acting in quite a different way.

Pushing my bike through the carport to the back garden, I was delighted to see my two little daughters playing in the back garden—one toddling unsteadily, the other rushing around full of energy. When they saw me they trotted and hurtled respectively towards me with excited cries of 'Dadeee! Dadeee!' as if they hadn't seen me for weeks. I marvelled at their enthusiastic welcome, and at the fact that this had once been the norm. But whereas they'd seen their daddy only a few hours before, I hadn't seen these two adorable little mites for many years in the natural way.

Katie heard the cries of the welcome committee and emerged from the back door. 'Ah good, you're home, dear,' she said with a smile. 'I've got dinner on the go, and Barbara's coming to baby-sit, so we shouldn't be late.'

'Shouldn't be late? Late for what?' I thought. That was the trouble with coming back into the past—you never knew what situation you'd be landing into. A bit like a blindfolded parachutist, you could be coming down in green pastures or in deep waters. Katie and I were obviously going out somewhere, but what for? A pleasant meal, just the two of us in some romantic bistro? Probably not—perhaps we were going to see a film, or watch a play. My last guess was almost spot on—apart from one small detail.

'Let's see,' I mumbled, fishing for clues, 'what time do we have to be there?'

Fortunately Katie was used to my often vague, slightly forgetful manner, and she sweetly replied (albeit with a somewhat puzzled look): 'About half-past six, love—same as the other nights. Curtain up is at seven-thirty, but you'll have wardrobe and makeup first.'

A cold shiver of realization went down my back. I *was* going to the theatre—not to watch, however, but to *act*! I then recalled that for several years I'd been a member of The Hardington Players, the local amateur dramatics society. I'd always enjoyed acting, ever since, as a child, I'd been involved in some of the sketches my mum had written for the Women's Institute concerts that took place once or twice a year in my home village. She was a 'dab hand', to use one of her favourite expressions, at coming up with playlets based on scenarios remarkably similar to events that had recently been the talk of the village. She had that enviable and uncanny knack of being able to portray characters closely resembling well-known local figures in such a way that to most of the audience it was patently obvious who were the subjects of the caricatures, yet without actually saying so—even to the extent that the 'victims' themselves could laugh at the pomposity, idiocy or peculiar mannerisms of the characters on stage without even realizing they were actually laughing at themselves.

For a moment my mind went back to various school plays in which I had acted, and I experienced a brief sense of satisfaction as I thought how well I had carried off some difficult roles in the past. But that feeling rapidly turned to one of horror as I contemplated the prospect before me: what on earth was the production I was to appear in tonight? Was it a musical? A comedy? A tragedy? Yes, I thought, it really *would* be a tragedy for me, being plunged straight into something I was totally unprepared for.

I was desperate for clues. I couldn't ask Katie outright—she'd think I'd totally lost my marbles (she might well be right, I thought). Then it occurred to me: yes, the kitchen notice-board: there was bound to be a flyer or programme there, to tell me what the production was. I made my way into the house and nonchalantly scanned the family notice-board. The usual things—details of toddler group and nursery events, notices about jumble sales, the weekly events leaflet from church and four or five strip cartoons from the daily paper. There were even my monthly astronomy notes from The Times, which a neighbour regularly passed on to me. I began to think my luck was out, but then I noticed, partly obscured by a bus timetable and a list of useful tradesmen's phone numbers, a glossy advert for The Hardington Players' production of... I brushed the bus timetable aside to reveal the title... Oh no! 'The Architect's Dilemma'.

Horrors! Of all the dire plays that I have ever had the misfortune to be involved with, that was the dreariest, the most ghastly, boring, banal and just plain awful load of tripe ever to be written. The Players had had a very successful run of lighthearted plays that had gone down really well with the local audiences, and the chairman of our little company had made the bold (or with hindsight, foolish) decision that while we were on a high, we should try something different for a change. Different? No kidding! 'The Architect's Dilemma' was the product of that most un-memorable playwright, Oscar Partington, a dour Northerner whose works could well have accounted for the familiar, if largely inaccurate, expression, 'Ee, lad, it's grim Oop North!' For me this play was the one most memorable for its awfulness and the one I most wished to forget.

It had been The Players' custom to put on their performances midweek—Tuesday, Wednesday and Thursday nights—ostensibly to provide local entertainment on the quieter nights of the week, but realistically because there was no way we could compete with the greater attractions on offer at weekends in the city centre. We used the modest-sized but well-equipped theatre in the local high school, whose services were provided for a nominal fee, partly because it provided good experience for some of the students who were undertaking drama studies, as they helped with the makeup, wardrobe, lighting, scenery and so on.

I recalled with a sense of shame how badly our production had gone. My role was that of the architect's assistant—a fairly major part, in fact. And although I had delivered my words and actions superbly (I had thought), and my fellow actors had, largely, performed equally well, the plain fact is that when your working materials are rubbish, the end product will also be rubbish—and that is certainly what the audiences thought of it.

The first night's performance had been attended largely by most of the school's teaching staff, who, along with what might be termed the more erudite members of local society, had made at least a pretence of enjoying the production, feigning appreciation of the deep meaning of the events and situations portrayed. But we could all sense very clearly by the quiet, polite applause and the furtive whisperings of the swiftly departing audience, that our best efforts had failed to impress, to put it politely.

Night two was attended by a modest number of local residents—so modest, in fact, that the auditorium was less than half full. By the end of the performance it was only quarter full, the rest having made their escape from purgatory during the interval. The half-hearted applause lasted all of about eight seconds, and it seemed to take even less time for the theatre to be cleared completely. The local pubs did a good trade that night, as the bewildered, disillusioned theatregoers sought to extract a modicum of cheer from an otherwise pretty ghastly evening.

The final night was the worst of all. The organizers had done their utmost during the preceding day to publicize the play, getting local shops to display 'Last Night' posters, and handing out vouchers to people on the street, valid for half-price admission. One of the older actors, who didn't have a day job, even dressed up as a town crier and paraded the local shopping precinct, hollering his invitations, until he was moved on by a copper on the beat, after several shopkeepers complained he was causing a nuisance.

At least the theatre was full that night—but a significant proportion of the eager audience consisted of the local rabble, whose main purpose in life seemed to be to cause chaos and disruption wherever they went. That night was no exception. Within five minutes of the start (which constituted such a mind-numbingly boring dialogue between the architect and his assistant that it was a wonder anyone was left in their seats), the boos, whistles and catcalls were well under way. And thus it continued right throughout the first two acts. Unfortunately the actor who played the title role had a speech impediment, and couldn't pronounce his R's properly. Equally unfortunately his assistant (played by yours truly) was called Frederick, and in a memorable early line where Tarquin the architect praises his colleague, the actor (whose name I withhold to spare his embarrassment), declares: 'Fwedewick, my good fwiend, you are twuly bwilliant—you are a vewitable light fwom Pawadise!' at this point someone in the audience called out something that suggested the actor himself was from a different spiritual realm. From then on it was all downhill— even though we had felt things couldn't possibly get any worse.

At the interval the director decided to cut our losses by omitting Act 3 completely and going straight into the final act.' They're hardly likely to realize,' he reasoned, and no doubt he was right. This did, however, anger some of the actors, who claimed that their finest lines (and for some their only ones) were in Act 3, but their protests were brushed aside. The decision succeeded in reducing the boos, catcalls and missiles launched at the stage from an hour to thirty minutes, but that was little consolation. The whole production was an absolute fiasco, and the critics in the local paper and on BBC Radio Roxbury were entirely unforgiving in their derision. The reputation of the Hardington players was well and truly blackened forever: several of its members resigned, and attempts at recruiting new blood failed miserably. The company was forced to disband without any further productions being staged.

As I contemplated the appalling situation I had landed myself in, it suddenly occurred to me that, although I had once learnt the script off by heart, I had long since forgotten (or rather, deliberately chosen to forget) my lines. My appearance on stage this evening was destined, it seemed, to become even more of a disaster than it had been the first time around. How could I escape this ordeal? I decided to feign illness.

'Darling,' I groaned, 'I'm feeling really, really sick—I don't think I'm going to be able to go tonight.'

'Oh, don't be silly,' replied my practical (and, I thought, unsympathetic) wife, 'it's just a bit of stage fright, that's all. Have a bite to eat, to settle your stomach.'

'It's no good,' I protested, 'I feel really dreadful. They'll just have to use my understudy.'

'There isn't one, remember? Jim Protheroe had to drop out when his mother had a bad fall, and he had to go back to Cardiff to look after her. Richard was *his* understudy too, so he can't play your part as well, because you both appear in the same scene together. Come on, love, you'll be all right.'

It was clear my doom was writ. I couldn't escape. Tentatively I asked, 'Where did I put my lines?'

'Oh darling, you don't need those—you've been word-perfect these last two nights.'

'Um...er...' I mumbled, 'well, it wasn't really *my* lines I was worried about—I thought...er...Mike Elsdon fluffed one of his lines and nearly miscued me.' I managed to pluck from my uncertain memory the name of a mate I was pretty sure had been a fellow-actor, though I guessed from Katie's puzzled look that I may not have hit the nail quite on the head. Fortunately she didn't question it, but answered my original question.

'I suppose they're in the usual place—your desk in the spare bedroom.'

'Yes, of course—that's where they'll be. I just want to check that bit.' Then I added: 'Uh... you go ahead and start your meal without me. I'm going to the bath-room—my tummy's still playing up a bit.'

I climbed the stairs and went straight to the aforesaid desk. To my joy, there was the script in the top drawer, with my lines highlighted. I grabbed it and shut myself in the bathroom. Sitting on the toilet seat, I leafed through the seemingly endless pages. Waves of horror flooded over me in realization of both the amount of lines I was supposed to know and the supreme awfulness of the material. Coming back to it after so many years seemed to reinforce my pained memory of how dreadful the whole 'work' had been. However we had agreed to perform anything by Oscar Partington, let alone this load of codswallop, I simply cannot imagine. I vaguely recalled numerous evenings of poring over the script to learn my part, and the many rehearsals we all had to attend. I must have known these words really well, but to try to re-learn them now in a mere half-hour, if that, was a hopeless task.

For some reason my mind flipped back to the time when I was about eight or nine, and I was taking part in one of those Women's Institute variety concerts back home in Devon. Villagers young and old, from all walks of life and degrees of status were invited, coaxed, and virtually press-ganged into taking part. Those who could sing or play instruments provided musical items, and those who couldn't produced decidedly un-musical items. There were sketches and playlets, some serious and some quite comical, as well as recitations as diverse as Penelope Lambert-Smythe delivering a Shakespeare sonnet in a very affected, pseudo-highbrow manner, and six-year-old Gillian Williams stumbling her way through 'January brings the snow, makes our feet and fingers glow...'[1]

On one such occasion my turn involved being dressed as the French singer Maurice Chevalier. Equipped with a cane, and a straw hat perched jauntily on my head, my task was to sing one of his well-loved numbers, 'Louise'[2]. With my mum at the piano, I sauntered onto the stage, and at the given signal launched

---

1. A Calendar, by Sara Coleridge (1802 – 1852).
2. Louise, by Richard A. Whiting, 1929, from the Paramount motion picture 'Innocents of Paris'.

into the song in my best pseudo-French accent: 'Ev'ry leetle breeze seems to wheesper Lou-eez; Birds in ze treeez seen to tweeter Lou-eez; Can eet be true, some-one like you could love me, love me?' I started well, and was continuing confidently, when, halfway through the second verse, I felt a stab of horror—I couldn't remember what came next! I'd learnt those words so well, and had sung them two or three dozen times, but at the vital moment my mind went blank! What was I to do? Should I stop, look embarrassed and ask my mum for a prompt? No doubt if I had the largely tolerant and sympathetic audience would have smiled sweetly and muttered something like, 'Aw, bless 'im, the little love,' while a significant minority would snigger audibly.

What happened next was little short of a miracle. Without a pause I carried on singing—I just opened and closed my mouth, exhaled my breath rhythmically and modulated my voice—and the words just seemed to flow! It was as if for a few seconds I was on automatic pilot: I was mentally unaware of the words I was pro-ducing, but from somewhere deep in my subconscious what I had learnt issued forth. I picked up again on the next verse and completed the song apparently flaw-lessly, to a vigorous applause, and to my own sincere re-lief. I was at a loss to explain this phenomenon, unless by some merciful divine intervention I was being spared the embarrassment of failure before so many spectators at such a tender age.[3]

---

3. This anecdote is true! It really happened to the author in the 1950s. Only the county name has been changed (it was in Somerset).

As I relived that event, I considered my current predicament and prayed fervently that the thespian muse would not desert me this night. Perhaps by some even greater miracle I might manage to prevent a certain disaster developing into a complete and utter fiasco. I began to feel strangely calm, although not without a few butterflies in the tummy, as though to validate my excuse of feeling unwell. At that moment I heard a voice calling up the stairs.

'You all right, love? You've been in there a long time.'

I flushed the toilet to continue my pretence. 'Just coming, dear!' I washed by hands, as they were genuinely rather sweaty.

Going down to the dining room, I declared myself to be feeling much improved and tucked into a delicious beef casserole with dumplings. There was no point worrying about what might happen tonight, I reasoned. Things could scarcely go worse than they had done on the original occasion. I may as well fortify myself with good food and drink, and press on boldly.

The children were duly led off by Katie to brush their teeth and dress for bed. I followed to read them a story and say a short bedtime prayer. Barbara the babysitter arrived at that moment, popped her head round the door and called, 'Hiya, girls! I'll be downstairs if you need me.' The girls obviously knew her well and demanded a hug and a kiss each. I vaguely recognised the lady and tossed a nonchalant greeting in her direction as though I was used to seeing her quite often.

Katie drove us to the High School, and I was gripped by a curious mixture of trepidation and excitement as we entered the building—as though I was embarking on a kind of unreal adventure. I was greeted by Ron the director: 'Hello, Billy!' I felt his enthusiasm was somewhat forced. 'It's going to go a lot better tonight—I can feel it in my bones!'

'I certainly hope so,' I responded, but thinking, 'Oh no it won't!'

'OK, I won't hold you up, you'd better get your costume on. Wardrobe's left it in your dressing room— you know which one that is, don't you?'

No, I thought; 'Oh yes!' I said.

Katie went off to help the students who were doing the makeup. I set off in the direction very helpfully indicated by a sign that read DRESSING ROOMS. This led to a corridor with five or six doors on each side, labelled with numbers. Not having a clue which was supposed to be mine, I took the logical step of starting with No. 1. Tentatively I turned the handle and opened the door. At first the room appeared to be empty, but as I looked round I came face to face with a young actress. She possessed a beautiful, angelic face with piercing blue eyes, framed by wavy, shoulder-length blonde hair. But she was completely naked from the waist up!

'Oh, Mr Draper,' she giggled, 'you *are* a saucy one!'

Hugely embarrassed, I blurted out: 'I...I...I'm so sorry.... I seem to have the wrong room.'

Showing no sign whatever of bashfulness, in fact almost flaunting her charms with relish, she approached me, moving round to the direction in which I had averted my eyes. 'That's *quite* all right, she purred, 'I don't mind a bit! Yours is the room opposite, by the way.'

As she said this she pointed with one hand but curled the other around my arm. At this point many other men would have lingered awhile. However, my face had turned bright red and felt like a furnace as I tore myself hastily from her grasp. 'Yes. Um…of course. Thank you. Very sorry…. Er…got to go,' by which time I was out of the door and bursting through the one opposite.

'Phew!' I gasped, adding to myself, 'That was some encounter! …Mind you, she *was* pretty!'

I donned my costume and headed back to where I had seen Katie go. I found the makeup room and one of the young ladies beckoned me to a chair in front of a wall of mirrors and lights. I was more than a little disconcerted to find that that the person sitting next to me, being attended by my own wife, was none other than the fair damsel I had just met in a state of semi-déshabillé. Nadia, as I discovered her name to be, gave me a huge smile; I returned it with a polite nod of the head. I tried hard to ignore her, but my eyes kept straying to her reflection in the mirror, whereupon she would grin and wink at me. She even made one or two flirty comments, and I noticed the frowns they evoked on the face of my beloved.

Relieved that Nadia's makeup session was outlasting mine, I quickly left the room and followed signs to the backstage area. I had at least remembered which side I should wait for my entrance in Act 1. However, I had not remembered how restricted and cluttered the back-stage area was, and still partly blinded by the bright lights of the makeup room, I stumbled over some ca-bles. As I fell, I grabbed hold of a wooden strut, which came away in my hand. Cursing under my breath and muttering that Health and Safety would not have al-lowed this mess in my own century, I picked myself up and surveyed the damage. The strut had been attached to the back of the set, and to a wooden base. I tried to push the nails back into the holes from which they had been wrenched, but with little success, so I left it. Examining the cables, I noticed I had dislodged three plugs from their in-line sockets, so I replaced them as I thought they should go.

It was a nervous few minutes standing in the wings, listening to the hubbub of the waiting audience, which was punctuated at frequent intervals by some raucous cackle or guffaw from the more 'common' members of the theatregoing fraternity. Eventually I could hear a ripple of excitement corresponding to Ron's arrival on the apron stage to make the customary opening announcements. The hubbub died down somewhat, but the reduction in volume served only to accentuate the periodic heckling of those whose presence was not primarily aimed at an appreciation of the performing arts.

The curtain rose to reveal the architect bent over a desk in a squalid, dimly lit room, wielding a pencil and a setsquare. For a moment there was silence from the audience. I was carefully timing my entrance. I had been instructed to wait for a reasonable length of time so as to achieve a more dramatic effect, as the architect toiled away at his craft. I would have preferred an earlier entrance, but the director deliberately held me up. At the point when a voice from the audience hollered: 'Geddon wiv it, then!' I decided to ignore the director and step forth.

I delivered my opening line: 'Greetings, my dear Tarquin. I perceive you are labouring long.'

The voice called out: 'Flippin' obvious, innit?'

The craftsman unbent himself and declared, 'Indeed, I pway you to excuse my pweoccupation; I am twying to wesolve a difficult pwactical pwoblem.'

'I've lost me false teeth!' called out the wit in the audience.

'Then allow me to assist; it often helps to apply a fresh mind to a situation,' I continued.

There followed a few moments where the architect and I both pored over the plans and conducted an animated but indistinct exchange, with much pointing and shifting of instruments, until I, the ever-resourceful assistant declared, with an air of triumph: 'There! I think you will find that's your problem solved!'

This evoked the memorable quote:

'Fwedewick, my good fwiend, you are twuly bwilliant—you are a vewitable light fwom Pawadise!'

At this point the worthy playwright had directed that the architect's declaration should be dramatically emphasized by a burst of light as the stage lighting came on full. Such had been the case on the two previous nights, but this time, no doubt aided by my incorrect reconnection of the cables I had tripped over, there was a vivid blue flash and the stage was plunged into deep darkness. A pungent smell of burning plastic proceeded to envelop actors and audience alike, by which time the theatre had erupted into uncontrollable fits of laughter.

A couple of stagehands appeared, holding large torches, which they trained on the two of us from raised vantage points at each end of the apron stage. Although in themselves quite powerful, their illumination was relatively weak in that setting. In view of the circumstances there seemed little point in trying to maintain the supposedly serious nature of the play—the atmosphere just wasn't right. I therefore attempted to inject a little humour into the situation, by turning to the audience and saying: 'This brings a whole new meaning to the term "light entertainment"!'

This produced the response I had hoped for—a roar of laughter—so I decided to ham it up a bit more, and with a few more quips I succeeded in maintaining the air of jocularity. Fortunately, my fellow actor in the title role caught on to what I was doing and quickly joined in with some of his own wit, which, I don't mind admitting, was considerably sharper and more copious than my own, and he deliberately exaggerated his speech defect with even more comical effect.

We were aided immensely by an unforeseen incident that occurred at the close of Act 1. Due to the almost complete blackout, there was a good deal of stumbling about backstage, and frequent bumps, crashes and muttered oaths could be heard coming from behind the set. We had reached the decisive moment where the architect, whom the inspired Mr Oscar Partington had portrayed as a somewhat tortured, self-doubting soul, turns in mental anguish towards his trusted and supportive assistant and wails: 'Ah me! I am doomed to diminish into obscuwity, for my best designs are of no account, and my stwuctures insignificant!' At this dramatic juncture my encouraging response was: 'Fear not, my dear Tarquin, for you shall have a noble and lasting reputation—as lasting as these splendid, solid buildings you have erected in this city. This very house itself shall stand for many a century as a memorial to your honour and expertise!'

As it happened, the juncture was even more dramatic than anyone could have foreseen, because another unfortunate soul tripped over one of the supporting struts holding up the scenery, and the whole rear panel collapsed forward onto the stage. By some miracle of positioning, the architect and I were standing in the very spot where the window of the 'solid' house fell. It was the only flimsy part of the set, made of a fine net curtain material, with rectangles painted on it to look like small panes. As we were facing the audience, we didn't see it coming, and even the gasps of the onlookers failed to alert us to the descending structure. The thin material broke easily as it hit our heads, and as the set collapsed about us, we were left standing amid the wreckage—still illuminated by the noble stagehands, who had valiantly remained at their posts. However, when we noticed the side walls of the set beginning to teeter unsteadily, we took the prudent step of running for dear life—to the tumultuous applause and cheers of the highly appreciative audience.

As several more stagehands rushed on and hastily began to shore up the rickety scenery, the director appeared and announced that the interval would take place now, and that complimentary drinks would be served in the lounge. The auditorium of course emptied very effectively, and in the time it took for the audience to partake of their tipples and filter back into their seats, the electricians had succeeded in locating the anomalous circuitry, reset the fuses and got the lighting back under control. A new set had been due to be lowered into place for Act 2 in any case, in front of the supposedly more permanent original one, so the fallen panel was simply removed. It should have been left for Act 4, but Ron the director said it wouldn't really matter.

The extended interval enabled Ron to gather all of us thespians together for an impromptu conference, to decide how best to play the remaining three acts. He had at last realized that the drama as it had originally been conceived was a total disaster, and we should achieve far greater audience satisfaction by continuing as things had gone so far, albeit unintentionally, that is, as a comedy. He made a few suggestions with regard to certain scenes, but advised us mainly to 'play it by ear and improvise: I'm sure you've all got good acting ability in you—just let it come out, and do what comes naturally!' Then he added: 'And *enjoy* yourselves!'

Enjoy ourselves we certainly did. Whereas Act 1 had been mainly a dialogue between the architect and myself, each of the remaining acts involved several players at a time, and we all chipped in with our own jocular contributions. There followed a string of puns, double entendres, risqué remarks, deliberately ironic comments and hoary old chestnuts that could well have come from the cheapest Christmas crackers or the raciest music hall performances. At one point the playwright has the architect looking distractedly round for some blueprints. 'Oh dearie me,' he mutters; 'now where on earth did I put that thing?' As his faithful assistant, I am supposed to respond helpfully by saying, 'It's just there behind you sir—on the table.' Instead, I called out in an exaggerated manner: 'It's be-HIND you!' motioning with my hands to the audience to encourage a response. They reacted admirably, chorusing: 'OH NO IT ISN'T!' 'OH YES IT IS!' I replied, and so on.

In Act 3 I came face to face with Nadia again (thankfully, fully costumed this time). On this occasion her line to me was one of appreciation for the extent to which the architect's work had been very largely influenced by myself. I should, she reasoned, be worthy of at least as much honour as he for the wonderful buildings that had resulted from what were supposedly his designs, since I had done much of the work for him. In reply I was supposed to say, 'I confess there is much in what you say, for I have been responsible for some splendid edifices.' However, I had always found that last word difficult to get my tongue round, and usually stumbled over it. On this occasion I decided to replace it with a synonym, but I did so without full consideration of the particular word I chose. My claim that I had 'been responsible for some splendid erections' just about brought the house down, and the fair Nadia played up to it wonderfully well—in fact, rather *too* well for some people's liking—mainly Katie's.

Anyway, the play proceeded to an excellent conclusion, due very largely to some brilliant ad-libbing by the rest of the cast, particularly when in one of the typically dry and boring lines a client of the architect's is commenting on the excellence of workmanship as his future residence is in its very early stages of building. As he peers into an imaginary trench to examine the footings, he comments, 'My word—what admirable foundations!' at this, one of the onlookers, in the form of the delectable Nadia, saucily lifted her skirt to reveal her foundation garment—and a pair of very shapely legs besides. This evoked a chorus of wolf whistles from a very appreciative audience, but more was to come from the remarkable Nadia. The script required the architect to reply: 'I am so glad to hear you say that, for it is oft what is hidden from view that is of greatest importance, yet for few thereby is their interest aroused.' This gem of wisdom he delivered, pronouncing the last word 'awoused', of course. But before the client could make his response, a sultry female voice declared: '*I'm* aroused!'

The final few lines were completely lost in an eruption of cheers, laughter, applause and any other expression of appreciation you care to mention. At curtain call each actor received an extravagant reception, but the longest and most tumultuous was saved, naturally, for Nadia. We returned to our dressing rooms on a wave of euphoria, and soon after I had flopped into a chair in mine, filled with a curious mixture of relief and exhaustion, along with exhilaration and thankfulness that the performance had surpassed my wildest dreams, I was jerked out of my dazed but happy state by a knock at the door. It opened as I was still rising from the chair, and there once again was Nadia. She greeted me with open arms—literally—and gave me a huge hug. It was quite a long one, as I felt powerless (or maybe unwilling) to escape from her firm grip.

'Thank you *so* much, Mr Draper,' she said, 'I've never enjoyed myself so much!' I wondered what I in particular had contributed to this lady's enjoyment, but as she was kissing me warmly on both cheeks it seemed neither opportune nor relevant to ask questions.

Back in my normal clothes, and with most of my makeup removed, I rejoined Katie and we walked to the car and I let her drive home. I was experiencing what one might well call a case of post-dramatic shock syndrome: so stunned that I was virtually speechless. Katie, however, was affected in the other extreme, and even if I had wanted to speak, I doubt if I could have got a word in edgeways. 'You know, Billy,' she told me, 'you absolutely saved the day! I don't know what streak of brilliance prompted you to turn that verbal dirge of a play into a comedy, but it worked a treat! After the debacle of the previous two nights I *really* thought we were all on a hiding to nothing. I actually could have died when that Burntwood Estate rabble turned up—why, they're absolutely guaranteed to wreck anything, and they seemed intent on demolishing the performance tonight. Mind you, talking of demolition, I had to laugh! The way that set collapsed, leaving you two standing in the middle of it, couldn't have worked better if you'd rehearsed it a hundred times! And how the lights....

'...Wake up, dear, we're home.'

I had succumbed to an exhaustion-induced slumber while Katie had been prattling on. She almost had to heave me up the stairs to the bedroom. Not bothering to brush my teeth, I half-undressed and slumped into bed, lulled quickly to sleep by the animated but distant chatter of Katie and Barbara as the latter was regaled with a verbal re-run of the performance, doubtless in fine detail.

Although I slept like a rock, when I woke next morning my muscles still felt tense after all the physical and emotional exertion of the previous evening. I climbed out of bed, and after a refreshing shower, dressed, took a freshly made cup of tea to Katie and told her I felt like a walk in the fresh air, to wind down a bit. Although our newspapers were delivered, it was too early for the paper boys and girls to have begun their rounds, so I made my way to the newsagent's to collect our papers in person.

'Looks like you did a good job last night, then, Billy!' Mr Edwards the newsagent commented, in a manner uncommonly cheerful for such an early hour of the morning.

It being a Friday, the Roxbury Echo was on sale, and as I looked at the copy handed to me, I was amazed to see a picture on the front page of myself and all my fellow actors under the headline: "Hardington Players' surprise success". Being directed to a review on page 8, I hastily unfolded the unwieldy pages and scanned the paragraphs of glowing adulation as I walked along, apologizing to a lamppost that I blundered half-blindly into.

"Reports of the first two nights of the Hardington Players' latest production being excruciatingly boring and greeted by a barrage of catcalls were decisively refuted by last night's performance of Oscar Partington's little-known drama 'The Architect's Dilemma'. Whatever the tenor of the previous evenings' offerings may have been, last night's audience were treated to a brilliant reworking of what is generally held to be such a dense and impenetrable work that most drama companies touch it at their peril.

"It is not known who exactly was responsible for the ingenious adaptation of the play into a work of comedy—indeed at times a farce—but it was carried off with such spontaneity that the overall effect was a degree of freshness seldom found in amateur dramatics. Although the playwright's style of sentence sounds decidedly quaint and pompous, the lines were delivered in such a way as to accentuate their comical nature, and the actors' delivery was exemplary in their ability to bring out nuances of meaning that were surely quite unintended by Partington.

"It is perhaps unfair to single out any one individual for particular praise—from the architect himself, and his witty assistant, right down to the roadsweeper who uttered only a few incoherent grunts, all were marvellous. But I do feel it appropriate to make special mention of the perky young actress Miss Nadia Melgrove, whose contribution was notable for its charm and humour."

And so the article continued, three columns of unqualified praise from 'Our Dramatic Arts Reporter,

Calvin Shawe'. I couldn't help nourishing a feeling of intense pride that I had been the one (albeit not entirely by design) who had initiated the turnaround of the evening's events—and possibly the fortunes of The Hardington Players themselves. When I got home I showed the article to Katie, who was by now up and about, and feeding the girls their breakfast.

'That's wonderful, dear,' she responded, 'I must show that to Daphne and the others this morning.'

I had no idea who Daphne was, nor what she and Katie would be doing with 'the others', but it didn't really matter, as I had no real reason to stick around. I bustled about and made noises about having to get off to work, then kissed Katie and the girls goodbye and went off in the direction of the shed to get my bike.

I set off towards Clunmore, fully intending to buy another copy of the Roxbury Echo as I went through town. However, I was so preoccupied with thoughts of my triumph that I was halfway up Clunmore Rise before I realized I'd sped past three newsagents without making the intended purchase. Never mind, I thought, I could always consult the Echo's archives via the Internet when I got home.

It never ceased to amaze me how, by heading for a particular location and focusing my thoughts on the time in my life associated with that place, I could so effortlessly span the space-time continuum and arrive in a totally different decade, or century, even. The funny thing was, it wasn't always obvious where the changeover occurred—there was usually such a gradual transition that it could be several minutes before it had dawned on me exactly where, or rather, when, I was. This time was no exception—it wasn't until I noticed a new-style car registration that I knew I was back in the 21st century.

Katie's greeting was a nonchalant 'Hello, dear,' as I entered the kitchen. 'How's your day been?' she asked, routinely.

'Oh, you know,' I answered, as coolly as I could, 'pretty much as usual. Uh...I'm just popping into the study to check my e-mails.'

Waiting for the computer to boot up, my eye caught something new on the shelf above—a clutch of what appeared to be pamphlets that hadn't been there the last time I was in that room. I pulled a few out and discovered they were programmes—from none other than Roxbury Players' productions! Leafing through a few of them, I soon discovered that our little company had gone on to achieve glowing accolades for our regular offerings. They were mostly comedies or lighthearted dramas, and I noticed too that the chairman, who had been responsible for choosing the ill-fated Partington play, had resigned from his position after that near-disaster. The cast lists remained pretty much the same, however, and I was intrigued to see that I had apparently appeared in half a dozen further plays up until the time we moved to Clunmore.

As soon as I was online, I entered 'Roxbury Players' into a search engine and was amazed at the proliferation of references. I checked a few and was agreeably surprised to see how the company had enjoyed continued success—right up to the present time. Furthermore, several of my fellow thespians had gone on to even greater things. I was particularly delighted to see, for instance, that a certain Miss Nadia Melgrove had been signed up for several dramas on television, and then gone on to appear in various West End productions.

'Well, fancy that!' I exclaimed.

'Fancy what?' said a voice from behind me, as Kate came to tell me dinner was ready.

'Oh…I didn't realize what a big star Nadia Melgrove had become.'

'Huh!' snorted Kate. 'I'm surprised *you* hadn't cottoned on to that, seeing how you used to be her number one fan! Such a flighty little minx, she was!'

Sensing I had touched a very raw nerve, I hastily logged off. 'Mmmm,' I enthused, 'that dinner smells absolutely *delicious*!'

CHAPTER 8

One good turn...

It's a weird and alarming experience to wake up and find that you're not coming out of a normal night's sleep in your own bed, but that you're in some completely different place, surrounded by strange faces and pulsing machinery, some of which is attached to you by wires and tubes. When it happened to me I opened my eyes expecting to see the morning light filtering through our bedroom curtains and the familiar pictures on the wall, and to hear the cat's cheerful 'Prriaow!' as she gave me her usual morning greeting. But as I blinked to try and clear the sleep from my eyes, I saw the indistinct shapes of three beings dressed in white peering down at me. I tried to lift my hand to rub my eyes but found there was something restraining it. I tried the other hand but that too was held fast.

'I think he's coming to, Doctor!' I heard a female voice cry.

What was that, 'Doctor'? What were these people doing in my bedroom, and why was there a doctor present? Why couldn't I see properly? Where am I? What was I doing here? I tried to cry out, but only a faint gasp escaped from my throat. One of the beings wiped my eyes with something, and as my vision cleared slightly I could make out the form of a nurse, plus two other females who appeared to be a physio and a technician of some sort. Although I had spent most of my working life in hospitals, my mind was currently too muddled to distinguish the different professions represented by these young ladies. Another female face came into view.

'Yes—the sedation's wearing off now. That's good,' she said. This was obviously the doctor, a pleasant but businesslike young registrar with a South African accent. I later came to know her as Dr Ruth McAllister.

Over the next few hours the expert attentions of the ward staff helped me to regain at least a semblance of normality. The feeding tube was removed from my nose and I was given some fresh water to drink, which enabled me to speak again, albeit rather huskily. Various monitors and other encumbrances to my freedom of movement were removed, and as my physical state improved, so did my mental condition. As my mind began to clear, my memory slowly returned—then I started to piece together the events leading up to the situation in which I now found myself.

I had popped over to Friar's Morcombe, a village to the southeast of Clunmore, to see my old mate Ray Turville. He was several years younger than me, but he'd had to retire early due to some kind of infection he'd contracted a couple of years ago. It had left him weak in his left arm, and he walked with a limp. However, it hadn't stopped him supplementing his disability pension by undertaking a number of little jobs that came his way, and he especially enjoyed tinkering around with old cars. We'd been neighbours many years ago, and we still enjoyed the occasional get-together for a natter over a glass of beer or cider.

His latest project, which this time was for his own benefit, not someone else's, was restoring an old Triumph Herald. He told me he'd spent a couple of months on it, and I must say, it looked splendid. All the dents and scrapes had been bashed out or filled in, and the paintwork positively gleamed. The chrome bumpers glistened in the sunlight.

'The only trouble is,' bemoaned Ray, it's missing the distributor, and I can't get a replacement for love nor money.'

'Aren't there dealers who can get them? What about Motorists' World?'

'Not a chance, mate—they tell me it's way older than anything they cater for.'

'Have you tried scrap dealers?'

'Yeah—been to all the scrap yards for miles around; nothing doing, I'm afraid.'

'What a pity,' I commiserated, 'we used to have a car exactly the same model as that. It served us well for many years. *That* one ended up on a scrap heap, unfortunately.' This set me off on a new train of thought, then tentatively I ventured, 'Actually…there is *one* other scrap yard I can think of. I might just be able to help you out.'

Without elaborating on my plan, I continued my social visit with Ray and his wife, commenting now and again how lovely it was to see a Herald in such good condition, and how it reminded me of so many happy hours of motoring we'd done in our old banger. Its registration letters had been OTT (a good old Devonshire registration), so naturally it had acquired the nickname of Otto. I embarked on what I have to admit was a

lengthy account of various journeys, incidents and experiences we'd enjoyed or endured with Otto. To most
people this would have seemed unspeakably boring, and
in fact, Ray's wife Sylvia offered to make us a cup of tea,
just as her eyes appeared on the point of glazing over, and
she seemed relieved to be able to get away. Ray, however,
was lapping it all up, taking in every little detail, and even
getting me to elaborate on certain points.

I enjoyed a bit of social chitchat with the Turvilles,
although Sylvia, as usual, seemed subdued and not over-
communicative. She was actually Ray's second wife, his
earlier marriage having ended in divorce. Ray had had
no children from that marriage, and although he and
Sylvia would have loved children of their own, she had
rather sadly become infertile after treatment for cervical
cancer just before they had got married. Ray had so
many interests that being childless was not too great a
problem, but for Sylvia it was a bitter blow, and
although she had made Ray an excellent wife, and they
obviously loved each other very much indeed, you could
sense that there was something missing in their relationship. For Sylvia there was a continual aching emptiness
in her heart, and a very real sense of unfulfilment.

Eventually I said my goodbyes and took my leave,
promising I'd do my best to get the part Ray needed to
complete his restoration. That was a Sunday evening,
and the next morning, I set off as for work as usual,
having first grabbed a haversack from the cupboard
under the stairs. I tossed a few tools into it as I went to
the shed, then grabbed my trusty bike and pedalled
off once again in the direction of Upper Meadow
Close, and effortlessly crossed the divide between the
centuries. When I got to our old house I found no-one in.

I wondered where Kate (or rather, Katie) was, but it didn't take long to find out—there was a scribbled note from her on the shelf in the hall that read: 'Taken girls to Berrington for shopping & things. Get yourself some food – we'll eat out.'

This was actually a bonus for me, as it made my mission much simpler: I had not landed in another awkward situation (although in retrospect, the acting adventure had turned out to be great fun), and this was, after all, a serious business trip. Having achieved the time switch, there was no cause to hang around the house—I had not long since had breakfast (although I noticed from the kitchen clock that it was twenty past ten here), so I needed nothing to eat or drink.

I returned through the front door and considered how best to get to Dormington Magna, the village where our dear old Otto had found its final resting place several years ago. I could have cycled, but it was just a bit too far on this occasion, so the bus seemed the most sensible option. Stepping briskly off down the avenue, I turned left at the end and walked up the slight incline past the Parklands Clinic. I hoped no-one would see me, or I would be expected to come in to do some processing— or to attend some ghastly boring meeting that happened to be taking place that day. Fortunately I was able to make it unnoticed, and continued to the Broxville Road junction. The Broxville bus passed through the Dorm-ingtons on its route, so I took up my stance at the bus stop and waited. According to the timetable, the next bus should be along in less than ten minutes.

It was turning into one of those glorious early spring mornings, when only a few fleecy white clouds occa-sionally passed in front of a bright, warm sun, helped on their way by a moderate, slightly cooling breeze. Neighbouring gardens were awash with the colours of spring flowers, and there was a robin in a tree above my head, singing exquisitely. Absorbed thus in the beauty of my surroundings, I failed to notice a car draw up next to me, until a voice that seemed strangely familiar, called out, 'Hey, Billy! Fancy seeing you here! Where you off to?'

Jerked out of my vernal reverie, I focused my eyes on the occupant of the car, who was leaning across the passenger seat to peer out at the half-open window.

'Well, bless my soul!' I exclaimed, 'If it isn't Ray Turville! What a coincidence!'

'Coincidence? Why so?'

'Oh...um...I just...er...I was just thinking about you a moment ago, and suddenly there you are!'

'Can I give you a lift anywhere? I'm on my way to Broxville to fetch some equipment for my boss. You going that way?'

I told him I was, as a matter of fact, although just as far as Dormington Magna. I couldn't get over how much younger he looked than at our recent meeting in his 21st century home, and again how odd it was that to him I apparently looked the age I had been back in the eighties. This was a paradox I never managed to explain.

'So what's your business in Dormington, then?' enquired my old mate.

'Oh...er...I was going to have a look in one of those antiques shops there—see if I can find a little trinket thingy for Katie, to add to her collection, you know.' Dormington Magna, and to a lesser extent Dormington Parva, abounded in antiques shops, which drew connoisseurs from many miles around (it seemed ironic that sources of those treasured old items should be in such close proximity to an unsightly junk yard full of rusting old hulks). I hastily concocted an excuse for my errand, hoping it would sound plausible, although in fact Katie wasn't really a particularly avid collector of antique items. I did fleetingly call to mind some advice I'd been given as a teenager – 'If you always tell the truth, you'll have no difficulty remembering which version of the story you last used.' The trouble was, if I'd told Ray the truth, namely that I had come back from a couple of decades in the future to do him a favour, he'd probably have turned the car round and headed for the nearest mental hospital. Fortunately, he swallowed the line completely, and took up on the subject of my relationship with Katie.

'You certainly married a gem there, Billy. I wish I had your luck.'

This would have been about a year after he had split up with Charlotte, a charming lass with stunning auburn hair and green eyes. She'd had a very gentle nature, and had suited Ray wonderfully, but some issue relating to her parents that I had never fully understood had soured the relationship and what to me had seemed the perfect couple had gone their separate ways. Since then Ray had kept very quiet about the business, and about relationships in general, but now he seemed ready to open up a little.

'I had a date last night,' he began, 'well, if you can call it that. There's this girl who works in Accounts at our Berrington branch. I've been going over there now and then to help out in the workshop—they're a bit under-staffed, you see. Anyway, we'd sat next to each other a couple of times in the canteen, and got chatting, like. Well, I tells her I'm keen on speedway, among other things, see, an' she starts asking me about it, so I says "Why don't you come with me next Thursday night, then you can see for yourself?" "OK, I will," she says.

'What did she think of it, then Ray?' I enquired.

'Well...I don't think she really *liked* it, exactly, but she showed interest, and thanked me politely for the "fascinating experience" afterwards. Oh, and the other thing was, during one of the breaks she said she had to go to the toilet, but when she came back, she had a couple of drinks she'd bought, and gave me one, along with a chocolate bar. "How much was that, love?" I asks her, fishing for my wallet, but she says, "No, that's all right— my treat!"'

'She sounds nice,' I responded, 'What's her name?'

'Oh, Sylvia,' he replied, in a matter-of-fact way. I stifled a gasp, pretending to clear my throat. Sylvia—his future wife!

'Only trouble is,' he went on, 'she's...how can I put it? Well, she doesn't strike me as being all that exciting, if you know what I mean. Don't get me wrong—she's a nice enough girl, and she's obviously got a generous nature, but I...well, I sort of like someone with a bit of fire in them, d'you know what I mean?'

'Well, I...' I hesitated, not knowing if I wanted to agree with him.

'Now, that Melanie in the Roxbury stores, she's a completely different kettle of fish—a real feisty lass, that one. I took her to that adventure park they've just opened up in Berrington—you know, next to Dwarfland. Anyway, she wanted to go on all the scariest rides, and she tackled that assault course there—the hard one, mind, not the dead easy one. She's game for anything, she is. Then back at home I was showing her that old scrambler bike I've got—the Villiers, and she even had a go on that! She'd never ridden a motorbike before in her life, but after I'd showed her what to do, she just shot off like a rocket! Amazing! She went all round the field at the back of our house, and took off over some bumpy bits. Mind you, she took one corner a bit too fast and came off when she hit a muddy patch. Didn't bother her, though—she just got up and laughed like a drain!'

I managed a half-hearted chuckle. If I wasn't mistaken, Ray's first wife had been called Melanie. I hadn't really known her, because Kate and I had moved to Clunmore by then, and we lost touch for a few years.

Ray continued babbling on: 'I'm not really sure what to do, though—I'd intended asking Melanie out again this weekend, but Sylvia's asked me if I'd do her a favour and have a look at her car (she knows I like mechanical things). It's making an odd noise and she's not sure if it's something serious or not. She's offered to pay me to look at it—of course, I wouldn't take anything from her. I've half a mind to tell her she'd be better off taking it to a garage. I don't really know what to do—there's a stock car race on Saturday over at Pinkton airfield, and I was gonna ask Melanie to go with me. On the other hand, I don't really want to let Sylvia down. What do you reckon I should do?'

Poor Ray—he'd always been a very decisive guy, and to be fair, he still was in most respects, but when it came to women, he seemed to have lost his confidence. I'm sure the break-up with Charlotte had unnerved him more than he was willing to let on.

'Well,' I began, 'it's really up to you in the long run. I can quite see your dilemma, though.' I didn't want to barge in too hastily, or it might have had the effect of making him more determined to go the way he was inclined. 'Melanie certainly sounds like fun, I must admit. The only thing is, though…' (this was my attempt to sound nonchalant, as though it was merely an incidental thought). 'The thing is, I knew this bloke once— he was quite a bit like you, as a matter of fact….' (It *was* him, of course.) 'He was in a very similar situation. Remarkably similar, now I come to think of it! Anyway, *he* had two potential girlfriends, a nice, staid, comfortable one and a really lively one who liked to live it up a lot. He chose the lively one and they got married. They had a brilliant time at first—always going out to nightclubs, sporting events (yeah—*they* were keen on speedway, as it happened), adventure holidays—you name it, they did it. But after a while, poor Ray…er…I mean, Reg, he just couldn't keep up with the lifestyle—she was just *too* much for him. What's more, his wallet couldn't keep up with it either, and before too long they were getting into serious debt. Mind you, that never stopped her! She seemed to have an insatiable appetite for adventure, and she started moaning at the poor bloke for not satisfying her desires.'

I didn't really know the story behind Ray and Melanie's bust-up, so I made up the tale as I went along, embroidering on what seemed the most likely scenario. So I continued the saga.

'Anyway, in the end they were almost coming to blows over the whole business, and it led to a very acrimonious divorce. And do you know what? The one person who most helped him to pick up the pieces was the other girl—the quiet, steady one! They got married and had a very happy life together. True, it wasn't all partying and the high life, but she was a good little homemaker, and she used to let Reg go off on his jaunts whenever he wanted to. It's a funny old world, isn't it? Still, as I say—it's your choice, mate. You've got to live your own life, and I wouldn't expect you to make every decision the way I might. Just be a bit wary of Melanie, that's all I'm saying.'

Ray didn't answer immediately: he was looking a bit pensive, as though he were chewing over the matter. Then the twinkle returned to his eyes, and he dismissed the subject lightly, joking that he'd probably end up marrying the girl next door who was several years younger than him, and always seemed to idolize him.

By this time we were passing the turn for Dormington Parva, and it was only a few hundred metres to the larger of the two villages. As we reached the turn, I said it'd be fine to drop me off there; I'd just walk into the village. Somewhat to my annoyance, however, Ray insisted on taking me right into the village—away from the scrap yard!

'Which antique shop did you want, mate?' he asked.

'Oh, any one,' I answered, a little abruptly—'the first one. I'll work my way along the street if I need to.'

Not only did Ray drop me right outside the door of Angela's Antiques, he wouldn't drive off until he'd watched me go in. That's just what I didn't want—buying antiques was not my scene, and it certainly wasn't my intent. However, once inside, I felt obliged to wander around, under the watchful eye of the proprietor (or her husband, perhaps, as this large, but smartly dressed gentleman could hardly have passed for an 'Angela'). I had intended to look disappointed and take my leave, saying they hadn't got the item I was seeking, but my eye was caught by a pile of old magazines, among them some copies of 'West Country Steam', a railway magazine I hadn't seen for many years. One of them featured the Atlantic Coast Express, which used to travel close to my childhood home in Devon, on its way to Padstow.

There were three copies, and although rather tattered and dog-eared, I couldn't resist buying them, such was the feeling of nostalgia they evoked in me. I presented them to the watchful gentleman, who peered at them a little disdainfully and declared, 'I should be doing you an injustice, sir, if I were to take your money for these. I feel almost inclined to pay *you* to take them off my hands!' Although I tried to protest that I was perfectly willing to pay for the magazines, he insisted he wouldn't think of it. They were clearly in such a poor state that it was a wonder he hadn't already thrown them out. He produced a large carrier bag—one of those sturdy paper ones with cord handles, bearing the name of the shop in what could be termed antique letters. I couldn't help thinking he considered the bag (which of course was a free advert for his shop) to be of far greater value than its contents.

As I was thanking the gentleman profusely while edging my way to the door, there was a commotion from farther inside the shop, and a woman's voice (I assumed it was that of Angela) cried out: 'Stop that man! Don't let him get away!'

Immediately a young man with a holdall came charging through the shop towards the front door. Before I could react to try and stop him, he had roughly pushed me aside and made his getaway. I fell back against a freestanding display of sundry trinkets and knicknacks, and sprawled onto the floor with all the little artefacts cascading around me. The shopkeepers rushed to my aid, but I shouted, 'Don't worry about me, I'm okay—get after *him*!'

While the smartly dressed gentleman tried in vain to pursue his quarry, Angela helped me to my feet and apologised for the unfortunate occurrence. I assured her it was quite all right, and it hadn't been in any way her fault. Her partner returned, somewhat out of breath, panting that the blighter had got away, but insisting that he'd got a good enough description of the felon for the police to be able to catch him.

'Did he take much?' I asked, as I helped to pick up the fallen objects (which were fortunately all made of metal, so nothing was broken).

'Just a few bronze figures and a couple of candle-sticks, I think,' replied the lady. 'They weren't real silver, so they weren't worth a great deal.'

With a few parting pleasantries mixed with further apologies from the shopkeepers, I took my leave and turned back towards the scrap yard.

I was greeted at the gate by a stout, swarthy individual with a beer belly filling out his tattered, oily overalls. He was unshaven with greasy black hair, and a half-smoked cigarette appeared to be attached to his lower lip. 'Whatcha want, then?' he growled.

I explained as politely as I could that a previous car of mine had ended up in this dump, but if he would allow me to look for it and remove the distributor, I should be most grateful.

'You'll be lucky, chum—most of 'em don't last more'n a year of so. Them that's any good gets broken up fer spares, an' them that ain't gets crushed into tiny lit'l cubes.' He made a gesture with both hands to illustrate the size of the cubes.

'Well, would it be all right if I took a look round for it? You never know—I might be lucky.'

'Suit yerself, mate, but yer does it at yer own risk, see? 'Cos most o' they old cars 'ave bin stacked up in piles, an' I can't guarantee they're all that stable.'

Leaving the carrier bag in the care of the scrap merchant, I ventured forth. I trod warily around among the heaps of old wrecks—many had obviously been involved in horrendous road accidents, while others just looked old and clapped out—just as my old banger had been. My eyes were scanning both vertically and horizontally, but without any sign of the object of my search. Oh, what a blow! It seemed I would have to return to Ray empty-handed. As I was heading for the exit, my searching eye caught sight of a battered number plate, partly hidden by a tarpaulin. My heart leapt as I read the letters: OT.... Could it be? Was it too much to hope for? The car bearing the number plate was perched on top of two other cars, both the obvious victims of a nasty smash. Carefully I climbed up and tugged at the tarpaulin. It was old and rotten, and tore away in my hand, and as it did so, it revealed what I was hardly daring to hope: the number plate read OTT 57.... The end of the plate had broken off, but it didn't matter—I could see, this was it: this was Otto!

Having pulled away the rest of the tarpaulin, I was then faced with a difficult task: getting the car's bonnet open. On those old Triumph Heralds the bonnet constituted the whole of the front cover of the engine—the radiator grille, the top and sides. There were two large metal clips, one on each side, that had to be undone, and the whole thing hinged up and forwards. It wasn't too hard to release the clip on the side next to me, but to get to the other side I had to climb right up and over the bonnet and carefully descend the other side and find a footing on the mangled hulk on which Otto was resting. I managed it, but was somewhat alarmed when the stack began to shift under me. However, I succeeded in open-ing the bonnet, and was agreeably surprised at how well preserved the engine and all its attachments were—although the battery was covered with a white powdery substance, presumably the remains of the battery acid.

Removing the distributor was remarkably easy, and I stowed it, along with the attached plug leads, into my haversack, along with my tools. It did occur to me that it might well have been easier to use a distributor from another model of car and adapt it if necessary, but then, Ray was a stickler for authenticity, and nothing but the true original would have satisfied him.

What happened next I can only surmise, because that is the last thing I can remember.

My attempts to glean information from the physios and nursing staff about my condition and the cause of it proved frustratingly negative. They all kept avoiding the issue and fobbing me off with statements like: 'Oh, you don't have to worry about that right now—you just need to get plenty of rest to help you get better.' It reminded me of those medical dramas you see on television, where the distraught relative asks: 'Is he going to get better, doctor?' and the answer they get is something like: 'Oh, he's in the very best hands', or 'We're doing everything we can'. You wish that for once they'd come right out with it and say: 'Nope. Sorry chum—he hasn't got a chance' or: 'Yep. We're a brilliant bunch here—after his seven-hour operation he'll be as good as new. He'll be walking out of here tomorrow morning!' But of course, they have to be cagey to cover their backs. Any hint of a definite statement and if it doesn't turn out exactly as they say, they'd be sued for malpractice, unprofessionalism, breach of contract and any other kind of litigation you can imagine. So there was little I could do other than rest back on my pillows and await 'someone in authority'.

Eventually authority arrived in the form of Dr McAllister. I was a trifle irritated by her initial, slightly condescending tone. 'Well, then,' she chirruped, 'how are we?'

'How are *we*?' I responded. 'As far as I can tell, *you* seem to be fine. I'm not too bothered about '*we*'—it's *me* that I'm concerned about!'

She countered my irritable riposte with a disarming smile and a gentle reply. 'I'm sorry, Mr Draper, I didn't mean to upset you. It's just that it's good to see you awake at last. I'm merely checking on your progress.'

'Well,' I answered, a little too sharply, 'I appear to be alive, at any rate, but it would be nice if someone would actually tell me what happened to put me in here…and why my left leg's killing me!'

'Certainly, Mr Draper. By the way, it *is* Mr Draper, is it?'

'Of course,' I replied, thinking, 'Why should she think I wasn't?'

Dr McAllister explained clearly that I had apparently been climbing over some old cars at a scrap yard when the stack had shifted and toppled over. I had been trapped by my leg and lost a great deal of blood through a deep and very nasty gash. I had then gone into hypovolaemic shock and lost consciousness. It could have been very serious, but fortunately an ambulance was

nearby, returning from a routine patient transport journey, and the crew were able to respond very swiftly when
called. I'd been kept under heavy sedation for five days
and been given a blood transfusion.

Five days? I thought—that sounds really serious. Why
had I bothered with that wretched distributor? My next
thought was how soon I'd be able to get out of this fix.
But there was another thought troubling me.

'Excuse me, doctor,' I enquired, 'why did you ask me
if my name really was Draper?'

She hesitated. 'Oh…just routine protocol. Your registration procedure was incomplete, as the documentation
we found on you was somewhat limited. One of the
nurses will be along shortly to help you complete the
process.'

This should have set alarm bells ringing, but at that
moment my mind hadn't taken in the full significance of
what the doctor had said. In answer to my next query
Ruth McAllister informed me that it would be a few
more days before I could be discharged, as there were
some 'complications'.

The doctor excused herself, and after some indistinct
whisperings outside the curtain drawn across my bay, a
nurse bustled in with a clipboard in her hand. She was
tall, dark, and to complete the desirable trinity, attractive. Her badge bore the name Kowalczyk. Now it
happened that I was used to meeting many Poles in the
course of my own hospital work—a number of nurses,
domestics and a few doctors were of that nationality,
and, being a bit of an amateur linguist, I delighted in
greeting them with some of my limited repertoire of
Polish phrases.

'Dzień dobry!' I said, 'Jak się masz?'

Her reaction was puzzling. Instead of looking pleased at my attempt to speak her language, she frowned, plonked herself down on the bedside chair and said, 'I need to ask you some questions.'

Her English was very good. I noticed it had an Australian twang. Perhaps she's worked there, I thought.

She proceeded to ask me my full name, address, telephone number, marital status, next of kin, GP details and so on. Rather than irritate this cheerless individual further, I rattled off my details with great alacrity, much as a serviceman would recite his name, rank and number when questioned. I did venture to ask her what were the 'complications' necessitating my continued detention.

'There is some infection in the wound,' she replied, tersely. 'We need to get it under control.'

'Oh dear, it's not MRSA, is it?' I asked.

'Is it *what*?' she queried.

'MRSA,' I repeated, surprised that she seemed ignorant of the condition. 'It's a bug—most of us carry it around with us anyway—it's only when it gets inside us that there's a problem.'

'A bug?' She frowned. 'Who is responsible for this ...bug?'

'Oh, never mind,' I replied, realizing that, although methicillin-resistant staphylococcus aureus had first been identified in the sixties, it had not become a hot issue until towards the end of the twentieth century.

My inquisitor rose from the chair and swept out of my presence. As she departed she turned and shot a frosty glare at me as I ventured to bid her 'Do widzenia!' I lay back with my eyes closed, turning over a number of puzzling thoughts. There was one issue I considered I'd resolved after a while, namely that Nurse Kowalczyk was probably the granddaughter of a Polish migrant to Australia, and thus spoke no Polish herself. Other more disturbing revelations occurred essentially by accident.

I lay there for quite some time, not moving, as I was finding it quite tiring after such a period of unwonted inactivity, along with the pain of my injury. Still rearranging a number of conflicting and puzzling thoughts in my mind, I became aware of whispered voices nearby.

'He's very still—do you think he's lost consciousness again?'

'No, I think he's just asleep; pretty deeply, though, I reckon. See—his heart rate's down below fifty. You'd expect him to sleep a lot after what he's been through. Best leave him alone—do him good to rest. When he's a bit more with it, hopefully we'll solve some of these anomalies.'

Anomalies? What anomalies, I thought. I was inclined to ask them what they meant, but felt it advisable to keep my eyes closed and maintain the pretence of deep slumber. Being used to taking a lot of exercise (mainly through cycling practically everywhere), I had a strong, slow heart rate, as most athletes do, and although the rate increased momentarily as I overheard this conversation, the overall pulse rate helped to consolidate the pretence.

The whispers ceased, but not long after, I became aware of more voices approaching—hushed, but sounding earnest. The speakers were obviously of the opinion that I was oblivious to their conversation, but due to my keen sense of hearing, plus the supreme advantage that I was actually wide awake, I was able to discern almost every word. The first speaker was none other than the unsmiling Nurse Kowalczyk.

'...some kind of delusional disorder, Doctor. The details he gave me are a complete fabrication. He *doesn't* live at the address he gave. We checked, and the residents have never heard of him.'

'Yes—we tried when he was admitted. The personal data in his wallet gave an address in Clunmore. The phone number was correct, but when we rang it the man who answered denied all knowledge of this Mr Draper.'

'Well, he's certainly suspicious. He tried to speak to me in Russian or something. And he kept saying something about being bugged. He reckons most of us carry a bug around with us; I reckon he thought I was a Russian agent or something. Was there anything unusual in his belongings?'

'Well, we *did* find some sort of electronic device, but I think it was a new type of calculator. Not one I've seen before—made by a company called Nokia, I think it was.'

'D'you think he has a hypoxia-induced psychosis?'

'Not primarily, no—cerebral hypoxia won't have helped, but the condition must have been pre-existent, otherwise how would you explain the wrong identity on his person *before* the accident?'

'So he was already deluded before his injury? Should he be sectioned, do you think?'

'Actually, I was thinking more in terms of the police.'

'The police? Why?'

'It's my belief he's a thief and a fraudster. Putting together the pieces of the jigsaw puzzle, it seems to me that he was trying to steal something from that scrap yard. The ambulance crew reported that the proprietor of the yard had not given him permission to enter—he said he must have sneaked in while his back was turned.'

At this point I nearly gave myself away with a snort of disgust. The cheeky swine! Of course he'd given me permission! Someone else just covering his back, obviously!

The doctor (I recognised the voice of Ruth McAllister) continued: 'He's obviously concocted a false identity, just in case he gets caught or questioned. Didn't you think it's odd that he hasn't had a single visitor? Now if your nearest and dearest failed to come home one evening, wouldn't the local hospital be one of the first places you'd call, just in case he'd had an accident? No, you mark my words—he's a criminal all right. I'll get the law onto him first thing in the morning. I'll lay odds he's got a record!'

As the two women moved away and began discussing their next case, I lay there horrified. What an idiot I'd been! (Though in my defence I reasoned that my mind was still recovering from the coma I'd been in.) I'd given the address that wouldn't be mine for a few years from that time; and yet—if I *had* given my UMC address, my family would come rushing to my bedside, and not only would it cause them much concern over my condition, but also I'd have difficulty explaining what I'd been up to. One thing was eminently clear, however: I had to escape—and get back to my own time without delay. I decided it would be best to wait till night-time, when staffing resources were at their lowest, and I could slip away more effectively into the dark.

I sat up, and when dinner was brought round, I made sure I got an extra large helping, as I needed to build up my strength. It was some sort of stew, with dumplings and potatoes (not a very well balanced meal, I thought). Nevertheless, I stuffed it down me, despite its relative lack of flavour—and the treacle pudding that followed. Again, not well balanced, but just right to give me energy, I thought. I was surprised at how much of an effort it was to carry out even small actions. I checked my locker, and fortunately all my belongings were there. I stuffed them into the carrier bag along with the railway magazines, ready for a quick getaway.

After a seemingly endless evening, a solitary nurse came on duty for the night shift and she did a round of the ward. It was L-shaped, with a number of side bays, of which I was in one. She peeped through the curtain at me and asked: 'Are you all right, Mr Draper?'

'Fine,' I replied, 'but very tired. I'm hoping to get a really solid night's sleep.'

'Good for you,' she replied. 'I'll leave you in peace, then.'

As soon as she had gone round the corner, I swiftly but quietly leapt into action. First I had to remove the monitors attached to me. My inside knowledge of hospital equipment enabled me to silence them so that the alarm wasn't activated when I switched them off. I carefully removed the drip from my left arm, covering the injection point with a plaster I'd found in a tray on my locker. Then I began to dress. There were no trousers—doubtless torn to shreds and soaked in blood—but I was pleased to see that my shoes were still in a reasonable state, although pretty mucky. My shirt was rather heavily oil-stained, and my underpants were torn but wearable. There were no socks, but I could make do with the surgical stockings I was wearing. With the hospital robe wrapped round me, I crept (or to be precise, limped) furtively out of the ward and along the corridor. I'd ascertained from the logo on the nurses' ID badges that this was 'my own' hospital, the RRI, so I knew my way around. I made my way to the laundry department to get myself some reasonable clothing.

To my annoyance there were some laundry staff at work, so I had to make do with what I could glean from a large wire cage outside the department. I opened the side of the cage as quietly as I could and managed to extract a pair of trousers. They were a couple of sizes too big, and I had no belt, but they would have to do. I also found a plain blue work shirt, which was better than the one I had on. I quickly put them on and made my departure via the deliveries entrance. I threw my stained shirt into a skip and hobbled out into the street.

Getting back to my bike at 26 UMC could be tricky, as I wanted to avoid being seen if at all possible, so I set out to walk. It was going to be a long haul—forty minutes' brisk walk normally, but my current physical state was far from normal. However, as I took a short cut across a piece of waste ground near the railway station, I noticed a bicycle discarded among some brambles. With difficulty, and not without some scratches on my hands, I managed to drag it out. The back tyre was almost flat and the handlebars were bent, but it was rideable—just about. This was a great stroke of luck, I thought, as I wobbled off in the direction of my former home. It had occurred to me to go the other way— straight to Clunmore, but I'd got the distinct impression that in order to go back and forth in time I needed to be on my own bike. Besides, this old thing was really uncomfortable, and only two of the gears worked, so going that far would have just about finished me off.

I heaved the rusty old bike through a gap in the hedge opposite the end of UMC and made my way painfully along the avenue to my former home. Not surprisingly, it was in darkness. I carefully tried the door of the car port that we grandly used to term the garage. Alas, it was bolted on the inside, so I had no option but to go through the house. I turned my key as quietly as possible in the lock and crept through the hall and the kitchen, not wanting to wake my sleeping loved ones upstairs. The eerie thought occurred to me: Was 'I' up there, asleep beside Katie? Or had my eighties self somehow changed places with me? I'd never managed to explain this anomaly, and I decided it would be prudent not to try to do so now. Nevertheless, the prospect of there perhaps being two of me in the same house at the same time made me shiver all over. That, combined with a very real sense of fear, along with my being far from healthy, had a distinctly chilling effect.

With my teeth fairly chattering, and my knees trembling, I extracted my bike from the shed and carefully wheeled it through the house. I emerged from the front door and turned the key as I drew the door to, rather than make a noise by just pulling it shut. Unfortunately, I lost my grip on the bike, which fell over, knocking several milk bottles flying and evoking a loud squeal from a nearby cat. Almost immediately a light came on in the front bedroom. I was on that bike like lightning, and off down the street. I glanced back and saw the curtains move, but I think I got away without being recognised.

With my haversack hung over my shoulder and the carrier bag hanging from the handlebars, I pedalled through the city. The nightclubs and late-night cinemas were in full swing, and the streets were quite lively with young people. No-one gave me a second glance as I swerved around the groups of revellers. My leg was getting extremely painful, and most of my muscles were aching terribly. I also felt extremely fatigued, and wondered if I could actually make it home. I also wondered how Kate would react on seeing the state I was in.

I made it to the foot of Clunmore Rise, but gasped at the thought of the steep one-mile climb ahead of me. I pressed on, though, and as I did so, the task seemed to be getting very gradually more manageable. The pain in my leg was definitely decreasing, and I felt myself getting marginally stronger with every minute that passed. Another change I noticed was that it was getting gradually brighter all around me. Gosh, I thought, is it nearly sunrise already?

However, it then dawned on me (to use a possibly appropriate metaphor) that the sun—somewhat pale, and shrouded in mist—was *ahead* of me, not behind in the east! The mist quickly dispersed to reveal strong afternoon sunshine, and my watch confirmed that it was around the time I would normally be coming home from work. To my relief, the time transition had occurred, and I was back in my own century! I thanked heaven over and over in my relief. I also expressed my sincere thanks that the pain in my leg had now entirely ceased, as had my muscular fatigue.

Forcing myself to suppress my emotions, I breezed into the house and called out to Kate as I passed the dining room door: 'Hi. Love. Just popping upstairs to clean up a bit.' I didn't want her to see me in the unusual clothing I'd acquired.

A few minutes later, and looking much more like myself, I came down to help my spouse put away some very tasty savoury pancakes. 'I'm just gonna pop over to see Ray after dinner,' I said.

'What again?' asked Kate. 'You were there only last night.'

'Yes, well, he asked me to try and get him a car part, and I got one in…in…my lunch break. I'm just taking it over to him.'

Kate cheerfully assented, and soon I was drawing up outside Ray's house in Friar's Morcombe. I could see Ray round the side of the house, almost inside the open bonnet of his Triumph Herald.

'Hi, Ray!' I called out, 'look what I've got for you!' I triumphantly pulled the distributor from the haversack and held it before his eyes.

He looked rather less enthusiastic than I'd expected, and addressed me rather hesitantly: 'Oh, that's jolly decent of you, Bill. … Actually, though, …' He began to look really awkward. '…I hope you didn't go to too much trouble. I've been trying to contact you all day, but your mobile must have been out of range or something. I was trying to say don't bother—I've managed to get one on eBay. I should get it in a day or two!'

This was simply beyond belief! Too much trouble? I could damn well tell him what trouble it'd been! But somehow I heard myself saying, 'No, mate…no trouble at all. Tell you what, why don't you keep this one as a spare? You never know when it might come in useful!'

I was just about to turn and leave, when, in the field behind the house, I saw a little girl of about seven or eight come running from an old barn, calling out, 'Mummy, Mummy, come and see! Molly's had her kittens!'

'Who's that?' I asked, thinking they'd got visitors.

'Oh, just our little one,' Ray replied. 'She's been so excited since she realized her pet cat was pregnant. She's made her nest over there in the barn.'

Just then the girl came running back out, swiftly pursued by an almost equally excited Sylvia. 'I must see this,' I said to Ray, and turned to follow them. Ray muttered something about there not being that much to look at—just balls of fluff, but it wasn't the kittens I wanted to see.

I crept in on the delightful scene—a little girl enchanted by the wonderful sight of those new little lives, and a supremely proud and happy mother, looking far more contented and fulfilled than I'd ever known her to be. 'How wonderful!' I exclaimed. The mother and child no doubt thought I was referring to the kittens, but little did they know that *they* were the object of my wonderment. I was ecstatic—both proud and humbled that I had been the instrument of their loving together-ness, for I realized that Ray must have taken my advice and chosen the staid but more loving, faithful Sylvia, rather than the exciting but fickle Melanie. Sylvia was now Ray's *first* wife, and they had obviously married before Sylvia's cancer treatment. So this, then, was the product of their union—a delightful little poppet with sleek sandy/auburn hair and the most strikingly beauti-ful green eyes.

While I was standing there, admiring this little marvel, my thoughts were arrested by Sylvia's voice: 'We'd better leave them in peace now, Charlotte—we mustn't disturb them too much.'

'Charlotte!' At first I was surprised, but began to understand over the next half an hour, as I stayed for a cup of tea. It was obvious from the tender way Ray dealt with his daughter, the endearments with which he addressed her—and the adventure playground he'd built for her—that he absolutely doted on his little girl, and he had apparently transferred his frustrated affections for his former girlfriend to the father-daughter relationship (although I noticed he obviously thought the world of Sylvia too),

Eventually I had to tear myself away from this scene of matrimonial harmony and domestic bliss. As Ray saw me out to my car he said, 'I must pay you something for the distributor.'

'No, Ray,' I replied, 'keep your money—I've already been generously repaid for my efforts.'

Ray looked puzzled, as well he might. He was totally unaware that his life's history had been rewritten. He shrugged and waved me off.

As I motored home, musing on the unexpected but very satisfying outcome of my journey back through time, I once again experienced that eerie sensation of having new memories gradually form in my mind. I recalled going to Ray and Sylvia's wedding—not at Roxbury Register Office, but at Hardington Mountford Baptist Church—and, fittingly, Sylvia had been a radiant, beautiful bride. Several years later at the same church Kate and I had attended Charlotte's dedication service. It was so strange being able to hold two quite different memories in my mind at the same time. (That's partly why I want to get all this down in writing while it is still fresh in my memory, in case I later forget the details.)

Anyway, there was another little surprise in store, because when I got home, I found Kate relaxing in an armchair reading one of her dolls magazines. This seemed a good way to unwind and spend an hour or so until our supper and nightcap, so I retrieved from the hallway the carrier bag containing the railway magazines and pulled them out. As I did so a metal object fell out and landed on the floor at Kate's feet.

'What's this, dear?' she asked, bending over to pick it up. Then she gasped.

'Why, darling—that's fantastic! Wherever did you get this? Mum used to have one like this, and of all her little knicknacks, this was the one thing I'd always wanted to inherit when she eventually passes on, but a few months ago when we went to visit her and Dad, it wasn't there. When I asked her what she'd done with it, she just said, "Oh, I've had a clear out. I decided there was too much junk around the place, so I took a load of stuff to a jumble sale!" I was heartbroken—I really liked that little sculpture.'

I peered at the object she was lovingly holding. It was a little figurine—in pewter, I think—of an elderly lady and gentleman sitting side by side on a park bench. I had to admit to myself that it was quite sweet.

'Oh that...' I wracked my brain for a plausible explanation—not only of my alleged motive for acquiring it, but also how it got to be in the bag in the first place. Could the proprietor of the antiques shop have been negligent enough not to notice it in the bag before he put in the magazines? No way! Then of course, I realized— in the kerfuffle of the escaping shoplifter, that display of trinkets had scattered all over the place—and this very one had fallen into my carrier bag! What a fantastic act of Providence!

'Oh yes...I got it in an antiques shop. Not usually the sort of place I frequent, I must admit, but somehow I sort of felt obliged to go in. I thought that little thing looked familiar. Funny, really, isn't it? A random visit to a shop and I find the very thing you've set your heart on!'

'Well, it was very thoughtful of you, darling, that's all I can say.' Kate was genuinely delighted, and she showed her gratitude by being extra loving towards me that evening and in the following days.

I smiled to myself. My 'one good turn' for Ray had resulted in his inadvertently doing one in return, by bringing Kate and me a little bit closer to each other, so both our marriages have been strengthened in consequence.

CHAPTER 9

Just a little slip

It was the August bank holiday and we'd been watching 'The Great Escape[1]'—yet again. Truly one of the cinema greats, even if it tends to suffer from overexposure. Now there's one part that always strikes me—it's where Bartlett and MacDonald (Richard Attenborough and Gordon Jackson), having escaped from the POW camp, are making their way across country posing as French businessmen. Back in the camp, they'd been drumming it into all the other would-be escapees, to keep speaking in German or French, and, if apprehended, not to let themselves be tricked into speaking English. However, when they themselves are stopped by German authorities, and have kept up a convincing performance, one of the Germans dismisses them by saying, 'Au revoir...Good luck!' At this, Bartlett unthinkingly replies, 'Thank you!' and of course the game is up. Such a little slip, but what dire consequences were the result. Well, alas, I made a slip of similar proportions, with an (almost) equally serious outcome.

As usual towards the end of summer, Kate was draw-ing up a list of Christmas gifts for various relatives.

1. The Mirisch Corporation/United Artists.

Having been a schoolteacher, she was a very organized person, and knew exactly who was who, when everyone's birthdays were, and the sort of things they were likely to appreciate as gifts. Some of our relations live abroad, and to save exorbitant airmail costs, we try to get parcels sent off by surface mail well in advance of Christmas or birthdays. On this occasion Kate had got most items sorted, but was looking a bit troubled.

'I know what I'd *like* to get Aunt Clarice, but I haven't seen one in the shops for ages,' she complained. (Aunt Clarice had emigrated to Vancouver twenty-odd years ago, and although she loved her adopted country, she delighted in any object that reminded her of the UK.)

'I'd like to get her one of those egg baskets—you know, the sort of wire ones, shaped like a chicken. They used to sell them in Meecham's hardware shop in Hardington, but unfortunately they went out of business a couple of years ago, and I haven't seen those baskets anywhere else.'

Meecham's had been a brilliant little shop—quite old-fashioned, but a virtual gold mine. It was simply packed from floor to ceiling with every commodity imaginable, from bags of coal to bike parts, can openers to copper kettles, dinner plates to dimmer switches, fertilizer to four-inch nails. Forget Do It All or Texas Homecare—if you wanted a tap washer (and not a pack of five), or a spare bulb for the inside of a fridge, you'd go straight to Meecham's and be sure you'd get one. Sadly, however, the increasing cost of rates, combined with old Mr Meecham's wish to retire, meant the end of this great little shop.

However, at the mention of the name my ears pricked up and my eyes brightened. 'Well, funny you should say that, dear,' I chirped, 'I'm sure I saw one in a shop just the other day' (A *very* 'other' day, I thought to myself— about two decades 'other', in fact.)

'Oh, marvellous,' replied Kate, 'do you think you could see if it's still there? I'd be ever so grateful.'

'No problem,' I breezed, 'I'm going that way tomorrow, as it happens—I'll call in and see.'

I'd certainly make sure it would happen—although I'd acquired a few misgivings about this business of delving into the past, I felt this was a legitimate use of my very unusual 'gift'. I'd be helping at least two other people, and I had no selfish motives about the venture.

So, next morning I gave my spouse the usual parting peck on the cheek and set off. 'Aiming' for some point in the early eighties, I rode in through the gate of Parklands and reported for duty. Unfortunately I'd picked a very inconvenient day, as almost the whole department was preparing to go off to a conference in Broxville, a town some 40 miles to the south, where a new Neurological centre had been recently opened in the Fleming Memorial Hospital there. I could see no way of avoiding this 'outing', which no doubt I would have enjoyed had I not got a hidden agenda. And so I reluctantly had to climb aboard the Parklands minibus along with all my old colleagues and take part. I must admit, I did so with rather bad grace, not really taking in the details of the learned presentations, or participating in the animated discussions that followed. Unfortunately my lack of enthusiasm did not go unnoticed by my colleagues, and some of them commented on my unwontedly quiet mood. When asked if I was all right, I muttered something about not having slept well, and feeling off-colour. As I did so, the tantalizing thought occurred to me that if

I were to keep up this pretence, it might encourage a prompt getaway from the meeting, to enable me to get back before closing time. To my supreme joy, it worked! I heard one of my colleagues saying, 'We probably hadn't better hang around too long—Billy's obviously sickening for something.'

So, with suppressed elation, I rode back to Roxbury in the minibus, trying to make a little conversation (which was difficult enough, as my heart wasn't in the situation at all), while not seeming *too* lively). At length we were passing through the suburb of Hardington Mountford. As we were approaching a convenient lay-by just around the corner from Meecham's, I suggested: 'Why don't you drop me off here? It'll save you going out of your way, and the fresh air will do me good as I walk home.'

'Are you sure?' they chorused.

'Positive!' I replied, nursing my secret missive within me.

So I was duly dropped off amid calls to 'Take it easy', 'Look after yourself' and 'See you tomorrow!' Not if I can help it, was my unspoken response to the last greeting.

Waiting till the 'bus was out of sight, I bounded round the corner to Meecham's. But what was this? Usually the pavement (which, fortunately, was quite a wide one) was piled up outside the shop with bags of potting compost, water butts, potted flowers, kitchen utensils and a whole lot of other stuff. But now the pavement was bare—not a thing on display. I checked my watch: 4:50—another 40 minutes till closing time. Then I realized my error: it was Thursday—early closing day! What a cruel hand fate had dealt me! I'd gone to the trouble of coming back to this day, endured, rather than enjoyed a jaunt to Broxville and the opportunity for social chit-chat with our counterparts there, not forgetting the medical talks given (which I would probably have found interesting, had I been concentrating on them). Then I'd acted the miserable, unwell colleague rather than enjoy the informal debriefing session on the way back —all for nothing!

Well, one thing I had to do now was go home—but which home? I decided it might as well be the one in the time zone in which I found myself now, so I walked briskly off, making the detour to Parklands to collect my bike, and then pedalled the short distance to Upper Meadow Close. Still cursing myself, or Fate, or whatever I could think of, for my misfortune, I strolled in round the back to be greeted by my darling Katie. Surprisingly, she hadn't got anything cooking, as was usually the case (we normally had a meal soon after I arrived home, to give the girls a reasonable time for theirs to settle before bedtime). When I queried this, Katie replied, 'Why, don't say you've forgotten? We'd planned to go out this evening.'

'Oh, er...' I mumbled.

'On the river, of course you remember—Sally's been getting quite excited about you hiring a boat to row us down to that nice pub where we can have dinner.'

'Yes, dear, of course I remember,' I lied, 'sorry—I was just a bit preoccupied with something we were discussing at work.' I was grateful for her explanation, which had given me just enough information to bluff my way through the situation.

And so, grabbing the essential commodities for a summer evening's outing (Katie had of course, got everything ready, and the girls dressed and prepared appropriately), we all bundled into the car and set off for the boathouse. (On my way out of the door I'd grabbed some post that had arrived that day—I wasn't sure why—probably more out of curiosity than anything. It was a fortunate move, as it turned out.) The River Roxe approaches the city from the north, passes through the centre and then off to the southeast, after which it meanders lazily through lush meadows grazed by herds of indifferent cows. Skirting the edge of Berrington, it then takes a definite southerly turn and heads for the coast. There are two boathouses in Roxbury: the main one is just north of the city centre, and particularly popular with local students and visiting tourists, as it passes close to some of the colleges and other notable buildings. However, we usually preferred the smaller one, in Hardington itself. Hardington Mountford was originally a self-contained village, once the site of Mountford Manor, home of Lord Mountford. But like so many similarly sited villages, it had long since been swallowed up into the suburbs of the expanding city. However, there was still something of a 'villagey' feel to the place, and the river, with its rather quaint, old-fashioned boathouse, was a popular local venue for families, couples, anglers, walkers and joggers. You would not infrequently see an artist on the bank there too, capturing on canvas an idyllic rural scene, which, it seemed, had remained unchanged for centuries. This was predominantly dairy farmland, and thus spared the ravages of intensive modern arable techniques.

'Come on,' urged Katie, as I parked the car and we all scrambled out, 'we don't need to queue—it's all booked and paid for!' In actual fact, there wasn't much of a queue, but it did gain us a few minutes. Katie handed in the booking slip and we were shown to our boat. While the girls were having their safety jackets put on (Sally, looking very cute in hers, was eagerly helping mummy get baby Hazel into her mini-sized one), I checked my hastily grabbed mail. Two items: the first was an advert for double glazing (there was a very handy bin nearby), and the second was a new cheque guarantee card from the bank (it wasn't as yet a combined cash and Maestro card—that would come in a decade or so). I popped it into the inside pocket of my jacket for safety.

'We're ready, Daddy!' cried an excited little Sally. 'Weddy, Daddy!' echoed Hazel.

I steadied the boat as the others climbed aboard, and once they were safely settled at the stern of the boat, with little Hazel in the middle and Big Sister acting very grown up as she helped guard her sibling lest perchance she should manage to get to the side and fall out, I pushed off from the bank. Soon we were proceeding downstream at a steady pace. I settled into a leisurely pace—there was no need to hurry as it was a bright, early evening in midsummer and we'd got the boat for three hours, plenty of time for our little excursion, and we'd be back well before it began to get dark.

I must admit, until that point I'd still been nursing a mild feeling of resentment at having been denied my primary aim of this trip back in time. But as I drank in the sheer delight of that experience— almost drifting aimlessly along, pausing to peer down into the pellucid waters of the dreamy River Roxe, and with the lambent flickering of the sunlight through the leaves overhead— it suddenly occurred to me that this, *this*, was a priceless jewel of far greater worth than some fowl-shaped wire basket! I relaxed my grip on the oars and just let my senses be filled with the wonders of an English summer. All around there were birds performing their distinctive songs—blackbird, chaffinch, skylark and wood pigeon, with the occasional rasp of a pheasant somewhere beyond a hedge. The mingling smells of sun-dried hay and cow parsley flowers scented the air, with an occasional whiff of cow dung—not perhaps the most romantic of substances, especially if you happened to step in it, but somehow not an entirely unpleasant 'fragrance', especially to one brought up in the country. A warm, gentle breeze was rustling the leaves of the riverside trees—willow, alder and aspen among others. And perhaps best of all, the visual images: the lush green grass, generous hedges, a cluster of rooks' nests in a copse, and best of all, the smiling happy faces of my lovely family—Katie, smiling rather wistfully, I thought, proudly watching over her precious little ones, Sally, equally proudly protecting her little sister, her chubby round face aglow as she pointed things out to her, and Hazel, eagerly imbibing this new experience, and exclaiming: 'Ook—moo-cow!' and 'Ook—man on boat!'

There was indeed a man on a boat, because, as the river was shallow (my recollection of school geography told me it was in the 'plain stage'), it was ideal for punting, and indeed, that was a popular pastime here. As the punters passed, I mulled over the fact that here, they punted in the Oxford style, that is, by standing on the sloping, slatted end of the punt—not surprising, as Roxbury, with its university and colleges, has strong links with Oxford. Further downstream in Berrington, however, they preferred the Cambridge fashion, the pole-pusher standing on the smooth end of the punt. Well, I suppose Berrington is a few miles nearer to Cambridge, but I suspect it was really because the residents of Berrington (although it does have a sizeable college of further education) have always maintained something of a rivalry with their larger, and less industrialized neighbour.

In view of my earlier irritation at having my 'shopping excursion' interrupted by family affairs, this experience taught me a valuable lesson. So often we have some event or project to look forward to—maybe it's a long-awaited holiday, or starting a new job; or even just the things we intend to do at the weekend—and we get so preoccupied with the future that we neglect to savour and enjoy what's happening *now*, even if, in my present case, the particular 'now' I was experiencing was one that had occurred a couple of decades ago. We're probably all familiar with the phenomenon of 'wishing one's life away', and I vowed there and then to try henceforth not to let that happen to me: whenever I'd be anticipating some future event, I'd try nevertheless to get the most out of the present, like enjoying the sight of blossom, or of children playing, while I'm cycling home, rather than having a blinkered view of what I'd be doing when I arrived.

Before long we rounded a bend and found ourselves at the riverside pub in the sleepy little village of Melbury Magna, and we coasted in to the side and tied up our craft. The Plasterer's Arms was a popular stopping off point for rowers, punters and canal boaters. The canal ran the other side of the pub, with a disused railway beyond that. Of course, with such a name, there were plentiful jokes about going to Melbury to get plastered, but this hostelry was noted more for its excellent food that for any drunken revelry. We sat out at one of the dozen or so picnic tables by the riverside to enjoy our meal, and I certainly savoured every moment, and every morsel, of this particular 'now'. I need not describe it in detail—suffice to say we all thoroughly enjoyed this welcome departure from our usual evening routine. Katie handed me the chequebook and I went inside to the bar and paid the bill. I marvelled at how cheap it was back then.

Although the return journey was technically up-stream, it seemed no harder to row, as the waters were flowing so gently, as though they themselves could not be bothered to summon up more than the watery equiv-alent of a summer evening's stroll. The children were tired in the car going home, but it was a cheerful, satis-fied tiredness, not the grizzly, fractious kind that can make travel such a pain with small children on board. In any case, it was a drive of only a few minutes to get home, and before very long we'd got the girls (taking one each) undressed, given them a quick wash and packed them off to bed in their 'jammies'. They were asleep within seconds. The two of us then went down-stairs and just chatted about our successful and thor-oughly enjoyable outing, agreeing that we should do it again some time. After a light supper we too were ready to slip gratefully into our bed.

Next morning I awoke on such a wave of euphoria that I almost forgot my original quest—how trivial that wretched basket seemed now! In truth, it might have been as well to give up the idea at that point, but I was deter-mined not to return to the future empty-handed. Kissing my wife and daughters goodbye, I set off for work—except that I didn't go to work straight away. I'd decided I would go to Meecham's first, make my purchase, and then proceed directly to my 21st century job at the RRI.

In five minutes I was there; as usual, the shop was open bright and early. I went in, went straight to the corner of the shop where I knew the chicken-baskets would be, selected one and took it to the counter. I'd expected to see old Mr Meecham himself, or else his son Clive, but it was a stranger who came through the doorway from the back of the shop.

'Bill not in today?' I asked.

'No,' replied the new guy, 'family's all gone on holiday for three weeks. Gone to Bill and Jean's niece's wedding in America. I'm Bill's cousin—on t'other side of the family, like, so I never got an invite. You know him well, do you?'

'Oh yes,' I replied, 'I'm one of his regular customers,' and I proceeded to tell him who I was, and that my wife was quite friendly with his daughter-in-law. 'Just this then, I added,' producing the article.

As he quoted the price and I fished in my purse for a £5 note, I was quite preoccupied with the thought of Bill Meecham and his family, who'd never had more than a day trip to Bournemouth in all the years I'd known them, gadding off to America for three weeks. And that was when I made that fateful slip—the £5 note I handed over was a 21st century one! It never occurred to me at first, so I was puzzled when the assistant took the note, stared at it with a frown and said, rather coldly, 'Just one moment,' and then stepped smartly through the doorway to the back, taking the banknote and the basket with him. At first I thought he was going to wrap it up for me, or maybe he'd spotted a blemish on the article and was going to replace it. Neither explanation seemed very plausible, so I edged towards the door to try and find out what he was doing. I could hear him speaking on the telephone.

'Yes, officer, it's definitely a forgery—never seen one like it before—smaller than the proper ones, and quite a different design. Bill told me to be on the lookout. He said he's had one or two dodgy notes recently … What's that? Yes, he's still here, but you'd better come quick. I'll try and stall him for a while.'

I was horrified. What a silly mistake! I made a swift move towards the front of the shop, but the assistant was back before I could leave.

'Oh, Mr Draper, sir,' he addressed me in a falsely amiable way, 'I'll just pop this in a bag for you,' then he continued, 'By the way, I'm sure you'd be interested in this new line we have over here.'

He indicated for me to follow him to another part of the shop, but I decided a swift exit was called for. 'Oh, yes,' I replied, then: 'Oh, hang on a moment—I think someone's knocked my bike over.'

I turned and marched quickly out of the door, leapt on my bike and pedalled off at high speed, with cries of: 'Oh, Mr Draper, you've left your…' fading in my ears. Oh, what folly! I should have realized I couldn't make today's purchase with tomorrow's money. I'd paid last night's dinner bill with a 'period' cheque backed up by an appropriate cheque card. It had been so automatic that I never gave a thought to what would happen when it came to cash!

The shop assistant must have phoned the police again immediately, and got them to radio the nearest patrol car as to my mode and direction of travel, because I was soon aware of a flashing blue light, reflected in the windscreen of an oncoming bus. They were after me! I took a swift left turn into Rockall Avenue, but I was aware that my pursuers were not far behind.

Then my heart sank—another patrol car was heading *towards* me—I was cornered! Suddenly police officers had jumped out of both cars and were advancing towards me.

'Richard Olwen Draper,' intoned one of the officers, as he grabbed my lapel (I had hastily dismounted with the irrational thought of making a run for it; your mind entertains all sorts of silly ideas like that when put in a spot). He continued: 'I am arresting you on suspicion of passing forged banknotes. You do not have to say anything, but...'

'Okay,' I interrupted, 'I'll come quietly. Let me just put my bike in here.' I had noticed that, by sheer chance (or was it the merciful provision of some higher power?) we had stopped right outside number 35—the home I had lived in for ten years before we'd moved to Upper Meadow Close! I couldn't be sure that what I was about to try would work, but it was at least worth the attempt, especially as I'd previously managed to go back to my old workplace at the Dunkirk. Without waiting for the man in blue to respond, I jerked myself from his grasp and swiftly wheeled the bike through the gate and into the side entrance. Then, rather than return to the long arm of the law, I sprinted through to the rear of the house and, muttering to myself, 'June 1976,' I darted in through the back door. Fortunately it wasn't locked, and I was able to gain immediate entry to the kitchen.

'Why, hello, Willie,' came the surprised cry of my beloved, who had miraculously become even younger than when I had left her that morning...or, well...the *other* morning (you know what I mean). 'What are you doing home from work so early?'

I muttered something about not feeling well, and being sent home, as I rushed into the living room to peer out of the front window. To my amazement (I had still not ceased to be amazed at these time shifts), the Law had gone—no cars, no uniforms, nothing! I tentatively went into the hall and opened the front door—just a crack at first, and then, rather gingerly, wider, until at last I went right outside. I looked all around, not really knowing why—I had obviously succeeded in travelling several more years back in time, and had left the cops behind in the future. There was my bike, sure enough, in the passageway where I had left it—I couldn't really explain why that had not been left behind, although to be honest, I didn't scrutinize it enough to rule out the possibility that it hadn't been my 1976 bike, as that was just where I used to leave it when popping inside for a short while.

I went back inside. 'Whatever is it, love?' my wife enquired, her face betraying her obvious concern.

'Oh...' I stammered, 'd-d-dog; ... this huge dog went for me as I came up the road. Nearly sent me flying.' It was a pretty reasonable off-the-cuff lie, but it happened to be just the right thing.

'That'll be that wretched rottweiler from number 42—always breaking out, it is. Causes havoc. Sylvia Wetherby's even reported it, but nothing's been done.'

'Um ... Kathy,' I faltered, having to collect my thoughts and find the right name for my spouse for this particular phase of our relationship, 'I think I should lie down—I need a rest.' This was quite true—I certainly *did* need time to recover from the shock I'd experienced, as well as to try and work out the best way to undo the trouble I'd inadvertently caused myself.

'Of course, dear,' came the sympathetic response. You go on upstairs and I'll bring you up a nice mug of milky coffee.'

I lay there for a while considering my options, but my ruminations were interrupted by the angel of mercy—my beloved—ministering to my fevered disposition with a delicious cup of smooth, mild, milky coffee—just the way I'd always liked it. She sat on my bedside for a while, gently talking to me in hushed tones. To be honest, I didn't really take in what she was saying; I was just letting myself be soothed by her dulcet voice. And it obviously succeeded in lulling me off to sleep, for I woke several hours later, and at first I was so disorientated that it gave me quite a fright, and it took me a few minutes to piece together all that had happened to me over my last day or so. Having convinced myself that it had not all been a dream (the very fact that I was in *this* house now was clear proof of that), I resumed my thoughts as to how to put right the things I'd done. As I saw it, the options, and their probable outcomes were:

- Just return to the future and hope everything would have blown over. No good—the Law had been after me and I'd absconded. They knew my identity and address, so they'd be round there like a shot, frightening the wits out of my loved ones and almost certainly arresting my 'former' self. I could only hazard a guess at the eventual outcome— probably yet another abrasive encounter with the Major-General of 36 The Willows!
- Return to Meecham's the day after my fateful slip (since I knew I couldn't relive the day itself) and

attempt to present some plausible explanation for what I'd done. Hopeless—the Meecham cousin would have been informed of my escape, and would be primed to take appropriate action if I should return.

- Return to Meecham's the day *before* my inadvertent misdemeanour and pre-empt the situation.

The latter, I decided, was the only feasible option. I got up, pulled on my trousers (I hadn't undressed completely) and went downstairs. Kathy was sitting in an armchair reading a book.

'Hello, love,' she said, soothingly, 'Are you feeling better?'

'Yes, thanks,' I replied, but I'd like to pop out for a walk—I think the fresh air will do me good.' My aim was to get swiftly on my bike, pedal to the hardware shop and project myself forward to my target date. But I was to be thwarted yet again.

'Oh, that's a good idea,' was the reply, 'I could do with blowing away the cobwebs a bit too—I'll come with you.'

'Oh NO!' I thought. 'Oh...yes,' I replied, 'er... that'd be nice!'

And as a matter of fact, it *was* nice. It had been a really long time—in any decade, or century, even!—since I'd gone for a gentle stroll with my wife, just the two of us together, hand in hand. There were some fields at the end of the road (a kind of rural oasis within the city), and a path under trees beside a stream, so it was a very pleasant place for a leisurely amble. We chatted about trivia—I let Kathy do most of the talking, as I had to be very guarded as to what subjects I chose, limiting my repertoire to events no later than the year we were in. Once again I learned the value of appreciating the 'now' rather than wanting to skip ahead to some future event or project.

Well, to cut a long story short, I spent the night there (and then), and the next morning after breakfast bade my spouse adieu and prepared to pedal off. Before leaving home, however, I asked Kathy if she had a fiver. When she asked what I needed it for, I invented an excuse about collecting for someone at work. She expressed some surprise about it being an awful lot of money, but I said not to worry—I'd repay her somehow. I set off and headed straight for Meecham's and concentrated my thoughts on the day before my previous visit. However, to my surprise when I walked through the door, I found myself face to face with Bill Meecham himself!

'Oh!' I exclaimed, 'I didn't expect to see you here!'

'Who on earth *did* you expect?' he asked, 'I do happen to be the proprietor!'

'I guess you must be off to the airport soon, then?' I queried.

'Whatever *are* you talking about?' he asked, looking extremely puzzled.

'Oh, sorry,' I muttered, 'I've obviously got the wrong end of the stick. Er…is that today's paper?' added, indicating a copy of the Daily Mail on the counter.

Receiving an affirmative reply, I picked it up and looked at the date. I was still in 1976! No wonder old Bill looked puzzled! But what had gone wrong? Why couldn't I make the time transition? Had my 'season ticket' expired, as it were? Could I no longer go back and forth between the millennia? These thoughts had me extremely worried, and I made some hasty excuse and left the shop.

Not knowing exactly in which direction to go, I free-wheeled somewhat aimlessly down the road, lost in thought. And then it occurred to me—all my previous time transitions had taken place when entering my various homes or workplaces. For reasons I couldn't at first figure out, other places, like shops, would not act as 'time portals'. Maybe it had to be somewhere that had had a very close association with myself for a sustained length of time. I wondered whether, in fact, it would work if I entered our old church—or even the house I grew up in.

Anyway, eager (possibly even desperate) to prove this theory, I decided to head for the Parklands Clinic. Once again concentrating on the day before the fateful Meecham visit, I took a deep breath (not knowing what situation would greet me) and walked in through the door.

'Ah, Richard,' the boss greeted me, in a more than usually genial mood, 'I'm glad to see you're early today. I've got a pleasant little job for you later.'

Pondering what this 'pleasant little job' Dr Strickland had in store might be, I greeted my colleagues, and received their cheery greeting in return. It soon transpired that we were to have a little party for Jean, one of our secretaries, who was retiring after twenty-three years in the department. The girls had brought various edible goodies, and I was to be entrusted with the job of going out to an off-licence to buy the booze. Most of the staff liked drinks that were light and sparkling, but the boss insisted on dry sherry.

I accepted the task willingly, for I knew the off-licence was only two shops away from Meecham's. So I set off on my errand joyfully, and bought the booze and stowed the bottles in my pannier bags. Then I went to Meecham's.

Sure enough, there was the cousin serving, and he greeted me as though he had never seen me before—which of course, for him, was true.

'Yes sir, what can I do for you?' was his brisk greeting.

I chose a small item that I knew would cost only a few pence: 'I need a half-inch tap washer, please.'

He produced the article and I fished in my purse for a coin of a suitable date. Then I asked if he had any wire baskets shaped like a chicken. He made a positive response, strode to the place where they were kept and produced one. I then fumbled in my purse, frowned and remarked, 'Sorry, I don't seem to have enough on me. I'll have to get it another time.' Then came my redemptive strategy. Withdrawing the 'futuristic' £5 note, I added, just a trifle hesitantly, 'Um, actually, I wonder if I could impose upon you to help me. I'm conducting a survey on behalf of the Royal Mint. It's just a part-time job I have; doesn't pay much (even though they print loads of money!' (He gave a faint chuckle) 'I'm doing it more out of interest than for any personal gain. Anyway, they've been trying out new designs for some of their banknotes, and I've been asked to show some to members of the public and get their reactions.

I handed over the note and proceeded to take a small notebook from my jacket pocket and scribble in it as he made comments. He thought it was a nice, bright, clear design, although he said the smaller size would take a bit of getting used to. I thanked him for his opinions, took back the note, and as I replaced it in my purse, and then remarked, in what I felt was a suitably jocular tone: 'I must be careful to keep it apart from the *real* money—I very nearly tried to pay for some groceries with it!'

The Meecham deputy gave a little chuckle, and as I was replacing the purse in my pocket, I said, nonchalantly, 'I'll probably pop in tomorrow for that chicken-basket thing. It's a present for my wife. In fact, I'd be grateful if you'd remind me to hide it in the workshop when I get home!' He looked visibly puzzled by this remark, but I had made it deliberately, because I planned to come back a couple of days later and retrieve it. You see, I couldn't just buy it there and then, as I knew I'd be coming in for the same item the next day, and... well, *I* knew what I was doing, or at least I thought I did! I just hoped that somehow both I and the shop assistant would sort of automatically act to the rewritten script tomorrow. I returned to the retirement party (I might as well enjoy myself, I thought), then went home to 26 UMC.

It was a pleasant enough evening with Katie and the kids, and I went to bed knowing that the following day would be the one in which we'd enjoy an evening on the river. Since I could not, by the quirky laws of time travel, revisit that day, I figured I'd wake up on the morning of the day after. And so it proved to be! I was over the moon, and my womenfolk couldn't understand why I was in such a good mood! I enjoyed my breakfast and all the usual morning activities, then bade my loved ones goodbye. Making my way out to the workshop, where I kept my bike, I paused to peer around, and, yes! There it was! Barely covered with a piece of newspaper on the bench was my prize—the chicken-basket! My ploy had worked, and I'd successfully avoided being suspected of forgery, being chased by the cops and all the rest of it— *and* I'd put the basket where I would find and retrieve it. At that moment I suddenly had a strange thought. I pulled the purse out of my pocket and examined its contents. The £5 note of the future was still there, but the other one—the one I'd scrounged off Kathy—had disappeared! The purse was bulkier too, for it now contained some more coins—the change for the basket! It was so amazing, but I didn't stop to ponder; I hastily stowed my prize (as though it were some hard-won sports trophy) in my pannier bag and sped off. But I didn't bother to go to work—I simply pedalled at top speed back to Clunmore, thought-targeting my return for the evening of the day I had last left home. As I walked triumphantly in through the back door (noticing with relief that nothing had changed as a result of my adventures) and through to the living room, I found Kate sitting, reading the newspaper.

'I managed to get the basket, love,' I announced, holding it up for her to see.

'Oh, good,' came the matter-of-fact reply, 'I hope it wasn't much trouble.'

'Of course not, darling,' I replied, 'No trouble at all!'

Awarding myself an early night, I lay for a while in bed ruminating over the strange experiences I had just had. I ought to go back sometime and repay the £5 I'd borrowed from Kathy. But as I marvelled at the fact that I'd managed to return not just one but *two* phases back in our history, I was gripped by a frisson of excitement tinged with fear at an even more ambitious possibility.

CHAPTER 10

Back tracking

The thought that was buzzing around in my head was: If I could return so effortlessly to the home before last, could I just as easily go back even further to the one before that—to 29 Valley Crescent? It seemed perfectly logical that I could, and yet there was always that lingering doubt as to whether there were some limit—in time or space—beyond which I'd be unable to pass. In fact, I'd already come up against such a barrier in the Meecham's debacle. A couple of weeks after that see-saw adventure in the past (I had just about recovered my wits and my nerve, although arguably not my good sense), I was pondering this question at breakfast one Thursday morning. Kate was reading the newspaper and commenting aloud every few minutes, but I wasn't taking it in.

'Oh no,' she'd say, 'council tax set to rise 7% next year—that's all we need!'

'Hmm, really?' I'd mumble, 'That's a shame.'

'Oh, that's dreadful—a four-year-old boy's drowned in the canal at Melbury Magna.'

My ears pricked up momentarily, as it was local, but my mind drifted off again as Kate continued: '…While his parents Alan and Sue Fairburn were getting ready for an afternoon trip to a theme park, little fair-haired Callum somehow managed to open the garden gate and toddle down a lane to the canal. His father Alan told our reporter that Callum had always loved to see the brightly coloured canal boats go chugging past, and...'

Somewhat insensitively, I'll admit, I replied, 'Oh well, unfortunately these things do happen,' and I rose hastily from the table and announced: 'Right, I must be off—got lots to do today.' Kate gave me a slightly disapproving look but said nothing. Before leaving, however, I popped upstairs, not only to brush my teeth but also to go to the cupboard where I kept my rather neglected collection of coins and notes. I had once been a very keen numismatist, and had built up a considerable stock of, among other things, pre-decimal British currency. Over the years the enthusiasm had waned; however, being something of a hoarder at heart, I'd held on to my collection, 'for the grandchildren' (none as yet) or because 'it might come in useful some day.' Well, this *was* that day! I was determined not to be caught out with the wrong money again!

With the usual parting pleasantries, I set off, ostensibly to go to work. That had in fact been my first intention—I'd got quite a backlog of processing to do at the RRI—but as I got into town I changed my mind and carried on through to the far side, to the Smallbrook part of Hardington. Coasting down the steep hill towards Valley Crescent at the bottom, I noticed how the trees on each side of the road were beginning to show the first tinges of autumn colouring. I liked autumn—after the heat of summer it was refreshing once again to feel the chill of the morning air, to be dampened by showers, and feel the wind that swirled and played with the yellow, orange, red and brown leaves. But then I liked winter too—unlike many folk who moan about the cold and the dark nights, I really enjoy the romantic scene of a dim light glistening on the wet streets and pavements, and snow—I *love* snow, whether fluttering down from heaven or lying thick across the countryside, deadening all the usual noise and bustle into subdued quietness. But spring is great too, as the countryside wakes up, shakes off the damp, dark shroud of winter and the trees, hedges and roadside verges begin to burst into life again—hawthorn and horse chestnut being the front runners in producing new, tender green foliage. And of course, the birds all seem to sing so much louder and persistently, welcoming the warmer, lighter days. But summer too is wonderful— long, bright days and balmy nights, rich green fields and deep blue skies; holidays, seaside; long walks in the coun- try, or leisurely cycle rides along quiet lanes.

Which season should I choose? I wondered. In the end I decided to plump for winter—it would make a refresh- ing change from the long, hot summer we'd been having. So I chose a date in early January 1970. In fact, the date more or less chose itself, because in thought I declared (slightly arbitrarily): 'A Tuesday in early January, 1970' as I climbed the steps at the back of the row of shops to gain entry to our maisonette, the one above the middle shop. This time the magic cut in rather earlier than I'd expected. I thought I'd have to get to the door, but, as if to reassure me that my experiment *would* work, I was aware of a fairly swift drop in temperature, an uncanny rapid darkening of the ambient light, and a much softer quality to the sounds around me. I was forced to look up, and as I elevated my gaze above the brick parapet of the stairway, I beheld a wondrous sight—the whole neigh- bourhood was covered in a thick blanket of snow. Now,

I know a lot of people complain bitterly (to use an appropriate adverb!) about 'the white stuff', but I *love* it! It makes the whole world look clean, bright and beautiful. OK, so it's cold, but what fun you can have in it—making snowmen, having snowball fights, riding sledges, and then coming indoors to a mug of hot chocolate with your face and hands all aglow. I wouldn't want to live permanently in a hot country, where there was no relief from endless, baking sunshine, and never the experience of seeing the hoar frost on bare twigs, or drawing in your breath on a winter's morning and feel the icy draught go down into your lungs—and then see your breath as you exhale. I feel desperately sorry for Australians sometimes! Sadly, in the 21st century, it seems we don't get nearly as much snow as we used to.

The snow on the stairs and walkway, partly impacted by the feet of others before me, crunched in a satisfying way under my shoes. Then another sound came to my ears—a most melodious one: music; in fact, singing. I stopped to listen, and then saw a small bunch of people, wrapped up in thick overcoats (in fact, I was wishing I'd got mine). They were carrying an old-fashioned lantern, and some had sheets of paper. What was this? I thought. They seemed like carol singers—but surely, Christmas was over a couple of weeks ago. I attuned my ear to their songs. Some were indeed familiar carols, but others I didn't recognize—and they were in a different language. Then it occurred to me—these were members of the local Russian Orthodox Church, reminding the neighbourhood that according to *their* church calendar, the Nativity (as they tend rather to call it) is celebrated 13 days after our Christmas Day. There were quite a number of Russian families in this area. Many had come over soon after the war, and settled in Roxbury. They had generally integrated well, but they kept up their old traditions, and their church was well attended. I didn't think Eastern Orthodox Christians normally went in for carol singing around the streets as we in the West do, but I suppose these folks had partly adopted some of our customs.

I deduced, then, that the date was probably January the sixth or seventh—the latter being the Russians' feast of the Nativity, the former being what is known in Britain as Old Christmas Day (harking back to the time before our calendar was changed). As I stood there, drinking in the sounds of those mostly unfamiliar carols, I thought to myself, 'Well—why *not* Christmas in January? It's no less logical than December.' No-one *really* knows the date of Jesus' birth, and it almost certainly was *not* in the winter, despite the well-loved carols and customs that insist it was. Shepherds would not be out on the hillside with their sheep in midwinter—it was more likely to have been autumn or spring. When the early Christians decided they should commemorate the birth of the Lord, they chose midwinter in an effort to replace the pagan feast of Saturnalia and other such festivals when the days started to become longer and lighter. It seemed fitting to celebrate the coming of the Light of the World at a time when it was becoming physically lighter. Whether this was a wise decision or not is perhaps debatable, as some of the old pagan customs have been carried over into the Christian celebrations, although they have mostly been invested with new meanings.

I thought of carols like 'In the bleak midwinter' and 'See amid the winter's snow', so obviously modelled on a typical European winter Christmas, and I recalled the alternative versions I'd once suggested, had they been written originally in Australia, where Christmas comes in the summer:

See, amid the summer's dust,
Born the One in whom we trust,
See, the tender Lamb appears,
Promised from eternal years!

Hail, thou ever-blessed morn!
Hail, Redemption's happy dawn!
Sing through all Jerusalem,
Christ is born in Bethlehem!

See, amid the maddening flies,
Jesus in a manger lies—
Cows and horses, by God's grace,
With their tails caress His face.

See, beneath the blazing sun,
God's new work on earth begun.
Shepherds cease from shearing sheep,
See the Saviour fast asleep.

[OK, so strictly speaking, the shepherds came by night, so the sun wouldn't have been blazing, but why let a little matter of authenticity get in the way of a good rhyme?!!!]

In the harsh midsummer,
Sunshine blazing down,
Earth was hot as fire,
Making all men frown,
Dust had settled, dust on dust,
Dust on dust,
Wise men found the Baby,
Worship Him they must.

(Tune: Cranham, by Gustav Holst)

The recollection of this bit of silliness made me chuckle, but inwardly I was thoroughly glad that Christmas (in our part of the world at any rate) comes in winter. It just seems so *right*, somehow. I'm sure our American and Canadian cousins would agree with that—'Chestnuts roasting on an open fire' and all that; and so what if some of our Yuletide customs aren't entirely biblically authentic? 'The Holly and the Ivy' still makes some good spiritual points, after all.

I jerked myself out of this cogitative aside and pressed on with my primary missive—to revisit the first of our homes as a married couple. Pulling the bunch of keys out of my jacket pocket, I selected one which seemed closest to the sort that would fit the lock—not too difficult, as both lock and key were of the Yale variety. I was only mildly surprised when the key fitted and turned effortlessly—I had experienced this phenomenon before. As I opened the door and stepped inside, I could hear music coming from the kitchen—it was the radio, tuned to the BBC Light Programme (later to become Radio 2, of course). 'Hi, love!' I called out, as I closed the door behind me.

'Oh, hello, Will,' came the cheerful reply, 'Dinner'll be ready in half an hour. You're a bit earlier than usual, aren't you?'

I glanced at my watch: five past five. Normally I'd have been kept at work till at least five o'clock, and by the time I'd collected my things, said goodbye to my colleagues, put on my outdoor clothes, unlocked my bike and pedalled home, it would be about half-past. I invented some scenario about having had to help with a difficult patient during my lunch break, so Dr Pritchard had (somewhat generously for him!) let me off early.

I looked at Kath (as I used to call her then). No, I *gazed* at her, for this was the stunning young beauty I'd fallen so helplessly in love with all those years ago. Not that she was any less beautiful in the 21st Century—but now her beauty was of a more mature, elegant kind. I fumbled in my mind for a suitable simile, and came up with that of a good wine—after a few years, and given the right conditions, it would blossom into something rich, full and sustaining, but in its youth it could be bright, sparkling and energetic. And thus was my bride whom I beheld before my happy eyes now (for she had once told me that a woman retains the title of bride throughout her first year of marriage).

'Why don't you go on into the living room, darling?' she suggested,' and put your feet up. Put on a record or something.'

As I entered the living room I was struck by the sparse appearance of the room. It was actually quite a large room (the only other ones on that level being the kitchen and the hall), and in it were a table, four dining chairs, one armchair, a small writing desk and a couple of book-cases, each half-full with a variety of books. A couple of pictures adorned the otherwise bare walls. There was also a record player, perched atop a small cabinet that contained a modest collection of records—about three dozen 45s and a dozen or more LPs. I picked one out—Mendelssohn's Violin Concerto. I'd bought it after our honeymoon the previous summer. For part of our fort-night away we'd enjoyed a touring holiday in Norway by coach, and this piece was one of the small repertoire of works that were being played over the coach's PA system as we travelled along. Ever since it never failed to remind me of the spectacular scenery through which we passed—the grandeur of the mountains and the mystic wonder of the evanescent morning mists clinging to the bottoms of the valleys as we passed above them. As that delightful music swept over me, I once again agreed with myself that this was surely the finest and most perfect of all the violin concertos.

My reverie was gently interrupted, however, by my sweet bride bringing in two plates of a delicious smelling lamb casserole, which she deposited on placemats on the dining table. We sat up and prepared to dine (I noted that 'nowadays' we hardly ever sit up at table for our meals—they're usually consumed off a lap-tray while we sit in front of that tyrant called television; you could hardly call that 'dining'). I thanked Kath profusely for such a tasty meal, into which she had obviously put a great deal of effort. She countered my comments by pouring out her thanks to *me*.

'I'm sorry, sweetie,' she added, somewhat sheepishly, 'but I just *couldn't* resist peeping! It's a really *lovely* present. You couldn't have chosen anything better—you're so thoughtful.'

It took me a moment to gather my senses. Present? January? Oh, of *course*—her birthday! It's not that I usually forget it (in fact, in all our years of marriage, I've never forgotten it—how could I, since it comes so early in the New Year, and I always have to wrack my brains to think of something else to get her straight after Christmas? In fact, I usually started to 'put my thinking cap on' at the same time as I would for Christmas presents.)

'Oh...oh...yes,' I fumbled verbally, not having a clue as to what it was I had apparently got her. 'So glad you liked it. What else did you get?'

'Oh, I haven't opened any others yet—I thought I'd better keep *some* for the day itself!'

From this I deduced that it was the 6th. I recalled that Kath's birthday was the 7th of January—Russian Christmas Day. I always remembered the date was special somehow. A little unsure what to say next, I ventured: 'Shall we go out tonight? For a meal, or something?'

'No, silly billy,' came the reply, 'we've got that arranged for tomorrow—surely you hadn't forgotten? And anyway, it's your AGM this evening.'

'Oh yes, of course,' I bluffed, thinking there was no 'of course' about it. AGM? AGM of what? What club, organization or society did I use to belong to back at this time?

Making an excuse to go out into the kitchen (to get the salt or something), I took the opportunity to scrutinize the appointments calendar I knew would be hanging up there (being a teacher, Kate was always highly organized). There it was, in black and white (well, actually, blue and white, as it was written in ballpoint pen): 'BRLR AGM'. There were no other clues, and I obviously looked quite pensive, troubled even, as I returned to the table.

'What is it, darling?' came an anxious voice across the table.

'Oh, er...nothing, really,' I mumbled, 'just something I heard at work today.' But I was still trying to puzzle out what those initials stood for. The 'BR' bit suggested British Rail, which, as it happened, wasn't far off the mark. I continued to eat in silence, giving Kath only half the attention she deserved, as she chatted happily about her day. All the while I was desperately trying to recall whatever it had been that I'd belonged to. 'BRLR...BRLR...' I kept thinking to myself. Then I tried 'BR...BR...' and '...LR...LR'. I tried to think of other

176

titles ending in the initials LR, and that was the key that unlocked the mystery. Of course—there was SDLR: South Dorset *Light Railway*; EVLR: Eden Valley *Light Railway*...and...I could think of three or four other light railways past and present. It thus didn't take me long to work out (or rather, recall) that BRLR stood for Berrington & Roxbury Light Railway, a quaint little line that had joined the two conurbations, running close to the River Roxe and the canal.

My face took on a somewhat brighter hue, as did my level of conversation. By and by, when there was a lull in the conversation, I ventured: 'Let's see, it *is* seven-thirty that the AGM begins, isn't it?' (I figured that most evening meetings began at 7:30.)

'Yes, dear—that's what you told me.'

'And,' I hazarded what proved to be a fortunate guess, 'it'll be in The Signalman's Arms, I suppose?'

'Why of *course*, love. Whatever is the matter with you? It isn't like you to forget something like that!'

'Oh, sorry dear—it's just been one of those days, that's all.'

'Do you want to tell me about it?'

'No, love; I don't want to bore you—you wouldn't understand anyway.'

That last bit was certainly true—in fact, if I'd even begun to try and explain, she'd have rushed me off to the local mental hospital to get me certified. No, actually, she wouldn't—she'd have been far too kind and loving for that. Her first resource would have been our local pastor, who'd have given me some sympathetic counselling, and a lot of prayer.

We finished our meal, and did the washing up together. I'd forgotten how enjoyable those little chores had been when tackled together, in the early years of our married life. I enjoyed the little chitchat we exchanged over the task, although I had to let Kath do most of the talking, as I was several decades out of touch with contemporary life. We continued our chat together over coffee in the living room, and I desperately wanted to tell her of the joyful times we'd share in at least thirty-five years of marriage—of the two lovely daughters we'd have, and the exciting holidays we'd have as a couple, and later as a family. I wondered about some of the difficult and sad times we'd experience, but was glad in a way that, along with details of the positive aspects of the future, I'd no need to burden her with the negative ones.

Presently the time came to think about setting off for the AGM.

'Why don't you take the bus, dear?' my spouse suggested, 'it's pretty icy out there now, and I don't fancy you slithering about on your bike,'

'Good idea,' I agreed. Fortunately, I could still remember where the bus stops were—our nearest was just round the front of the shops. With a swift kiss, I took my leave of Kath, having grabbed a thicker coat off the rack than the jacket I'd deposited there earlier, and made my way down the steps and round to the bus stop. As I stood there, I recalled in my mind the events of the last hour and a half. What most amazed me, as it had with all my other forays back in time, was how much more youthful my wife had been—and yet she seemed to see me as of the same sort of age when in reality I was considerably older! As I was further pondering some of the quirks and seeming inconsistencies of this whole business, I was brought back to reality (whatever *that* was!) by the arrival of the 6B bus. I climbed on board and asked the driver for a return to Vandyke Terrace, the nearest stop to the Signalman's Arms (as it still is today).

'One shilling, mate,' the driver said, gruffly.

One shilling! How cheap is that! I thought, as I handed him half-a-crown from my carefully prepared purse. A twentieth of a pound! Inflation had certainly taken its toll in the intervening years—what would 5p buy now? Well, in the twenty-first century, that is. I took the one-and-sixpence change and made my way to a seat. The bus was practically empty. Not many souls venturing out that night—too cold, and with Christmas and New Year behind them, nothing much to go out and celebrate. Most sensible folk were staying at home, sitting by their firesides.

The bus started off up the hill, but partway up it hit a patch of extra slippery ice and lost its grip. There were some gasps from the other passengers as we began to slither backwards, but as we slipped to one side the wheels gained a stretch of less impacted snow and by careful manoeuvring, the driver managed to get us up to the top (on the wrong side of the road, as it happened, but the roads were almost deserted anyway). This little extra adventure amused me somewhat—as it evidently did the other passengers, once they had regained their composure.

As we continued our journey I turned over in my mind the things I recalled of the Berrington and Roxbury Light Railway. It had been built towards the end of the 19th Century as an industrial line, to carry raw materials from the main line through Roxbury to its smaller neighbour, and light manufactured goods back the other way. As such it was a narrow gauge line, built to the relatively unusual gauge of two foot six inches, the only other examples of that particular gauge in the UK being, to the best of my knowledge, the Llanfair & Welshpool Railway and the Leek & North Staffordshire. Back in its heyday you would see the little pannier tanks chugging back and forth along the single line, hauling eight to ten trucks. There was a passing loop at Melbury Magna, and at some time in the twenties, I believe, some enlightened visionary had the good sense to initiate a passenger service along the route. It was a common sight to see the mixed rolling stock—a couple of passenger carriages plus half a dozen trucks. There were no appreciable gradients along the line, so one engine could manage the load with ease. By the early sixties, however, both passenger and goods demands were declining, and although the BRLR escaped the Beeching axe, it looked distinctly as though its days were numbered. Around the middle of the decade a group of enthusiasts managed to buy up the line and most of the rolling stock (largely thanks to a wealthy benefactor who was something of steam railway buff), and it was kept going partly as a commercial enterprise and partly as a tourist attraction. Being quite keen on railways myself, and steam railways in particular, I joined the BRLR Association and took part in some of their activities, but alas, not long after I'd joined, it seemed clear that we were fighting a losing battle, and, as our funds were well-nigh depleted and the future of the little line looked bleak, we reluctantly decided to call it a day. Hence the line was closed and all its assets were sold off—mainly to other private railway companies, or to enthusiasts who were keen to buy a bit of railway nostalgia. I remember thinking some years later, how short-sighted we had been, and how, in the late 20th and early 21st centuries, private steam railways had become a real tourist attraction, some of them even performing a valuable service to the community as commuter lines.

I vaguely recalled being rather upset at the closure of the BRLR, and wishing I could have done something to help save it. Well now, it seemed, was my chance—I would at least have a go. Nothing ventured... as they say. So it was with a certain amount of determination that I stepped off the bus at Vandyke Terrace and marched round the corner to the Signalman's Arms.

The chairman, secretary and treasurer were already there, propping up the bar along with half a dozen of the other members.

'Ah, good to see ya, Richard,' declared Jim Belton the chairman. Get yerself a pint o' summat; we're only waitin' fer Jack Wilshaw, Colin Bentley and Louise West, then we can commence.'

Presently Louise and Colin arrived, looking as if they were very much 'an item', and, armed with a pint of Whiteway's Devonshire cider, I accompanied them into one of the small function rooms, which we had hired (for a very small fee, Reg Polkinghorne the landlord being only too pleased to have our custom, since he knew we should be requiring a few top ups of our glasses and tankards).

And so the meeting got under way, with Mary Jackson the secretary noting Jack's absence and reading the minutes of the last meeting. These were agreed and signed as an accurate record, and the matters arising concentrated very heavily on the very disheartening financial report that Alan Carter-Wright the treasurer had presented. It was abundantly clear that our resources were at a very low ebb. After many minutes of heated discussion, Jim called the meeting to order, saying that item 5 of the agenda would be dedicated to a frank appraisal of the Association's future, and with it that of the line itself. We proceeded with item 4, a report on last month's visit of a group of rail enthusiasts from Czechoslovakia (this was, of course, before the 'Velvet Divorce', when Slovakia parted company with the western part of the former country), and as we did so, I began to steel myself for a robust defence of the line's right to survival, marshalling in my mind all the ammunition I could muster to fight my corner.

And certainly a fight it was. Alan was adamant that the current situation was unsustainable: he'd demonstrated beyond all possible contradiction (he maintained) that we were, if not spiralling, at least sliding fairly rapidly towards financial ruin, and that, regrettably, our only viable option was closure and dispersal of our assets at the earliest opportunity. I considered how readily, it seemed, treasurers of clubs, associations and suchlike would produce gloomy reports, and always look on the pessimistic side of the situation. I'd noted on previous occasions in other organizations, how, even when there was a healthy surplus in the kitty, the treasurer was always quick to foresee every conceivable eventuality that would require a financial outlay well in excess of the resources in hand. On this occasion, admittedly, there was at least some substance to Alan's arguments—passenger numbers had dwindled appreciably over recent years, and the volume of freight was at an all-time low.

After several minutes of corporate wringing of hands and gnashing of teeth, I decided to put my oar in and inject a note of optimism. Our recent poor performance was, I argued, largely due to our having gone about the business with the wrong attitude. We needed to adopt a much more lively approach—aggressive, even—to advertise the delights and the potential of our great little line. The newly created local radio station, Roxbury Radio, would be a good place to start. I suggested we ring up the station controller and ask to present a feature about the BRLR—being a fairly new station, Roxbury Radio was on the lookout for interesting local stories. If we could arrange an interview with one of us (I said I for one would be more than willing to offer myself for this), that would almost certainly generate interest around the city and neighbouring region.

We should canvass the opinions of local people as to what would be the most convenient times for commuter trains, and adjust our timetables accordingly. We would do well to contact the many light engineering and other businesses in Berrington, and persuade them of the value of sending their wares via the BRLR to link up with the main line in Roxbury—after all, I argued, the roads were becoming increasingly congested, and fuel prices were certain to rise steeply before long. (With the benefit of hindsight—or in the current situation, foresight—I knew that the seventies' oil crisis was looming, and I did my best to detail the political factors already becoming apparent in the Middle East, although I soon realized this was not proving a very convincing line of argument.)

I tried a different tack: 'We should promote much more in the way of leisure and novelty events at weekends and holiday times. Thomas the Tank Engine theme days, for example; cream tea specials in the summer, and Santa Specials leading up to Christmas—they're *bound* to be popular!' (I 'foresaw', of course, that this would indeed be the case within a few years; I just had to persuade my fellow enthusiasts to be, well, enthusiastic!) I went on to suggest 'Steam Experience' events, whereby individuals could pay to have a half-day's carefully guided 'tuition' in how to drive a steam engine.

I continued: 'We should aim to maximize our publicity: get some adverts in the local papers, distribute fliers, put leaflets in the tourist information centre. We could even have our own website.'

'Our *what* sight?' asked one of the members.

'Oh…er…never mind,' I muttered, having forgotten for a moment that I was some twenty years early for that particular development. I continued to wax lyrical, proffering every available reason why the BRLR was bound to succeed if we'd only give it a chance—and our dedicated support.

I could tell that I was beginning to win over some of the others, but I was not convinced the battle had been won. Needless to say, Alan the treasurer remained stolidly opposed, and when I proposed a motion that we should take a positive view of the future and put all our energy into preserving the line for posterity (it was seconded by Louise West), he spared no effort in trying to shoot me down in flames. One or two others took his side and gave him ammunition with which to do the shooting. In the end, Jim once again called the meeting to order (just as Reg Polkinghorne came in to take our orders for a much needed fresh round of drinks) and declared that we had given the matter more than enough airing, and proposed that we take a vote on the proposal that we should endeavour to keep the Berrington and Roxbury Light Railway open, adding the rider that we should review the situation closely, and give the venture twelve months to decide finally whether or not to continue operations.

In the event it couldn't have been closer: six for and six against (I was mighty glad that Jack Wilshaw hadn't turned up—I knew for sure that he would have opposed the motion. He was a miserable old s... No, I'd better not put it in writing or he might sue me for libel.) Anyway, it fell to the chairman to give the casting vote, and to my sheer delight it carried the motion. One or two of those who'd opposed it continued to grumble into their beer; others took the attitude that we might just as well give it a go, and came round to the idea. So, on the whole, we completed the rest of the business in a generally happy and positive mood, and agreed to hold the next meeting soon, in order to discuss our campaign strategies.

I shall skip lightly over the rest of the evening's jollities; suffice to say that a generous quantity of ale, and a moderate amount of cider, got poured down the throats of the BRLRA members' throats. Before very long the two ladies were tittering incessantly over their G & T's, and even old Alan, the miserable miser, got so thoroughly bladdered that he was slapping us blokes on the back and practically molesting the women, declaring in loud, slurred tones what an excellent meeting it had been, what a brilliant future our beloved railway had, and how Will Draper was a 'damn good fellow', and we should all congratulate him for his insightful perspicacity (except that it came out more or less as 'insh-eyeful pershy pink cashidy').

I made my excuses presently, and departed. After all, I didn't want to leave my little one all on her own for too long on the eve of her birthday. I rode home on a No. 6 bus and a cloud of euphoria. I was quite confident that

I had succeeded in preserving for posterity a valuable little piece of railway history—a veritable treasure that would otherwise have been lost forever.

As I mounted the steps at the back of the row of shops on which our home, and the neighbours', were perched, the snow crunched even more crisply under my feet, as the temperature had fallen to well below zero. Inside me, however, there was a really warm glow—due partly, 'tis true, to a fair measure of Whiteway's Devonshire cider, but mainly as a result of the splendid achievement I had wrought. As I went inside, Kath greeted me cheerfully from the living room, where she was doing some embroidery, while listening to a play on the South of England Home Service (later to be subsumed into Radio 4). Bidding me to get by the fire and warm myself, she popped into the kitchen and rustled up two mugs of hot milky coffee. She switched off the radio ('It wasn't a very good play, anyway') and proceeded to listen to my (somewhat abridged) account of the evening's business. When I told her the outcome of the vote, she seemed almost as thrilled as I was.

'Why, that's marvellous, darling— Mum and Dad used to take me for shopping trips to Berrington on that line when I was small, and I *loved* those little tank engines, and the sweet little carriages.' (She was, of course, a local lass.)

Eventually it was time for us to turn in, and we put out all the lights and made our way up to bed. It was about twenty to eleven. Although my mind was positively spinning with the thoughts of that day's —or actually, evening's—events, I very soon drifted off into the Land of Nod. This was probably at least partly the effect of the cider. About an hour later, though, I woke up again, with a distinct urge to visit the bathroom. This was definitely an effect of the cider.

As I emerged from the loo, I recalled that tomorrow would be Kath's birthday, and I pictured myself sharing with her the delights of that occasion. But as I did so, for some quite intangible reason, I began to feel that somehow that wouldn't quite be right. I wasn't able to put my finger on the cause of my unease, but in some way I felt it was right to let my other, former self experience that joyful occasion. So, very quietly, so as not to wake my beloved, I got dressed and stealthily slipped out of the house. I trod as warily as I could down the slippery steps and round to where I'd left my bike. There it was, covered in a layer of white rime from the frozen moisture that had settled on it. I tried to wipe off the saddle as best I could, but as I got on, the warmth of my body caused it to melt, giving me a wet bottom.

Although my day had effectively lasted only seven hours, I was feeling really tired—a product, no doubt, of my exertions at the AGM, and, of course—that cider! Furthermore, the unaccustomed cold (such as we're no longer used to in the 21st century), made me feel I wanted to be tucked up warm in bed—just like the one I had so recently left. So, as I pedalled warily up the hill, avoiding the patches of hard-packed ice, I decided to return to the Thursday I had left, but late at night, rather than at tea-time, as I would have done if I'd just come home from work. As I rode through the city, and 'thought my way' forward more than three decades, I felt the cold saddle grow warm, and my trousers become dry. The air temperature changed too, becoming so much warmer that I had to stop, remove my jacket and stuff it in my pannier bag.

I hadn't been too sure if I could specify my return time, but in fact, it did work the way I'd wanted, and I was able to creep into the house well after dark, disturbing no-one except one of the cats, and I was able to slide into a soft, welcoming bed beside Kath (no! I meant Kate! I really *had* to get these names right—it was so confusing!) and treat myself to the 'early' bedtime I felt I deserved, even though it was nearly midnight. As I snuggled down, my mind was wrestling with the insoluble puzzle as to how my 'other' self was (presumably) able to fill in the gaps when I was not present. I was trying to imagine him/myself back in the early seventies as a young twenty-something walking across the landing and returning to the bed I had recently vacated (or had he simply materialised in it at the moment I'd made the transition back to the future (or present))? It was as I was tackling the bewildering issue of whether he/I had just vacated *this* bed (for it seemed as if the sheets *had* been rumpled somewhat), that I was graciously relieved of the burden of this problem by that wonderful leveller of sleep, covering and enfolding me, and drawing me off into oblivion.

Next day being Friday, I put out the rubbish for the bin men and, after breakfast and the usual intra-marital pleasantries, I sped off on my trusty steed to the RRI, and performed a day's work, somewhat more brightly than usual, after the triumphs of the previous (half-) day. My colleagues even commented how unusually cheerful I was (although I really liked to think I was *always* cheerful!). Although I was dying to share my experiences with some of my closer colleagues, I knew I dared not. They would surely think I was either spinning a very far-fetched yarn, or had completely lost my marbles.

So, I travelled home again and plonked myself down in my favourite armchair to read the papers before tea. When I picked up the local weekly paper, the Roxbury Record, I let out an audible gasp and my eyes nearly popped out like organ-stops. For there, emblazoned across the front page was the headline: TWELFTH BUMPER YEAR FOR LOCAL RAILWAY, with an extensive article about the resounding success of the BRLR! As I scanned the article I learned how, after re-inventing itself in the early seventies, the little line had enjoyed gathering success ever since At first it was a matter of simply breaking even, which it began to do after a slightly uncertain start characterized by decreasing annual losses. After that it had begun to make modest gains until at last a short-term bridging loan had been paid off and eventually the operators began to see a small but increasing profit.

As finances improved, the Association had been able to invest in extra rolling stock, bought cheaply from another railway that had had to close (some engineering work had been necessary to convert the stock to the BRLR's unusual 2'6" gauge). On the principle that 'success breeds success', each new investment brought in more custom, and that meant greater revenue and hence more opportunity of further investment. The local Leisure and Tourism Board caught on to the idea and began promoting the line, safe in the knowledge that as more people came to visit this quaint little gem of steam working, it would generate more income for the shops, restaurants, theatres etc. of both Roxbury and Berrington—and villages such as Melbury Magna, Sutton Welthorne and Axtonborough along the line would also benefit, as passengers stopped off en route to sample the food and drink provided by the various pubs in those communities. Some far-seeing entrepreneur had come up with the idea of combined train and canal excursions— chugging along on the water in a leisurely manner in one direction, then returning by train (or the other way about). Local businesses too took up the opportunity to send a significant proportion of their goods by rail.

As I continued to read, I suddenly let out such a snort of disgust that it brought Kate scurrying in from the kitchen. 'Whatever is the matter, dear?' she enquired, looking alarmed.

'Well, of all the bloody cheek!' It took a lot to make me swear, but *really*!

'Listen to this!' I exploded, and proceeded to read aloud:

'The railway's treasurer, Alan Carter-Wright, 68, told our reporter: "It's so rewarding to see all the hard work that's been put in over the years paying off so well, and a complete vindication of the brave step of faith I took thirty-odd years ago in insisting that we continue to give this wonderful little line a further chance, instead of throwing in the towel and opting for closure, as had been proposed. Way back then, few could have foreseen what a resounding success our venture would prove to be, but I was one of the few—*very* few, I might tell you—who could appreciate what a valuable treasure we possessed, and should strive with all our might to protect, against all the odds. I can tell you, it's not always been easy—we've had to come through some pretty tough times, when even I began to doubt the wisdom of my decisions, and I've waited for many years, many years indeed, for this glorious mo-ment. It means now that I can retire from my post as

Treasurer of the BRLR, proud and satisfied with the tremendous legacy to our local communities that I have been able to pass on to those coming after."'

'Honestly! Of all the blasted impudence!' I thundered, toning down my language but not my mood. 'How can he have the brass neck to take the credit for something he was dead against?' *He* was the one who most vehemently opposed keeping the line open, and *I* was the one who had to work my guts out to persuade the members of the Association to take a positive line! If it'd been left to Mr Carter-flaming-Wright, there wouldn't *be* a success story now!'

'Oh, come on, darling,' countered Kate, as soothingly as she could, 'You don't know that—it was such a *long* time ago. He may not have actually been as anti as you think.'

'He darn well was, you know,' I argued: 'I remember that meeting as if it were yesterday!' (There was a great deal more truth in this statement than I was prepared to let on!)

'Well,' reasoned Kate, 'Life's like that, I'm afraid— there are the hard workers like you and me who seldom if ever get the thanks or credit we deserve, and the blatantly cheeky ones who do nothing at all and get treated like heroes.'

True though that was, it did little to pacify me, and in a great huff I threw the newspaper down in disgust. 'I've a good mind to write to the editor and jolly well tell him *who* was the prime mover in keeping the line open.'

'Now, you know that wouldn't do any good, dear,' said Kate gently, 'either it wouldn't get printed or people would think you were just trying to steal the glory from a successful man. I'd leave well alone if I were you—*I* know how hard you've worked for that railway over the years, and I'm sure all your colleagues do too.'

She was right, of course (as wives usually are), and strangely, upon hearing those words about my dedication to the railway 'over the years', I once again experienced that eerie sensation of having a 'memory', albeit rather hazy, start to form in my mind. I could 'remember' many of the special events we had held, and of how my two daughters, as little girls, had squealed with delight on their first Santa Special, when the train had pulled into the station and there was the jolly fat gentleman standing there in his red coat, calling out 'Ho ho ho!' to all the children.

After dinner, I got Kate to get out some of our photo albums, and I enjoyed 'reliving' in pictures the experiences I'd apparently had—as part of a trackside gang, shovelling ballast, enjoying the thrill of actually driving a tank engine, being in the welcoming party for a visiting member of the Royal Family and so on. This all cheered me up no end, and I would have gone to bed a supremely happy man, had not one small matter put a damper on things.

As I picked up the newspaper I had so peevishly strewn onto the floor, my eye caught a small headline on an inside page: TODDLER KILLED ON RAILWAY LINE. I continued to read with dismay:

'A four-year-old child was knocked down and killed on Wednesday when he strayed onto the tracks of the privately owned light railway at Melbury Magna. While his parents Alan and Sue Fairburn were getting ready for an afternoon trip to a theme park, little fair-haired Callum somehow managed to open the garden gate and toddle down a lane to the railway. His father Alan told our reporter that Callum had always loved to see the smart little tank engines go steaming past, and he was unfortunately struck by a workman's trolley when he stepped into its path. The workman, John Bentham, was unable to stop the trolley, and was treated for shock at the RRI. The child died at the scene.'

What a dreadful irony—only a day ago I had heard how poor little Callum Fairburn had drowned in the canal. He would have crossed path of the disused railway to get to it. My actions in the revisited past had prevented him from meeting a watery end, only for him to suffer a more violent one instead. For a moment I pondered how to return to the past and make a suitable amendment to history that could save this young lad's life, as I'd managed to with young Damien Winterton. But the more I turned the problem over in my mind, the more I felt—and I have no way of explaining this—that I should simply let things be. It seemed as if some unspoken voice within me was saying that there is a limit to how much tragedy in this imperfect world we can avert. Some things, apparently, are beyond our reach, and are simply destined to be.

CHAPTER 11

The boy who never was

After the shock I'd received over the Callum Fairburn business, the whole concept of time travel lost its appeal to some extent. It wasn't as if I deliberately vowed not to go back anymore—I just hadn't particularly got the desire. Yes, of course—my ventures back in time had indeed on the whole enriched the lives of myself and other family members, along with a lot of other people besides, but the realization was gradually dawning on me that there was probably going to be a limit to just how much I could achieve, and maybe I had come close to reaching it. There was also the increasing uncertainty as to what this was doing to my health—was it really good for me to be flitting back and forth between the decades (millennia, even)? Was I also perhaps shortening my life-span somewhat, by adding extra days unaccounted for by the natural calendar? Hence I did not go out of my way to return to former years.

It was, in fact, quite unintentionally that I travelled some thirty years back again. With Kate firmly involved in the activities of Dollybirds, and several other ventures that were occupying her increasingly active leisure time since her early retirement, I decided that I needed to broaden my own interests somewhat. I was still working, although I had cut down my hours somewhat. I was still a fair way off retiring completely, but I felt a gradual transition to that phase would be preferable to a sudden culture shock. So, I joined an astronomy club that met once a month in Walburton, a couple of villages further west (chosen by virtue of its lack of street lighting and other forms of light pollution, the curse of all would-be astronomers). Then there was the Roxbury Camera Club, a twice-monthly affair, and the Clunmore Natural History Society. Being a country lad at heart, I had always enjoyed the delights of nature, and there were certainly some fascinating flora and fauna in the neighbourhood—not forgetting the recent sightings of 'big cats' (a puma and a lynx had been allegedly spotted by ramblers on the heathland to the north of the area).

I really came to enjoy the natural history meetings, because each week without exception, some fascinating topic would arise, and I (as well as the other members of the group) would make some intriguing new discovery. One evening we were discussing the vast numbers of different beetles that frequented our gardens and neighbouring tracts of land. One of the favourites—particularly with the women members—was the ladybird (or rather, the range of varying patterned beetles classed generally as ladybirds: the seven-spotted variety, the two-spotted sort, the ones that were basically yellow rather than red, the 'inverse coloured' ones with red or yellow spots on a black background, and so on). Then I asked the others: 'Has anyone else come across the American mint beetle? This query drew the complete range of negative responses: shaking of heads, blank looks, puzzled expressions, murmurs of 'No', 'M-hm' and 'I beg your pardon?'

'The American mint beetle,' I repeated, and went on to describe how, many years ago this striking insect had appeared in our garden. Similar in shape to a ladybird but slightly larger, its wing covers were of a bright, metallic green hue—almost fluorescent, in fact. It lived, and fed, on our mint plants, and nothing else. I had mentioned it to Mrs Elspeth Merryweather, our neighbour across the garden fence. She was an ultra-keen gardener, and what she didn't know about matters botanical and horticultural was of little practical use. She replied, with a dismissive air, as if it were common knowledge, that these creatures were American mint beetles, and they had appeared in both our gardens shortly after she and her husband had returned from a holiday in the USA. She surmised that Victor, her spouse, must have brought back the grubs of the beetles in his trouser turnups or something. They were so beautiful that we positively encouraged them, and looked forward to their reappearance each year in the spring. I had even 'transplanted' some, along with the mint, when we moved from Rockall Avenue to UMC, although they didn't flourish quite so well there. And alas, when we moved again to Clunmore, my attempts to bring them with us again were entirely unsuccessful.

Naturally, all my naturalist colleagues were extremely keen to see some of these insects. Had I taken any photos of them? Could I direct them to any publication that described them? I had to answer no in both instances. Ironically, several years later, I discovered that Chrysolina menthastri, to use its scientific nomenclature, is not particularly American at all, and is actually quite common in parts of the UK. However, at the time, I was unaware of that, and took it for granted—wrongly, as it turns out—that the green-fingered Mrs Merryweather was correct in every detail.

When the others pressed me for more details, I initially gave a combination of gestures to indicate that there was nothing else, really, that I could do to satisfy their thirst for knowledge of this wonderful wee beastie. As I walked home that evening a thought occurred to me. It was mid-July: just the time when the mint beetle would be at its most prolific. It had flourished, as it were, every year at our former abodes, especially while we were at Rockall Avenue. If I were to go there tomorrow, the chances of my finding some live specimens were very high. I therefore resolved to do so.

It was actually quite convenient, as I'd got a spot of processing to do at Parklands, so I could nip across to Number 35 in my lunch break. This I did, and, leaning my bike against the wall in the passage-way between 35 and 37, and armed with a matchbox in my jacket pocket, I rang the bell and silently rehearsed my little speech:

'Excuse me, sir/madam; sorry to bother you, but I used to live here thirty-odd years ago, and there used to be some very interesting beetles that lived on the mint plants in the garden. I belong to a natural history association, and I...' Well, you can surely imagine the rest. I waited, but there was no answer. Once again I rang the bell, but with the same result. 'Oh well,' I thought, 'I guess that isn't surprising—a lot of these houses have been bought up and let out to students; they're probably out at lectures or something. Or it could be a young professional couple living here—these houses are popular with local health workers and teachers. They wouldn't be at home during the day.'

This effectively gave me the all-clear to carry out my beetle-hunting alone and unimpeded, so I proceeded through the passageway and let myself in through the back gate. As I did so, I began to find my mind drifting back to my previous visit, when I had escaped from the long arm of the law, and been pitched rather abruptly back some three decades. I quickly checked my wandering thoughts, as I wanted to stay firmly rooted in the present. I had more or less decided that, in the absence of any dire emergency, I would avoid further meddling with the space-time continuum, having experienced some of the unforeseen and undesirable consequences of doing so.

I made my way to the far end of the garden: it was of pleasingly compact dimensions—not so large and rambling as to be unmanageable, yet not cramped and pokey. I noted with great satisfaction that it had been kept neat and tidy: the lawn mown to a decent length and its borders straight and well defined, the hedge along one side nicely trimmed, the fence and shed in good nick and recently treated with wood preserver. The borders, too, were beautifully replete with colourful summer flowers. This was surely no students' residence! To my further satisfaction, there was the large clump of mint, over by the fence at the end. The compost heap I had kept next to it had been replaced by a modern plastic composting bin. For some reason as I stepped round to where the mint was, a memory popped into my head. It was a cat. A white cat—Mrs Merryweather's cat Snowball. He had been a real character, with one eye green and the other blue, and a kink in his tail where it had once got caught in a door. He had adopted our house and garden as an extension of his own domain (and probably claimed other territories adjacent to his own as well).

Almost always when I went down the garden with some peelings for the compost, or for some other purpose, Snowball would jump up onto the fence and greet me with that friendly little feline call of 'Prrriaow!' Of course, in due time Snowball had gone the way of all flesh and his passing had been deeply mourned by his owner (now a widow) and very much by ourselves. We missed him very much, and although he was no longer around, his memory lingered on.

Alas, I had done the very thing I'd resolved not to— I'd let my mind take me back to the time when our feline friend was very much on the scene, and the very next moment, there he was! In retrospect I should have been surprised when that moggie suddenly jumped up from beyond, gave his customary greeting and began to sharpen his claws on the top of the fence. However, so deep had I drifted into my reverie, that his appearance seemed perfectly natural and logical.

'Hello, old chap,' I said, reaching out to stroke his silky fur and tickle him under the chin, 'how are you today?'

It was just then that I realized that I had slipped, quite unintentionally, back in time. My instinct was to try and think myself back to the present, but experience had taught me that this was not possible—I had to enter, or at least, proceed towards, a 'point of transition', that is, another place where I lived or worked. Stuffing the matchbox (unfortunately, still empty) back in my pocket, I quickly retraced my steps back towards the gate leading to the passageway. I would mount my trusty steed and pedal bravely off back to work (in my own century) before I got caught up in the affairs of the seventies.

Sadly, however, my plan failed, for, as I regained the small patio (Snowball trotting briskly behind me), a familiar face appeared at the back door, and the voice of Kathy called out: 'Oh, there you are, dear. Come on in— your meal's ready.' My initial thought was to ignore her and make a dash for it, letting my 'other self' take over (I still hadn't figured out where he—or I—disappeared to when my later manifestation imposed upon his temporal territory), but that just didn't seem right somehow. Furthermore, my rudeness could well have untoward repercussions and get me into deep trouble again. So, my pace slowed swiftly to a stroll, and I walked in through the back door (followed, of course, by the cat).

'I've laid the table in the living room—your dad can't manage the high stools in the kitchen.'

What was that she'd said? 'Your dad'? Or were my ears deceiving me? Dad had died sixteen or seventeen years ago, but this, of course, was several years before that fateful day when Mum had very bravely phoned us up to say that her dearest one had slipped quietly away in his sleep. He had fallen off a ladder the previous day and suffered concussion. He was given a thorough neurological examination at the local hospital and nothing untoward was found. He'd then perked up considerably and was allowed home, but apparently there was some internal haemorrhaging that had not been apparent initially, and in the night his sleep deepened into a coma and with surprising swiftness to death.

Trembling with anticipation, I stepped gingerly into the front room. There, sure enough, was the familiar, stocky figure of my father. A thatcher by trade, he always had that healthy 'outdoors' look, and his jovial face was adorned with two bright, twinkling blue eyes. His bushy eyebrows sat underneath a huge mop of thick, black hair. I could scarcely believe my eyes—here was the father I'd missed for almost twenty years, back in my life again, as bright and as lively as ever! (I had, of course, met my late parents-in-law on the day of the Coventry opera debacle, but the full impact of their 'resurrection' had not struck me. Whether that was because they were not my own parents, or because the sheer awfulness of that situation had rendered the whole episode like a surreal, bad dream, I don't know. This, somehow, seemed quite different.)

'Hi, Dad!' I exclaimed, 'it's really great to see you again!'

His eyes returned an extra gleam at my unexpectedly fond greeting, but Kathy was quite bemused.

'Come off it, dear—you've only been outside five minutes, but you're greeting him as if you haven't seen him for years!'

She didn't realize how truly she spoke. Somehow though, Dad never batted an eyelid: he just beamed at me, and I fancied I caught a hint of a wink. It was just as though he knew that this was, for me, a very special moment. He was, indeed, a man of deep thought and great insight, and often when I had expressed what to most people would seem an outrageously unlikely notion, he had nodded approvingly, and if he had said anything at all, it was to agree that nothing was impossible, and that truth was often stranger than fiction.

'Oh, take no notice of me, darling,' I chuckled, 'it's just so nice to come in from the garden and see Dad here. Was it a tiring journey coming up, Dad?' I guessed that he had travelled up from Devon a day or two before on the Royal Blue coach. I chose what I felt was a fairly neutral question that might open up the conversation and give me some clues as to the situation.

'Oh, you know, son,' he replied, 'It weren't that bad—nice to zee the different zorts o' countryzide all the way yer.'

Dad was a real countryman at heart, and although his trade sometimes took him into the towns, and occasionally a city (since men of his trade were few and far between), he was never happier than when he was sitting astride a cottage in one of the pretty little villages in his native Devonshire, weaving the figure of a fox, or a pheasant, or some other rural symbol into the topmost strands of a thatched roof. He would stop now and again, wipe the sweat from his brow and survey the picturesque scenery around him. He would watch a herd of cows going in to be milked—they always knew the exact time to do so, without a clock, or a human agency to remind them. Or he would delight at the glimpse of shining blue as a kingfisher darted into a stream to grab its lunch. Maybe he would call down to a passer-by and have a brief chat from his lofty perch. Even when he wasn't working, his hobby—his whole life, even—was the countryside, and he liked little better (except, maybe, when he was lustily singing hymns in the village chapel) than to feast his eyes on the rich variety of rural terrain as he travelled about. He had his own little van as part of his trade, but on the odd occasions when he went further afield he would take the train or a coach.

As we continued to chat, I learned that Dad had travelled up to Roxbury two days before (a Wednesday), to fulfil his wish to see the home that Kathy and I had established there. We'd lived at 35 for a few years, but this was his first—and more than likely his only—visit. It had been the plan for Mum to come as well, but she had developed some sort of stiffness in her right hip, and she found it impossible to sit still for more that ten or fifteen minutes at a time. This was a recurring ailment, which, fortunately, struck only occasionally, though often at the least convenient time—like now. It would have been torment for her to make the long coach journey, so she had stayed at home and it had been agreed that the three of us would travel down to Tollington Raleigh on the Saturday (tomorrow, that was).

I found it wasn't difficult when Dad was talking (in his delightful Devonshire brogue) to steer the conversation in such a way as to pick up useful information about the current setting of time and place, so that I was able to answer in such a way as to appear that I hadn't, in fact, dived into the scene from many years into the future.

As we munched our way happily through the delicious meal that Kathy had cooked for us, various other thoughts occurred to me. I was reminded very strongly of that song 'The Living Years' by Mike And The Mechanics[1]—one of my favourites. The singer essentially tells how, after his father died, he regretted the fact that there were a lot of things he should have told him, such as how much he had really loved and appreciated him, despite some differences of opinion. He sings: 'It's too late when we die, to admit we don't see eye to eye', and in another place, 'I wish I could have told him in the living years.'

Well, I can honestly say that there were very few matters on which my dad and I didn't see eye to eye, and that when he was at last taken from us, I had no regrets about things I ought to have told him but had left it too late. However, over the years since then, there were

---

1. Written by Brian Robertson and Michael Rutherford.

scores of little questions I came to wish I had asked him while I'd still had the chance—about details of family members I hadn't been too clear about, or little incidents he or Mum had once mentioned briefly, and about which I'd been intrigued to learn further details but somehow hadn't got around to asking. Then there were matters of village characters and customs, now long forgotten. I proceeded to pour out a veritable torrent of questions, much to the bewilderment of Kathy, who asked why the sudden inquisition.

Dad, however, took it all in his stride, and furnished me with a valuable store of information which I would be able to commit to memory, or to paper for posterity, if only for my own satisfaction. Again, I somehow got the impression that he realized a lot more about the situation than might have been apparent, and in his knowing way, was only to happy to comply with the demands of the situation.

One major fact that came out in the conversation was that Kathy was three months pregnant. I had, in fact, noticed that her normally svelte figure was a trifle more plump than I'd remembered it, but had felt it prudent not to make comments about the lady's figure. However, it had not been long before that tell-tale glow and pride of the mother-to-be had asserted itself, and, in between discussions of how Old Bert Harwood used to lurk behind his chicken sheds with a shotgun in case the local lads dared to try scrumping his apples, there would be talk of antenatal clinics, mineral supplements, maternity clothes, 'healthy eating' and so on.

When, however, the subject moved on to plans for tomorrow, and in particular the journey we should all be making down to Devon to take Dad home and for

Kathy and me to stay the weekend there (Mum was naturally keen to talk women's things to the mother of her future grandchild), that alarm bells began to ring. It didn't take me long to recall why. This was Kathy's first pregnancy—we had deliberately waited a few years before deciding to start a family, in order to give ourselves a good chance to settle down together into marriage, and to enjoy the early years together without the encumbrance of offspring. Then, when we felt the time was right, Kathy was launched, as it were, on the road to motherhood.

Unfortunately, though, it was through being on the road in the most literal sense that sadly derailed the motherhood wagon (to mix my metaphors somewhat). The memories came back to me how it was as a result of so much travelling, on that long journey to Devon and back, that Kathy's pregnancy began to go wrong. Evidently all the shaking about on the roads (even though I am without a doubt the world's most skilfull and accomplished driver) had upset her system, and two days after our return poor Kathy had miscarried.

That had been such a sorrowful chapter in our relationship. Losing a baby—even one of only three months' gestation, whose identity is still unknown—is such a devastating blow, that, without a doubt, it constitutes a very real bereavement. I shan't dwell on the details—it's still too painful to reflect on it even now. Suffice to say, I recalled very vividly how badly it had affected Kathy— well, both of us, really—and it took a great deal of time for the wounds to heal. In reflecting on the whole issue, I was seized with a strong desire to prevent that tragedy occurring again (or rather, to prevent it happening at all, as it was still only potential).

I was pretty sure that if I were to advise Kathy not to travel down to Devon with us next day she would resist my attempts to 'mollycoddle' her. She had always been of a fairly robust constitution physically, and would not have expected any untoward effects of the journey. (This was largely why the miscarriage had come as such a shock to us all—it had been totally un-expected.) I therefore had to think of some stronger, or perhaps more subtle, form of subterfuge to avoid the fateful trip.

I shall not bore you with the details of my mus-ings—suffice to say my mind was severely exercised for perhaps an hour before a plausible scenario began to emerge. In that time, Dad had grown rather tired and, having transferred himself to an easy chair, was soon fast asleep. Fortunately also, Kathy had decided she needed to pop up to the shops for some things. 'I'll walk, dear,' she said, 'it'll do me good to get some fresh air.'

'Good idea, sweetie,' I replied, trying not to sound *too* enthusiastic, but nevertheless rejoicing inwardly that it would give me the necessary time to carry out my little plan.

As soon as she had left (and I'd watched her from the front window until she was out of sight), I went to the writing desk where I knew the address book was kept. Sure enough, there it was, and I flicked the pages over to the P's. The person I was seeking was Linda Pemberton, who had been Kathy's best friend at school. Yes—there was her phone number, too. I scribbled it on the palm of my hand, mentally noting that it was the old Coventry STD code, long before it became an 024 number. Step-ping out into the hall and gently closing the door so as not to wake Dad, I picked up the phone and dialled the number. An older woman's voice answered—Linda's mother. I asked if Linda were there by any chance.

'Who is it?' she enquired

'It's Willie Draper,' I replied, 'you know, Kathy's husband—Kat Willoughby as was.' I silently congratulated myself for remembering the nickname that Katherine had gone by at her school.

'Oh, hello, my dear,' replied Mrs P, 'how *are* you?' Before I could reply, she went on: 'Funnily enough, Linda's down your way at the moment—she's staying with Penny Wilson in Berrington. Penny has a job there, you know.'

I didn't know, but this was far better news than I could have wished for. Mrs P kindly told me Penny's phone number, and after a few more pleasantries, the call was ended and I was dialling again. It was Penny who answered.

'Hi, Penny,' I greeted her, 'It's Willie Draper. I gather Linda's there. Could I talk to her, please?' Penny passed the phone to her friend.

'Hi, Linda,' I continued, 'I wonder if you could do me a favour? You see, Kathy is three months pregnant, and…' (Here I had to pause as cries of delight emanated from the receiver, and I could hear snatches of animated conversation passing between the two young ladies.) 'The thing is,' I continued, 'My dad's here, and I'm driving him back down to Devon tomorrow. Kathy is intending to come as well, but I really don't think it's a good idea. She won't admit it, but she does tire easily, and I'm afraid the long journeys both ways will upset her badly. The trouble is, she's a determined lass, as you know, and she wouldn't take it from me. I was wondering if you could phone her up this evening and invent a reason to come over and see her tomorrow (it *is* a few years since you've seen each other, after all). Just don't take no for an answer, and don't let on that I've put you up to it!'

Linda was more than obliging: 'No problem, Willie. In fact, we'll *both* come—we've got the perfect reason to see Kat anyway—I've just got engaged!'

Brilliant, I thought, as I extended the appropriate congratulations, Kathy wouldn't want to miss any detail of Linda's beau—how and where they met, what he was like, what sort of wedding they were planning and so on. As an added bonus, Penny was also engaged—her betrothal being, in fact, at a somewhat more advanced stage than Linda's.

It was with a great sense of achievement that I put the phone down and returned to the sitting room to pick up the newspaper and reacquaint myself with 'news' that was some three decades old. I found it quite intriguing to see the sort of things that were occupying the minds of the journalists and politicians. Russia was still a kind of enemy power, there was (as usual) trouble in Northern Ireland, and people generally were concerned with the rising cost of fuel, housing, food and so on. *Plus ça change...* I thought.

Kathy returned with her purchases and I bade her sit down while I made a pot of tea (I had to search the kitchen cupboards to find where things were kept). I could hear Kathy chatting to Dad, who had woken up by now, and my heart fluttered a little as I overheard them discussing tomorrow's journey—where we would stop for coffee and meal breaks en route, and how we'd phone Mum from a village just beyond. Exeter to let her know we'd be arriving in 30 to 40 minutes.

I served up the tea, along with some fancy cakes I'd found, and joined the other two. When the phone rang I jumped—partly from surprise and partly for joy.

'I'll get it,' chirruped Kathy, and I held my breath as she slipped out into the hall. I heaved a huge sigh of relief as I heard her say, 'Oh, *hello*, Linda! Gosh—fancy hearing from you!' there were further animated cries of: 'Oh, *really*?' and '*Is* she?' etc. Eventually I heard the words I'd been hoping for: 'Well, OK, if you can't manage any other time…. No, it doesn't matter—I'm sure they won't mind. I can go down another time…. I'll ask him.'

Kathy then peered round the door, and in her most beguiling voice, addressed me: '*Willie Babe*' (She still used this more intimate nickname when entering her 'persuasive' mode). Her request that, if I didn't very much mind, could she not come down to Devon tomorrow because her two best friends from school were in the area and *really* wanted to come over because they had some *very important news* to share with me and she hadn't seen them for absolutely *years* was met with what I hoped sounded genuinely regretful and somewhat grudgingly assenting.

'Yes, that's fine,' I heard her say as she returned to the phone, 'tomorrow about lunchtime, then.'

The journey down to Tollington Raleigh was a really pleasant one, and doubly satisfying for the absence of Kathy; not that I wouldn't have enjoyed her company as well, but for one thing I didn't want her to be put at risk from the strain of travel, and for another, it was really great to have my Dad all to myself, just to chat to him as I hadn't been able to for almost twenty years, and also to glean further bits of information that had passed me by.

I needn't describe the weekend in detail: it was equally great to see Mum again, and to do with her as I'd done with Dad, asking about all those odds and ends you think of when it's too late to get it 'from the horse's mouth', as it were. I enjoyed being pampered by my mother, and she agreed with me that it was probably for the best that Kathy had not come too. There'd be plenty of opportunities for her to visit after the baby was born. I enjoyed being in the lush Devonshire countryside again, and on Sunday we sang Wesley's hymns lustily in the solid edifice that was the village Methodist chapel.

The drive back home that Sunday evening wasn't too bad either; it gave me ample time to reflect on the delightful experiences I'd had seeing my own parents again, when I'd thought I'd never see them any more this side of the grave. As I bade them farewell, it was with mixed feelings, as it seemed I'd been able, in a sense, to 'round off' our relationship in a more complete way before their inevitable demise a few years later, but at the same time there was a hint of sadness, as this very likely *was* the last time I'd see them on earth, as I'd more or less decided my time-travelling days were to end forthwith.

When I got back to Roxbury, I found Kathy tired but happy. Her two friends had, in fact, stayed the night, and the three of them had had a tremendous time together talking girlie talk nonstop. They were now fully up to date on all their recent histories, as well as details of numerous other mutual friends, and they had just about exhaustively analyzed the subjects of weddings, men, babies and a whole lot of other things it would be wise for me to leave to the reader's imagination.

After a well deserved night's rest, and the customary morning activites, I bade Kathy goodbye and set off on my bike for work. I had intended to head right back to the 21st century, but halfway to Parklands (where I still had some processing to complete) I remembered the original reason for my trip back in time, namely, my old friend Chrysolina menthastri.

'Bother!' I thought, realizing that I still had the matchbox in my pocket but with no specimens in it. As it happened, I was just passing the end of Upper Meadow Close at this point, so, in a split-second decision, I did a sharp left turn and headed along to No 26. Although the beetles had been less plentiful there, I felt pretty sure I'd find at least a couple to take with me to the next natural history society meeting.

In my eagerness, I hadn't thought too much about which particular date to aim for; I realized that my visit to Rockall Avenue had been sometime in the latter part of the seventies, so I figured the early to mid eighties would do. I would have preferred to go forward to my 'own' time, but I just felt it would be too awkward to face strangers there, and in any case, the beetles might have died out by then.

As it happened, I appeared at my former residence around midday, so my arrival took on the appearance of my usual lunchtime homecoming. I noticed a football lying near the front door, and as I turned my key in the lock (once again marvelling how "today's" key opened "yesterday's" lock), I stepped into the hall and almost went flying as I trod on a toy racing car. I was a mite surprised, because according to my calculations, Sally should have been only in the early stages of toddlerhood, and as for Hazel, well, she'd have been in mid-gestation.

In the kitchen was my beloved, who greeted me with: 'Hi, darling!'

'Hi, Kathy...uh, I mean Katie,' I replied, stumbling verbally over a gap of some six or seven years I had crossed in as many minutes. 'How ya doin'?'

'Fine, love,' she returned, giving me a beaming smile. Lunch is nearly ready. Timothy's playing with the lad next door.'

'*Who?*' I asked.

'*You* know, love, Ben Peters—Jane and Andrew's lad—they moved in last week, remember?'

'No, I meant *who* is playing with him?'

'Oh, come on, sweetie—*Timothy*! Don't tell me you've forgotten your own son's name! You get too wrapped up in that work of yours, that's your trouble! You need to get back into the real world sometime!'

Her tone was lighthearted, but her words really hit me for six. My *son*? I had a son? Still somewhat in shock, and, alas, without 'putting my brain in gear', I blurted out, 'But where's Sally?'

'Sally?' she asked, looking quite puzzled, 'Sally who?'

Realizing my faux pas, I did some swift mental gymnastics and replied, 'Uh...oh, um... Sally Whatsername, you know, your friend...Sally Grant—doesn't she come round to see you Monday mornings?'

'Oh, you mean *Polly* Grant!' Katie replied.

Well, considering the time that had elapsed since this weekly visit had ceased, I didn't think I'd done too badly in the memory stakes. In other respects, though, I could have done better.

'And yes, she *does* come round on Mondays, but seeing as today is *Wednesday*...!' there was a hint of sarcasm in her voice as it tailed off.

Of course! I'd made the silly (though understandable) mistake of assuming that, as I'd left Rockall Avenue on a Monday, it was also a Monday when I'd arrived here in the next decade. But as I hadn't specified a particular day of the week in transit, I'd taken pot luck, as it were.

My awkward moment was saved by the sound of the back door handle turning, and in burst a lively six or seven-year-old lad with a mop of fair hair and blue eyes, who was the spitting image of...ME! (When I was his age, that is.) 'Hi Mum! Hi Dad!' he called out, nonchalantly.

Hi Dad!—He'd called me Dad! Wow! This really was incredible! I loved my two beautiful daughters to bits, but to have a son as well—that really was the icing on the cake! I'd always sort of secretly fantasized about having a boy in the family: someone I could do boyish things with—playing masculine games, having man-to-man chats with and everything. Of course, in my dreams, he would have come after his two big sisters, but now he was going to be the big brother, and the girls would follow. Sally didn't appear to have come upon the scene as yet, let alone Hazel, and Katie hadn't looked particularly pregnant. Doubtless she'd wanted to wait a bit before increasing the size of our family, although I did think seven years was perhaps a rather large gap.

However, that fleeting thought didn't trouble me just now—I was too busy taking in the amazing fact that I actually had a SON! I was astonished by the likeness he bore to me, too—it was like watching a video recording of myself as a youngster (not that there *were* any video recordings of my childhood). I liked his name, too: Timothy, a good, sensible name. It means 'honouring God', I believe—a fine choice. And I knew for sure that his mum (and certainly his two grandmothers) would accept nothing less than his full name—no chance of 'Tim' or 'Timmy'!

It didn't take an Einstein, of course, to deduce that this great little lad before me owed his existence to my attempts—obviously successful—to avert the miscarriage that had threatened to disrupt so cruelly our plans to start a family. As I looked at him, I was absolutely thrilled with the outcome of my mission, and felt both proud and humble. I wanted so badly to shout for delight at my personal victory, and share it with my spouse, but I knew I had to hold it in, as she would never be able to understand what I was talking about.

'Come on, dear,' Katie's voice butted into my thoughts, 'whatever are you gaping at? It's only a blob of mud on his cheek. After all, you're the one who's always saying "Boys will be boys"!' Anyway, I want you to finish your lunch quickly and take him round to school. He couldn't go this morning, because there was a problem with the drains, but it's all sorted out now, and the secretary was phoning round to say the children should come back this afternoon. I can't go, because I have to be at the "Some Mothers do 'ave 'em" meeting at church. They've asked me to give a talk to the expectant and young mums about the problems of pregnancy and birth, and how to cope with them.'

I thoroughly enjoyed walking Timothy to school—it was a totally new experience to see the world through a young boy's eyes. Mind you, hurdle number one was to make sure I took him to the *right* school. You see, our house was on the border of two catchment areas, and there was considerable variation as to who went where. On either side of the dividing line, parents were given a degree of choice as to which school they could send their children to, and there was a fair amount of rivalry and difference of opinion as to which was the better. So I adopted the strategy of letting Timothy go ahead, by playing Follow my Leader. That pleased him greatly, especially getting his dad to do silly things like dancing a jig in the middle of the street (being a cul-de-sac, it had virtually no traffic), or 'tightrope walking' along someone's front garden wall! (Luckily they weren't in!) When the lad turned right at the end of the road (and I noticed with pride and satisfaction that he kept well in from the edge of the pavement), I knew at once which school we were heading for.

Being keen on photography, I naturally wanted to take some pictures of my boy, and I fished in my pocket for the little digital camera I carried around with me to enable me to snap the unexpected. Drat! It wasn't there! I must have left it by the computer after I'd downloaded the last batch of photos. However, our route took us past a row of shops, one of which was a chemist, so I made Timothy come in with me and I bought a disposable camera (making sure I paid with cash from my little store of old notes and coins that I kept with me *just in case...* Although I'd had no active intentions of burrowing back in time again, I felt I had to be ready for any eventuality, and I certainly did not wish to repeat my Meechams' experience!)

It did occur to me that both Katie and I would have taken masses of photos of our lad already, and they would be meticulously filed and labelled in our family albums, but for some reason I just wanted something a little more immediate. I took four or five of my son in various modes—posed and informal— and went with him inside the school. I saw the coat peg with his name above it, the drawer where his exercise books were kept, and the table where he generally sat. I greeted Mrs Hudson, his teacher, who told me what a lovely boy Timothy was—well mannered and considerate, helpful to the teachers and other children, and very conscientious with his work. I left the school fairly bursting with pride. I didn't go straight home, but lingered in a nearby park and tried to collect my disorganized thoughts. Time and time again I found myself so utterly dumbstruck at the thought of actually having a son, that I really did suspect that this was just a dream. And yet, it was so real, I couldn't imagine how I could ever have imagined all of this. I pulled a newspaper out of a nearby bin and checked the date—yes, there it was: 1981. I read some of the articles, and reasoned that, even with the best memory in the world, I could never have reconstructed in my mind the situations described in such intricate detail.

After what had seemed but a few minutes, I glanced up at the clock on the bandstand and realized it was only twenty minutes before Timothy was due to be collected from school. I hurried across to a telephone box and rang my home number (the one for the time zone I was in). When Katie answered, I reassured her that I hadn't forgotten our lad, and would be collecting and bringing him home.

He came running out of the school gate, delighted to be met by his dad for a change. On the way home I suggested that, after tea, we go to our local park together and have a kick around with a football. He readily agreed, and bolted down the snack his mum had prepared. Then he grabbed my hand and practically dragged me out of the door. 'Come on, Daddy! Don't be such a slowcoach!' Katie laughed at his eagerness, saying, 'What's got into you all of a sudden?' That remark gave me cause for thought.

We had a brilliant time in the park—after our kickaround (during which I let the budding striker score five goals between a pair of plane trees), we had a game of hide and seek, followed by an easy climb up onto a sturdy low branch of an oak tree, where we surveyed the scene beneath our feet—and just chatted. I realized to my joy that I had my MP3 player tucked away in one of my jacket pockets, and I set it to the 'voice record' function, gathering a sizeable sample of my offspring's general happy chatter. I took some more photos of Timothy, and got a passer-by to take one of the two of us together. I was enjoying this immensely, but eventually the time came for us to leave the park and return home. Timothy munched his supper (a bowl of Frosties) and I enjoyed reading him a bedtime story after tucking him in. It was a book about giants and dinosaurs—quite different from the tales of ballet dancers and pony riding I used to read to my daughters.

'I'm glad you had a nice time playing with Timothy this evening, dear,' said Katie as I went downstairs and joined her in the living room, 'he does love spending time with his daddy.'

'Yes,' I agreed, 'I'm glad I made the effort today.'

I then asked, 'And how was your day, love?' little knowing that her reply would settle some of my unanswered questions, and tell me a lot more besides—things I hadn't bargained for.

Leaning forward and switching off the television, she began: 'Well, it wasn't very easy, and I was quite nervous to start with.'

'Yes?' I prompted, sensing that I could catch up on some of our recent history that, curiously, I had shared in but of which I could remember nothing.

'Well,' she continued, 'I really didn't want to upset or unsettle those women who hadn't yet had their babies, but at the same time I felt it wouldn't be fair not to warn them of some of the difficulties that can arise. After all, I'd been specially asked to address this group, so I felt it was somehow my... well, my *duty* to sort-of tell it like it is.'

'Quite right,' I prompted, with an expression that demanded further details.

'So I shared with them how ill I was towards the end of the pregnancy, and about the pre-eclampsia and that (that was horrible). And that long, drawn-out labour. I tried to assure them it was exceptional, and not to let it worry them, but I could see a few anxious looks. Anyway, when I got to the emergency Caesarian, and how long it took me to recover after the birth, I began to wonder if I'd overdone the detail. Poor Nancy Green really *did* look green! She said she needed the toilet and left the room very hastily. I felt I oughtn't to say anything about Timothy being kept in the Special Care Baby Unit for three weeks, and how we were dying to pick him up and cuddle him, but weren't allowed to.'

As all this came tumbling out, some very loud alarm bells began to sound in my head. Katie paused and said, as a sort of aside to me: 'Still, I guess it was worth it in the end—look at the lovely son we have now!'

I smiled weakly, then winced as the words I was dreading finally emerged from her lips: 'They all sympathized wholeheartedly when I told them "Never again—

I wouldn't go through all that anguish for all the money in the world."'

'But I thought you'd always wanted a daughter?' I countered.

'Yes, I did,' she replied, with feeling, 'I'd have loved having a girl—or better still, two—I could dress up in pretty frocks, and take to ballet lessons, and do all the nice little 'girlie' things with.'

I could see a tear beginning to form in her eye. My heart began to be torn apart—I had just spent an absolutely wonderful few hours with the boy I'd always wanted, yet at the same time I'd somehow deprived my dearest one of what had evidently been her heart's desire. The pregnancy and birth I'd subjected her to had been such an ordeal that perhaps, after all, a miscarriage, traumatic as it undoubtedly would have been, might have been a marginally better option. Maybe Mother Nature—or God—actually knew best, and by meddling in matters that were not my preserve I had messed up some Divine plan. Or was I being silly? I really didn't know. All the same, I just wished I had let things be.

I quickly tried to comfort my beloved, then made her a hot chocolate and gently urged her to go to bed; she'd had a tiring day, after all. I then sat myself down in an armchair to try and think my way through this whole bewildering business. What on earth was I to do? I reflected that, although I had found the idea of having my own son very appealing, I really loved my two beautiful daughters, Sally and Hazel, almost more than anything else on earth—and yet, somehow, I'd wiped them both out of existence! How could I have done that? It was too much to get my head around. I dreaded the thought of going back to my 'real' life in

the 21st century to find no trace at all of their wonderful lives—the pictures Hazel had so skilfully
painted, the trophies for gymnastics, swimming and
pony riding Sally had won...Sally's charming boyfriend
Yancey and the sweet little cottage they had managed
to buy and do up. We would no longer be invited over
to Hazel's flat for an evening meal and generally to relax and have a nice chat now and again. And then
there was...

My mind was in turmoil; I couldn't think straight. I
tried to imagine how different our lives would be with
one son instead of two daughters. We'd be meeting his
girlfriends, watching him play rugby perhaps, study-
ing...oh, I didn't know—whatever blokes prefer to
study. But this was no good—I couldn't go on wallowing in speculation. I had to act, but how? Had I the right
to, as it were, play God and blot out one life to save two
others? Could I justifiably go for the lesser of two evils?
What would happen to Timothy if I managed to reverse
the course of history (albeit a history I had already al-
tered) and denied him his birth? Would it be that he had
never existed—except in my mind? Or would he be
given a place in heaven where, hopefully, I would meet
him again? I began to think of all those other billions of
babies who, down through the millennia of man's existence, had never made it to birth—those who had miscarried, those who had been stillborn, and those who,
through human intervention had been cruelly denied
their right to live. Would these all be given a place in
Paradise? Surely God would welcome them, since they
had not had the chance to choose between good and
evil. Perhaps that was partly what was meant by those
words in Hebrews, where it says that the inhabitants

of heaven include 'the spirits of good people made perfect'[2]

Maybe you, like me, sometimes find yourself in a the doldrums mentally or physically—feeling tired or under the weather, and you look at all the things waiting for you to do; lethargy has set in and you feel you can't begin to tackle them. Then you realize you have two options: to stay inactive and see nothing getting done, or to force yourself through the barrier of inertia and just get on with it. Once you take that step, the energy seems to return and you press on with renewed vigour. Well, I reached that point and determined to do what had to be done. I'd have loved to stay in that little tract of the space-time continuum and enjoy getting to know my son a lot better, but I knew that the more I did that, the less I should feel willing to restore history from the sidetrack along which I had sent it.

I didn't join Katie in bed, although I did sneak a last, loving peep at my little lad, peacefully asleep, probably dreaming about space rockets, racing cars or volcanoes. Then I put on my jacket and quietly slipped out of the door. It was dark as I pedalled off down the road, but as I turned right at the end and headed for the Parklands Clinic, daylight came upon me with startling swiftness as I 'aimed' for a time about a month before the date of my visit to Rockall Avenue, when I'd had that wonderful reunion with my dad. I decided to choose a Friday lunchtime, on the grounds that the afternoon was likely to be relatively free of heavy commitments. All I really wanted to do was to book a day off—the Monday following Dad's visit.

---

2. Hebrews 12:23.

However, the trouble with dropping unawares into a particular moment in time is that it's rather like parachuting to earth blindfold—you never really know what situation you're going to land in. And on this occasion, I'd chosen a day on which all the staff of Parklands had gathered to discuss in detail some future projections of the service we hoped to offer to the local community, and as a specialist unit, to a rather wider catchment area. The head of each department had to submit a statement which was to form part of a coherent policy for the whole unit. The snag was, my boss was apparently due to attend a prestigious conference in Rome starting the following day, and not only had he left early to pack and make his final preparations (as he was to deliver a major talk there), but in addition he had nominated ME to deliver a statement at the planning meeting outlining our department's position!

Fortunately I found some hastily scribbled notes on a piece of paper on my desk, so I grabbed that and hastened off to the seminar room. To my dismay, I was the first person who was aked to speak, and I'd had literally only seconds to read my notes—or *try* to. I couldn't believe how illegible my own handwriting of that time was. I was aware that it had changed somewhat over the years, but I must have been in a terrific hurry when I jotted these points down. Anyway, I launched into my presentation as best I could, and with a mixture of intuition, guesswork and pure flannel, plus frequent appeals to colleagues to corroborate and expand on my comments, I got through it, and even won the chairman's commendation for a good presentation!

But that was only part of the problem solved; what I really needed was to speak to the boss and ask him for a day off in four weeks' time. But since he had left, I supposed I would have to return to the department the previous day in order to catch him. Just then, however, good fortune smiled on me, as I noticed the figure of my boss scurrying past the window—he'd obviously come back for something. I jumped out of my seat and skidaddled out of the room so fast that my colleagues confessed later that they thought I'd been taken ill!

I just managed to catch the boss as he was starting his car, having thrown some files onto the back seat. In fact—he very nearly ran me over (I later caught myself wondering how that would have changed history; I never did manage to figure it out). As he wound down the driver's window, I started to make my request to take a day's leave on…

'Good heavens!' he cried, 'is that *all* you wanted? I thought something serious had happened. Just take whatever you want, lad—can't you see I'm in a hurry? I'll miss my flight if I don't…'

His voice tailed off into the distance as he revved the engine and shot away with a screech of tyres. Great! I'd managed that piece of the jigsaw puzzle—not many more to go now. Having popped into the department to ask the secretary to write my day's leave in the diary, I thought it polite to at least return to the meeting and try to look interested and involved, even though I felt it was the most irrelevant thing on earth right now.

I put up with another hour and a half of waffle, piffle, twaddle and balderdash (see how interested I was?), then a further half-hour of polite conversation and attempts at providing plausible responses to some pretty abstruse questions. I was dying to get away all the while, and, as I set down my wilting paper plate containing a partly-eaten sausage roll and my half-finished glass of apple juice, I made as if to go to the gents but slipped quietly out of the building.

Gratefully leaping onto my bike, I cycled back to Rockall Avenue and forward a few weeks to the Monday before my dad's coming visit. I said a silent prayer as I approached the door that I wouldn't land slap-bang into some other difficult situation, and this was followed shortly after by a word of thanks to the Almighty as my parachute came down safely, so to speak. It was a lunch time, and Kathy was sitting in an armchair, reading a book. I could smell something appetizing coming from the kitchen.

'Don't bother getting up, love—I'll dish out the grub!' I offered, going straight to the kitchen. As I brought in our plates, I announced, quite nonchalantly, 'I've decided to take next Monday off. I remember Dad sounding very interested when I told him about the country crafts musem out at Barfield Sowerby, so I thought I'd take him there on Saturday. Then we can go down to Devon on Sunday and come back Monday evening.'

'Whatever you like, dear,' she replied; 'you know best what'll suit your dad.'

And that was it: the dreadful deed was done—I had effectively condemned the one I loved best to a most heart-rending experience, followed by many months of sadness at what might have been (in fact I now *knew* what might have been!), before the first of our two beautiful daughters was born. But, I reasoned, I was only setting history back on the course it had followed before my meddlesome attempt to change it for the better.

After lunch, I kissed Kathy goodbye (with much more feeling than usual), and with a mixture of determination and trepidation, set off for the future—back to 36 The Willows, which I had left weeks ago, it seemed, but I knew I'd be returning on the same day that I'd left it. As I cycled, I pictured Dad arriving at our house and being enthusiatically greeted by the two of us; then, Dad and myself going to the crafts museum while Kathy entertained her old school friends; the journey down to Devon on Sunday, the tiring journey back the next day, and then... I deliberately turned my thoughts away from the repercussions of my actions, and back to...the present.

As I walked into the sitting room I was heartily relieved to see our daughters' graduation photos on the mantelpiece. 'Thank heaven!' I breathed.

'Hello, love,' murmured Kate from behind the latest edition of Costume Dolls Monthly, 'what you been doing today?'

'Oh, you know,' I replied, 'this and that.'

And that *was* that—almost. Soon after that we had our evening meal (I wasn't very hungry, being still quite full from a lunch I'd dished out myself a few decades ago), and Kate retired early when a headache unexpectedly came on.

A few days later I suddenly realized I still had the disposable camera in my jacket pocket, so I took it to a chemist in town. 'Oho!' he laughed,'You'll be lucky if you get anything worthwhile out of this, mate. Look at the date on it—it's years past its processing deadline!'

When I collected the prints a few days later, the chemist expressed his astonishment at how well the photos had come out. 'I can't get over it, gov—usually this type of film goes off completely after five or six years. I reckon this must be a record!'

I didn't comment; I just paid up and took the photos. I sped round to the nearest park and opened the packet. Unbelieveably there, before my very eyes, were the most beautiful images of my darling son, the son I'd secretly always wanted, the lad I'd loved and lost all within a few short hours—the boy who never was.

When I got home that day, I hid the photos in my treasured copy of 'Steam Railways of Bolivia and Peru' (I knew for sure that none of my family would ever find them!). But I kept just one of Timothy in my wallet— tucked away in a sort of inner fold. Now and again I'd take it out and peer at that little lad. It all seemed like a dream now. (In fact, that's largely why I'm writing this all down—for my own benefit, to keep the dream alive.)

One day, Kate found the photo. I'd lost my library card, and she couldn't believe I'd searched throughout my wallet in vain. I hadn't realized she'd got hold of it until it was too late. 'Who's *this*, love?' she enquired.

'Oh, some cousin or nephew,' I replied hastily.

'But he looks exactly like that picture of you when you were a boy.'

'Oh, *that* photo…' I fumbled verbally; 'Oh, yes… um, yes, it…yes, that *is* me. It was taken in some park by the seaside…in Torquay or somewhere.'

'But darling,' she countered, 'it *can't* be that old—it's in colour!'

'Ah, yes, but I'm not *that* ancient, you know! Colour photography was around long before I was born you know! I can't remember very well, but I think there was this man, you see—it was a bit of a novelty, and my dad had to pay him quite a bit to have it done. As a matter of fact,' I went on, 'I reckon he was pretty avant garde—d'you see how informal a shot it is? None of your carefully posed pictures with plastic smiles.'

I'm not sure Kate was totally convinced. 'Hmm, funny I haven't seen this before,' she said. 'Maybe you'd better get a copy made, to put in our album of us as children.'

Fortunately (or otherwise), another of her headaches came on, she went to bed, and the matter was conveniently forgotten. I was a bit worried about those headaches, though.

The irony of the whole episode was that, after all my original intentions, I never did manage to come back with any samples of the mint beetles. I could have kicked myself for not nabbing a couple while I'd had the opportunity, but at the time, I guess I'd had more important matters on my mind.

And sadly, when I tried to replay Tim's voice on my MP3 player, the sound was so distorted as to be unrecognisable. I cursed my luck, but consoled myself that I did at least have the photos. Maybe it was just as well I hadn't got anything as tangible as a voice—the whole experience had subjected me to emotional turmoil, and I reasoned it was best not to have too many reminders of that aspect. I little suspected, however, that I was to experience far worse before long.

CHAPTER 12

Lost

I don't want to sound unromantic but I'd never been particularly bothered about St Valentine's Day. In fact, deep down I'm a bit of an old softie, really. What I mean is, I don't see why couples should confine expressions of their deepest sentiments for each other to just one day in the year. If you really love someone, you ought to let them know it all the time. I don't mean by giving them extravagant gifts or taking them out for romantic meals every day of the year, but by doing little things for your dearest—putting yourself out for your partner, showing them your appreciation with words of praise; complimenting them on their appearance or the way they do things well—that sort of thing. Not that I'd ignored Valentine's Day completely—I'd usually manage to get Kate a card, and I'd receive one from her. Occasionally the date would slip our minds, and we'd just have a chuckle and say, 'Never mind, love!'

The trouble is, the media tend to go way over the top—the newspapers print all those lovey-dovey pictures of cute little animals or children cuddling up together, along with articles about how this guy hitch-hiked the length of America to be with a girl he met on holiday, or how Mabel Williams (96) and her husband Gareth (98) of Ystradgynlais or Giggleswick or somewhere have just celebrated their 80th wedding anniversary, and reckon they've never had a single argument in all their years together. You know the sort of thing, I'm sure. (I often wonder if someone makes up these tales, they sound so unrealistic.) The papers are full of those silly little love messages that say things like: "Dearest Snookums, you are the sunshine on my beach and the sugar in my coffee. With undying love, Twinklebum." Yeuk—pass the sick bowl, Alice, as my mum used to say! And the radio stations—I think they're the worst of all. At one end of the scale you've got Radio 3 and Classic FM playing romantic music from Tchaikovsky ballets and Mozart operas, and at the other end there's Radio One blaring out 'Love Is All Around', 'All You Need Is Love' and 'Love Is All That Matters'. I once facetiously sent in an anonymous Valentine request for 'I'm Sick Of You' by the obscure eighties group Goodbye Mr MacKenzie, just to be provocative, but they didn't play it!

Anyway, this particular Valentine's Day was no exception, and while shaving I was listening to BBC Radio Roxbury, and yet another of these done-to-death love songs was on the air. 'Lost In Your Love' by Tony Hadley (a founder member of Spandau Ballet, in case anyone's interested). How ridiculous, I thought—how on earth can anyone be 'lost' in someone's love? I suppose I was feeling in a rather pragmatic, cynical mood, and sometimes you can live to regret words or thoughts like that. Little did I realize I would soon find the answer to that rhetorical question.

I was working at Parklands that afternoon, and was packing up ready to go home when Dr Rayworth, one of the paediatricians, came and asked a favour of me. 'Oh, Bill,' he said, 'I wonder if you'd mind dropping this package off on your way home? It's just some journals I promised to pass on to Professor Trelawney.'

I glanced at the address: 23B Mill Street. He ought to know that isn't on my way home, I muttered under my breath. Still, it wasn't that far out of my way, and I was in no special hurry to get home quickly. I set off on my trusty steed, and was soon turning into the bottom end of Mill Street. I must have cycled up and down this street thousands of times during the forty-odd years I'd lived and worked in this city, particularly in the early part of that period. It had changed a fair bit over the years—one or two shops had closed, others had changed hands, new flats built where there'd been spaces and so on.

Number 23 was near the top end on the right, just before the parade of shops on that side. Leaning my bike against the wall, I made my way to the entrance, and then it suddenly dawned on me—this used to be where my old bedsit was, when I first came to live and work in Roxbury, but my goodness—what a transformation! The whole façade of the house had been completely reconstructed. The tatty red bricks had been replaced with smooth, mellow stonework, there were attractive modern but tasteful windows, and instead of a faded, peeling pale blue door, there was a small vestibule with three doors leading off it. Flat B was on the right, and I pushed the package through the amply sized letterbox. The left-hand door was, of course, that of Flat A, and the slightly larger central door had two letterboxes labelled Flat C and Flat D.

This is amazing, I thought—when I'd lived here, the landlady Mrs Morrison lived downstairs on the left with a back room and kitchen behind, and in the room on the right lived a lodger—a grumpy old man in his sixties who never seemed to do anything other than moan about anything and everything. For instance, I owned a motor-cycle, an Ariel Square Four—a beautiful machine, it was. When I first appeared with it, this moody old geezer took one look at it and sneered, 'Huh—gonna kill yerself, I suppose!'

I didn't even bother to try to explain to him that my primary purpose in acquiring such a handsome steed was to provide a means of swift, economical transport, rather than to propel myself hastily into the hereafter. I could find far cheaper ways of doing that should I have felt so inclined.

A creaky staircase had led up to my room at the back of the house and to the front one, in which a young Span-ish lad lived. Noticing that the door to flats C and D was not completely shut, I couldn't resist opening it a touch and peeping inside. A very smart new staircase led up to the next floor, and I was intrigued that it all looked so much more spacious than the old place had been. Perhaps the new owner had bought the house next door as well, and expanded into it. Whatever the explanation, my curiosity got the better of me and I simply had to climb the stairs and investigate what improvements had been made.

As my shoes sank into the plush new staircarpet (unusually plush, I thought), I called to mind the faded, threadbare one that had borne my feet, and doubtless scores of others, back in the sixties. The stylish natural wood handrail was a far cry from its predecessor, whose paintwork had been unevenly worn away by several hundred hands passing over it. And there was a pleasant fragrance in the air, in complete contrast to the stagnant atmosphere of my former abode. Momentarily I stopped and closed my eyes to experience again in my mind that lingering smell of stewed cabbage and stale cigarette smoke (Mrs Morrison was such a heavy smoker that not only her fingers but also the front of her otherwise white hair was stained yellow with nicotine). Yes, that was it—I could recall the fetid aroma just as if I were back there in my old 'digs'.

When I opened my eyes I got a huge shock—I *was* back in my old digs! Not only was the smell just as real as of old, but so were the faded, threadbare carpet, the creaky stairs—and the door to my old room at the top! Oh blast that overactive imagination of mine! Why couldn't I learn to control it? What if I were to close my eyes again and actively imagine myself back in the 21st century? Could I move forward in time as easily as I'd moved back? I tried it, but without success. I tried again, really hard, but all to no avail. The only way back was to cycle home to Clunmore. Oh well—I resigned myself to remaining in the past for a few hours until I could return to my own time. Meanwhile I might as well go into my room and see what was going on there.

Opening the door, I ventured in, and my eyes were immediately drawn to the single, bare light bulb hanging from the ceiling. I never did have the luxury of a lamp-shade. At the same time my ears had no difficulty focus-ing on the continual buzz of an electricity meter down in the far corner. Strange how, during the years this was my home, I'd got so used to that perpetual noise that I never really noticed it, but coming to it afresh (as I had done originally) it really assailed the ears. The bed was just as I would have left it—the covers hastily drawn up just before I'd dashed off to work—and there were my breakfast things in the sink. A simple table in front of the window served several purposes, one of them being a writing desk, and there was a fountain pen and writing pad lying on it. To the left of the table was a small chest of drawers, on which stood my old record player! On a nearby shelf was my prized collection of 45s: The 4 Seasons, Dionne Warwick, Fats Domino, etc. Some of these I still possessed in the future, but sadly, most of them had somehow got lost or disappeared over the years. Just for fun, I couldn't resist removing one of them (it was 'Big Girls Don't Cry) from its paper sleeve and writing on the inside of the sleeve: CU in 21st C. When I get home tonight, I told myself, I'll look for that message.

Just then I heard six short pips—the Greenwich Time Signal. Instinctively, I checked my bedside clock: it said the time was 20 past 5! How odd—the clock was ticking away, and I had no reason to suspect it was wrong. Then the pips went again! My ears told me the sound had come in through the window. I peered out, wondering if someone had a radio on in the garden—and then I saw the source of the signal. Sitting in a cage in next-door's garden was an Indian Mynah bird! Now I remembered—they used to put it outside for fresh air, and among its repertoire of mimicry was a perfect rendition of the Greenwich pips! The sights, the sounds, the smells—all these stimuli to my senses served to consolidate my presence right here again in the sixties—it was amazing. I noticed, incidentally, that whereas I had left the 21st century in chilly mid-February, I had arrived here and now in midsummer.

Having taken in so much, I began to feel, almost reluctantly, that I ought to set about heading back to my proper time and place. With a last visual sweep of the room, I turned towards the door. As I reached it, I caught sight of a folded piece of paper on the floor, just inside the door. I could see it had my name written on it. Curious, I picked it up and unfolded it. It was a note, written in a very neat hand:

'Don't suppose I can persuade you to change your mind. But just in case you do, I'll be outside The Blue Danube at six—H.'

This had me distinctly puzzled. What might I change my mind about? And who was 'H'?

It occurred to me that Mrs Morrison must have pushed the note under my door, so I trotted briskly down the stairs and tapped on her door. She opened it, the perpetual cigarette dangling from her mouth. 'What is it, my love?' she queried.

'This note,' I said, 'do you know who left it?

'Sorry, dear—didn't see them. Just found it on the doormat. Saw your name on it, so I just slid it under your door. Didn't know if you was in or not, so I thought best not disturb you.'

I thanked her and plodded back up to my room. Well, it was now only half an hour from the proposed meeting time, so I wouldn't have long to find out. My fertile mind briefly rehearsed the possibility that this was a cunning plot to catch me in a trap. I didn't realize how near the mark I was.

I spruced myself up a bit, and then had a thought: money—on this occasion I'd no 'old' money in my wallet and I knew I'd need some if I were to have a meal with 'Secret Agent H', and it would have to be pre-decimal money, too. I didn't want to make the same mistake I'd made in the hardware shop. Remembering that I always kept an emergency fund in a box under the bed, I stooped down and peered underneath. I was amazed at the piles of junk I'd managed to amass there! However, I located the container I needed, drew it out and removed the lid. Inside were three ten shilling notes, several half-crowns and a few threepenny bits. I figured that should be more than enough for a banquet, but just to be on the safe side I stuffed the whole lot into my trouser pocket and set off for the mystery tryst.

The Blue Danube, a neat little Viennese restaurant, was just around the corner in Mountford Avenue, and I had enjoyed many a meal there, from a light snack to a sumptuous nosh-up, with friends in the past. Unfortunately in the nineties the site was redeveloped, and in the new building that emerged the only eating-place was a somewhat featureless store restaurant, whose culinary fare was also largely featureless.

I arrived a few minutes before six, and decided I was rather too early, because the only person in sight was a young woman in her early twenties. But she was not *just* a woman—she looked as though she had just stepped off a plane from heaven! Boy, she was drop-dead gorgeous! She was a little taller than myself, with sleek light brown hair flowing down below her shoulders, and a figure to die for, supported by a pair of extremely shapely legs. The low-cut light summer dress she wore served to accentuate these features. As she turned towards me, I was captivated by her disarming smile and sparkling light brown eyes.

For a second or two I stood there immobile, gazing speechless in wonder at this vision of loveliness. I was jerked out of my trance by her quiet greeting: 'Good to see you, Will.'

The penny dropped instantly. That face, that voice—of course, I couldn't possibly forget:

'Harriet! What a fantastic surprise!'

'I think *I'm* the one who should be surprised,' replied my former girlfriend. 'I didn't dare to hope I'd ever see you again after that note you sent me.'

'Uh...note?' I mumbled, at a loss to recall what it was I might have written to suggest we'd broken up. The vaguest of impressions began to form in the mists of my mind, and quite quickly blossomed into a more explicit memory. Of course, now I remember—Harriet and I were very much an item after we'd met at a mutual friend's 21st birthday party. But after we'd been going out together for four or five months she revealed to me that she, along with the rest of her family, were all set to emigrate to New Zealand by the end of the year. Her father had two brothers living in the Christchurch area, and after a great deal of deliberation and discussion, the whole family, including Harriet and her two elder brothers, had decided to take the plunge and uproot from the UK and move to the other side of the world. Harriet's uncles had found suitable jobs for all three of the men, and there was even an opening for Harriet in her own profession as a beauty therapist. The fact that I had begged her not to go, and my own fatalistic acceptance of the inevitable parting, scarcely registered in my mind just now.

'Well, uh...*maybe* I might be reconsidering,' I heard myself say.

'That's brilliant, Will,' replied the personification of Venus before me, 'that's just what I hoped you'd say.' Before I had time to comment further, she added briskly, 'Come on, then—let's go in and have a celebratory meal!'

Without waiting for my assent, the graceful siren encircled my waist with a slender arm and fairly swept me into the restaurant. I felt as if I were being borne on angels' wings into seventh heaven. Could this actually be happening to me? Was I really being permitted to share my existence with this divine creature? This realization, this feeling of inexplicable delight was beginning to drive all other thoughts and considerations from my mind.

A waiter showed us to a table, and as I was about to take a seat to the left of my beautiful companion, she chuckled and half-whispered, 'Other side, silly!'

The reason for this quickly came to me: being left-handed, Harriet preferred me to sit on her right. That way, we could hold hands while eating, by holding our fork or spoon in our dominant hands. I suddenly had a thought, excused myself and went to the gents. I took off my wedding ring and put it in my wallet. I didn't want Harriet to feel it. This caused me a pang of guilt—I was cheating on Kate, wasn't I? Or was I? After all, the date was 1966—I wasn't due to meet Katherine for another couple of years. How could I be cheating on someone I hadn't yet met? And yet, I *had* met her—and married her, hence the ring. It was all very confusing. I decided not to torture my mind and conscience—after all, this was just a bit of fun—a little fling, if you like. I returned quickly to the table and ordered.

Although the Erdäpfelsalat, followed by Apfelstrudel we devoured doubtless tasted heavenly, the experience was nothing compared to the sensation of holding that soft, delicate hand in mine. I know it sounds corny, but it really did feel as though a current of warmth, of a kind of electricity, was flowing between us.

The meal over, I paid the bill, leaving the waiter a generous five shilling tip.

'What shall we do now?' I asked as we made our way out into the street.

'Let's go up Mountford Rise,' replied Harriet, 'to our favourite spot.'

'Yes, that's a good idea,' I said, 'it should be really nice there this evening.'

We walked round to my bedsit. My bike was still leaning against the front wall, so I wheeled it round the side of the house and opened the tall wooden double gate (it was never locked during the daytime). There was a lean-to shed at the back where I kept the bike, and I stashed it away in there (I didn't seem to realize at the time that it had reverted from my sleek 21-gear modern hybrid to my old basic bike with a Sturmey-Archer 3-speed). My motorbike was tucked away out of sight, and I brought it out and wheeled it through to the road. It started with my first thrust on the kick-start and Harriet climbed on behind me. We didn't need helmets—they wouldn't be made compulsory for another seven or eight years. We roared off down the road and were soon climbing effortlessly up the steep lane to the top of the hill. With Harriet's arms hugging me round the waist and the delightful sensation of her soft, curvaceous figure pressing into my back, I felt as though I were ascending to Paradise itself. I could happily have driven thus for a thousand miles.

At the summit we made our way through a gap between the bushes and came out to an open space that sloped away to the southeast. The ground was quite uneven, and our favourite spot was a convenient little hollow just the right size and shape for the two of us to sit in. That vantage point commanded spectacular views of the vale below and the distant downs beyond. But right now the only view I was interested in was this gorgeous vision beside me. Her light brown hair glistened with a lustrous sheen in the evening sun: being so close, I could see that individual strands were golden, sandy-coloured, and even of an auburn hue. As she nestled her head against mine, I breathed in the delicious fragrance of her hair; I couldn't tell whether it was apple or peach, but it didn't matter—whatever it was smelt delightful. Her eyes, being of an unusually pale brown colour, seemed to me like deep, mysterious pools that held strange secrets, and she had the cutest of dimples when she smiled. Her skin was lightly tanned, and adorned with a modest sprinkling of freckles; and it was so soft and smooth to the touch, that it was a delight simply to rest my hand on her arm.

I scarcely spoke, other than to utter the occasional monosyllable of agreement. I let Harriet do most of the talking—mainly because the sound of her voice had all the allure of a tinkling mountain stream, and the music of a song thrush or a nightingale. Indeed, there was, if I rightly recall, a skylark nearby, twittering a symphony from on high, but it was so united with the exquisite melodies of this most beautiful of human voices, that I could not distinguish one from the other. What we (or mainly, she) talked about, I cannot say—the whole experience was like being enveloped in a cloud of sheer delight.

And then she leant over to me and we kissed. It would be pointless even attempting to describe that moment adequately. I could fill a hundred of these diaries and not do the moment justice. It was a moment of exquisite ecstasy—a moment that seemed to last for a thousand years, and yet at the same time to be gone in a microsecond. All other existence save Harriet and myself was driven from my consciousness. There was no world outside—all the sorrow and suffering of mankind, all its joys and pleasures, all its achievements throughout the centuries, all its tragedies; none of these existed for me anymore. I wanted to stay here forever.

Alas, reality has a nasty habit of hitting you right between the eyes, or in the pit of the stomach, and as darkness began to surround us and a chilly wind sprang up to cool our ardour, we had to make the difficult decision to return to suburbia and to our homes. And so we remounted my trusty steed and sped off back down to civilisation and prepared for the tantalizing process of parting. I was vaguely aware of Harriet asking me what I'd 'be doing about the New Zealand business' and replying that I'd sort out something or other.

Having reluctantly torn myself away after another electrifying kiss, I sailed up to my room and, with my head swimming in a whirlpool of thoughts, impressions, sensations and aspirations, and with the minimum of bedtime preparation, I dived beneath the covers (and I didn't even notice how lumpy the mattress was!) One would have thought I'd lie awake for ages, turning everything over in my mind, mentally reliving and savouring the delights of that evening, but I must have been worn out by the emotional overload of the situation, because the next thing I was aware of was the cold light of dawn.

In fact, as a figure of speech that was far from the mark, because when I awoke my whole being seemed to be suffused with an enveloping warmth, and the sunlight pouring through my window seemed several shades nearer to a rosy pink than anything remotely cold. But far from merely lying there basking in the glow of my good fortune, it was the very fact of this blossoming relationship that drove me into action. I leapt out of bed, performed the customary morning ablutions and other necessary preparations for venturing out into the world, and pedalled enthusiastically off to work at the Dunkirk Memorial Hospital. By now my consciousness was no longer that of revisiting the past: this was *now*, and all awareness of work, life and anything beyond this time had become so completely squashed and buried by the forces acting upon me that for me they did not exist.

Dr Pritchard was amazed to see me arrive more than ten minutes early—he had not yet taken up his stance, peering at his watch to catch me crossing the threshold a quarter of a minute beyond the nine o'clock deadline. Although rendered momentarily dumb by my unwonted punctuality, he lost no time in finding me some work to do. But the reason for my eagerness was so that I could consult the latest professional journals that were delivered regularly to the department. I slotted effortlessly back into my old routine, just as though I had last worked there the day before. But as soon as the boss had disappeared up the corridor to join the ward round, I nipped into his office and took the latest journal from his desk. Thumbing through the job adverts from abroad, I quickly found the New Zealand section. It was disappointingly small, but to my delight I found a promising looking vacancy for a research technician in a small hospital a little way south of Christchurch. I made a note of the telephone number and a few other details, then quickly put the journal back on Dr Pritchard's customarily untidy desk.

Although the quality of the work apportioned to me that day constituted drudgery and boredom, the time seemed to fly by, so engrossed was I in my love for Harriet and my plans to be with her for the rest of my life. Logically, my early arrival that morning should have earned me a correspondingly early departure at home-time, but Dr P's logic did not work like that. His reasoning was that nine o'clock was the official starting time, and if workers chose to arrive before that time, they did so voluntarily; five-thirty was still the official leaving time.

I sped back to my little room, longing to be with my darling again that evening, but was devastated to find a note from her explaining that an aunt of hers in Berrington had suffered a stroke, and she was expected to go with her family to visit the poor lady. Apparently she had pleaded to be excused but had been unable to get out of the trip. She assured me we would meet again after work the following day.

The evening dragged by after that. I tried listening to my records but they had no appeal; I switched on my radio, tuning and re-tuning to various stations, but none provided anything remotely interesting. I went out for a walk; some of the shops were open late, and I took the opportunity to change a ten-shilling note into coins. I was counting the hours until nine p.m. when I could make the all-important telephone call to New Zealand.

At long last the time came when I could be sure that tomorrow's working day had begun on the other side of the world. I rang the operator and asked to be put through on an international number. Fortunately, this phone box was one of the few new ones that allowed international calls. I stuffed a handful of coins into the slot and waited for the signal to press Button A. Eventually a rather distant voice with a distinct 'twang' of an accent came over the wires. I explained about the job advert I had seen and quoted the name of the journal. The owner of the voice began to sound very excited and explained that they were desperate to fill the vacancy but had received not a single enquiry. I said I would very much like to fill the position, and briefly described my qualifications and experience. The fact that they were pretty minimal (my thought mode being that of my '60s persona) didn't seem to bother him.

His response sounded something like: 'Ixcellunt! Whin d'ya thunk ya'd be eyeball ta staaht?'

'When could I start?' I queried. 'Well, I guess it'd take me a month or two to clear all the formalities with the New Zealand immigration service. Having a definite job to go to will doubtless help to speed things up.'

We continued our conversation until the money had run out, by which time the hospital administrator had assured me he would do all in his power to 'ixpidite' the process, as well as sending me full details of the post I was applying for, along with an application form, plus details of the hospital, the town and the region as a whole. I virtually floated back to my room; I couldn't wait to tell Harriet the next evening.

At last that time came; this time we met in "Arturo's Caffè and Coffee Bar" further along from The Blue Danube. Harriet could see I was really excited. 'What's all this about, love?' she purred.

'What would you say,' I began, 'if I said I'd got myself a job in Ashburton?'

Her purr quickly changed to a growl. 'Ashburton? You're going back to Devon? I don't believe it—we were planning our life together and you want to go back to being a country bumpkin!'

This reaction fairly took me back, and I hastened to clarify the situation. 'No, no, dear—not Ashburton in Devon, Ashburton in *New Zealand*!'

Harriet swiftly regained her composure and her gentle visage. 'It's all right, sweetie—just my little joke. Of course I knew you meant the one in New Zealand. Er...where is it, exactly?

'It's just a little way south of Christchurch, in the Canterbury Plains.'

'Sounds great, how did you manage that?'

I went on to explain about the journal and the phone call. I wasn't sure if I'd be ready to travel out at the same time as her and her family, but I wouldn't be far behind. I even added the corny line about going to the ends of the earth for her. When she asked me a bit more about Ashburton (I'd nipped into the local library in my lunch break to do some research), she began to show her dissatisfaction again.

'An hour's drive, you say? *That* far from Christchurch? But that'll be *miles* away! I thought we'd be living in the same town at least. When am I ever going to see you?'

'Oh come on, love—it's not that bad. People think nothing of driving those distances over there. And anyway, we could set up home together somewhere in between Ashburton and Christchurch. There's places like...um, Rakaia, or Dunsandel.' I had pored over the map and memorized the route.

Again, her reaction took me by surprise: 'Well, *I* don't want to live in some crummy little backwoods hamlet. I want to be where there's at least a bit of life!'

'Well, look, sweetheart—it might not be perfect, but it's a start. There wasn't anything suitable for me in Christchurch itself, but once we're there I can look out for opportunities—there's bound to be something going eventually. This is just a way of getting my foot in the door.'

That seemed to mollify the fiery maiden, and we settled down to a shared plate of pasta and an espresso coffee each.

Over the next few days I continued to make my plans. The letter from Ashburton Hospital seemed to take an age to come, and I filled in the application form immediately and sent it back by return of post. I also contacted the New Zealand immigration authorities in London, and set that part of the matter in motion. I wrote a letter to my parents explaining my plans, and also a letter of resignation to Dr Pritchard, but decided to withhold them until the issue was firmly settled. Each day I toiled at my day job, but like Jacob in the Bible, who had to work seven years to win the hand of Rachel from his mean Uncle Laban, the time seemed to fly by, for love of my dearest one.[1] Each evening I couldn't wait to be with her, and as soon as I'd got in from work and attended to any essential business, I would hurry out to meet her, either at a prearranged spot or at her home. On the latter occasions I sometimes met her parents, and they seemed delighted that I was committing myself to their daughter in such a definite way.

As things began to come together, I had determined to post the letter to my parents one evening, and hand in my resignation the next day. However, on returning to my

---

1. Genesis 29:20

bedsit after work, I found a letter from the NZ immigration authority. They had returned my birth certificate with their compliments, but asked for an additional form of identification. I actually can't remember now what it was they wanted, because the ensuing sequence of events completely bowled me over.

Seating myself at the table in my little room, I took my wallet from my jacket pocket and began to remove its contents. Now, one of my failings (and I'll readily admit it) is that I'm a bit of a hoarder. Often it's deliberate, for example, I'll keep the ticket stub from a visit to the cinema, to remind me of a really good film, such as 'The Sound of Music'[2], which Harriet and I had just been to see a few nights ago. But much of my wallet's contents were till receipts, bus tickets and other trivia I'd stuffed in there and never bothered to remove. So, while retrieving whatever it was the New Zealand people wanted, I decided to have a good clear out—it was overdue anyway, because the wallet had become bulky and awkward.

Some of the bus tickets looked unusual, for instance there was one marked 'Stagecoach', and I couldn't remember where I'd got that one. It didn't seem particularly important, so I just tossed it in the bin. The till receipts suffered a similar fate, but again, I was puzzled by one from a shop called PC Supplies Ltd. I couldn't think where that shop was, and I was puzzled by the item description: 1 USB cable. The price was expressed in a peculiar way, too: £10.99. I assumed it meant ten pounds, nine shillings and ninepence, but that the nines had not been printed separate. That seemed an awful lot

---

2. Rodgers and Hammerstein/20th Century Fox

of money to pay for a cable, I thought—I presumed it was something I'd got for the boss. I'd have to remember to claim the amount from petty cash. What really had me puzzled, though, were the photos.

There was one of an elegant young woman dressed in an academic gown, holding a scroll. On the back was written: "Sally's graduation June 1998". I kept turning the photo over, looking at the picture and then the inscription. I could see a strong family likeness in the young lady's face, but I couldn't say that I knew her. What was really weird, though, was the date—1998. That was more than 30 years away!

That must surely have been a slip of the pen.

Another picture showed a rather younger girl holding a silver cup. On the back of that was written "Hazel with dance trophy November 1994". Again—sheer bewilderment seized me: I just couldn't place this Hazel, and another future date had me completely stumped. Then I got a real shock as I found a third photo—of a wedding couple. The groom was very obviously me, but who on earth was the bride? (She looked pretty stunning, as a matter of fact.) The inscription read: "William and Katherine, July 1971". I just couldn't believe it—had I been set up for some elaborate practical joke? Who was this Katherine I had allegedly married (or would do in the future)? I searched for other photos, but found only one—of a boy about six or seven years old, with no writing on the back.

I spread the photos out on the table and pondered, really not knowing what to make of them. Looking through the remaining items in my wallet, I found a library card, and several other small plastic cards, each measuring approximately 8 by 5cm. One had "Platinum

VISA" on it, another said "Mastercard" and another, "Nectar". They all had long numbers embossed on them, with my signature on the back. There was even one purporting to be a driving licence, like nothing I'd ever seen before. It had my name on it, and even my photo, but with an address that was completely unknown to me—in the village of Clunmore, which I vaguely knew was somewhere to the west of Roxbury. There was also a ring—a simple gold ring, though it looked well worn; a family heirloom, I presumed.

Hopelessly confused, I fished the bus tickets out of the waste bin. They all had dates way into the future—into the next century, in fact! So did most of the till receipts— what *was* going on? I stood up—and nearly toppled over, so unsteady was I feeling. I poured myself a cup of water and drank it swiftly. I paced up and down the room, then sat back at the table with my head in my hands. I prayed for help, for enlightenment, as it were— some explanation for this perplexing riddle. I thought I'd got the situation firmly under control, but then these people, these strangers, were pressing in on my tidy little world, and the articles from the future were making things decidedly untidy.

I told myself to stay calm. I focused my gaze on the wedding picture. I closed my eyes and the image remained—in fact, it became clearer, more vivid, more animated. I fancied I could hear voices—a confused babble at first, but then individual ones became more distinct. One in particular, saying, 'There, we've done it at last, darling. Now we'll be together forever!'

Then I took the graduation picture in my hands (they were shaking terribly). I imagined I could hear a clear, sweet young voice saying, 'Hey, Daddy—guess what? I got a first!' The picture of the girl with the dance trophy evoked a similar response, and I fancied I could hear myself saying to each one in turn, 'I am *so* proud of you!'

The picture of the little boy had the most surprising—and disturbing—effect on me, which I was at a loss to explain. As I gazed at that sweet little face I felt a cold shiver go down my spine; and then I felt hot and sweaty all over. My head began to reel, and I started to feel sick. I got up, went to the sink and splashed my face with cold water. I had another drink and sat down again. I picked up the photo and examined it again. The boy in the picture looked very much like myself at that age, yet in the background I could see a building I recognised as being in a local park, here in Hardington, yet I hadn't come to this part of the country until I was an adult.

I prayed again, more urgently. That was something I hadn't done of late. I suppose I hadn't felt the need, as everything seemed to be going so well. I sat back, closed my eyes and tried to calm the whirlwind of confusing, conflicting thoughts racing around in my brain. I deliberately made an effort to empty my mind, and as I consciously dismissed each mental demon, slowly, gradually, some positive images began to take their place. Little by little, congenial pictures and impressions began to insinuate themselves into my mind, and take shape.

There was Katherine—Kathy—Kate. I began to recall meeting her in a general way at the local Free Church, and how, on a young people's punting expedition on the River Roxe, the pole I was wielding got caught in some low branches, tipping me unceremoniously into the water. Unfortunately Katherine had been standing up at the other end, about to move to a more central section, and the punt rocked so violently that she fell overboard too. We helped each other to the bank, and to my relief and delight she just roared with laughter, and thought it was an absolute hoot. That was the beginning of a beautiful relationship, and I found myself reliving, as in a video replay, significant events in our subsequent life together.

The details of the other two inscribed photos also became clear—my very own daughters, at significant moments of triumph in their lives. It all came back to me, how thrilled and 'blown away' I'd been when they were born—one simply gorgeous little baby, perfect in every detail, then another two years later. I recalled the broken nights Kathy and I had endured, looking after our little darlings, the joy we shared as each learned to walk, and speak (and how, sometimes we were later to wish they would stop speaking for five seconds!).

Gradually the mist of confusion cleared, and my whole future life unfolded before me—except for one key factor: how did I come to be back here in 1966? Was I dreaming the whole thing? Was I ill or in some sort of coma? They say when you're drowning your whole life flashes before you—is that what was happening? I certainly seemed to have been drowning in some kind of mental and emotional delusion, but it seemed, I hoped, that I was coming to the surface again. However, there were still some pieces of the jigsaw puzzle to put into place, and I felt somehow that the last photo was the key.

I peered at the picture again, and tried to put a name to the face. At first nothing suggested itself; then...could it be Jim? No, but I felt I was close. Then it came—Tim; Timothy—and I remembered playing with him in the park. Then I recalled with a very cold shiver how I had succeeded in bringing him into existence, only to have to condemn him once again to obscurity, lest my two beautiful daughters should be denied *their* lives. And then it all came flooding back—how I had accidentally found I could travel back in time to my former home and life, and how I had deliberately done so on a number of occasions for a variety of purposes. At first these trips had resulted in beneficial outcomes, but later they had had disturbing consequences—and none more so than this current nightmare.

One thing was clear—I had to get myself out of this mess. How could I have been so foolish, so blind, so completely deluded...so, so...*lost*? Yes, that was it—I had been totally lost, just as the song had said: 'lost in your love'. Meeting Harriet like that, quite out of the blue, and her affectionate manner towards me, had sparked off such a sudden surge of emotion that I had been powerless to resist. I had been swept away on a tide of infatuation. Realizing I could have forfeited a lifetime of love and fulfilment—not to mention the joys of family life—with my precious Kate for an uncertain future on the far side of the world with a person whom I really didn't know at all, I swiftly picked up my wedding ring and put it back on my finger, vowing to rededicate myself to the true love of my life.

I had to think carefully how best to extricate myself from this very awkward situation. Although I realized I didn't actually love Harriet, I still had quite strong feelings for her, and I wanted to let her down as gently as possible. I also had to let the hospital authorities in Ashburton know of my change of mind. Taking an airmail writing pad from a drawer, I sat down to compose a letter. I also switched on the radio, as I liked to have some undemanding musical accompaniment when I was reading or writing. Considering how best to get out of the job I'd virtually committed myself to, I decided to plump for the story that, 'due to an unforeseen family crisis', I found myself unable after all to take up the appointment. (This was not a lie—the crisis had been of my own making.) I apologised profusely and expressed my hope that they would find a suitable candidate for the post. I also penned a letter to the New Zealand Department of Migration, explaining to them that my plans had changed.

As I was putting the finishing touches to the second letter, the radio presenter announced, and then played, the latest release by Dusty Springfield, 'You Don't Have To Say You Love Me'[3], which made me sit up with a start. Another shiver ran down my back, but this time a pleasant one—they were playing Our Tune! This was the song that had featured prominently during the formative period of my relationship with Kate. Though not all the lyrics were applicable, it was the words "You don't have to say you love me, just be close at hand" that appealed to us—just being with each other was a silent but powerful means of expressing our mutual affection. I suddenly had a crazy idea, and wrote a third letter, which began: 'I realize this is a very unusual request, but...'

I glanced at the clock: six-fifty. I was due to meet Harriet in ten minutes. I'd no idea how I was going to break the news to her, but it had to be done. As I walked round to Arturo's I decided the family crisis line was the best card to play—in truth, it was the only vaguely plausible one I could think of, I mean, I could hardly say,

---

3. English lyrics by Simon Napier-Bell and Vicki Wickham; Philips label

'Sorry, chum, but I'm ditching you for the love of my life I've yet to meet!'

As soon as she saw me, Harriet deduced something was wrong. Being possessed of a woman's insight, she immediately saw through my forced cheerful façade. She came straight to the point: 'What's the matter? What are you trying to hide from me?' I couldn't help but reflect how different Kate's approach would have been. Hers was a much softer, gentler nature, and she'd put me at my ease before coaxing out of me something she knew was troubling me. Harriet by contrast was rather more confrontational. There was no point beating about the bush: I just came straight out with it.

'Harriet,' I said, 'I can't go to New Zealand. I'm sorry, but it just won't work. My mother's health is deteriorating and this is not the right time for me to go gadding off round the world.' (This was a teeny weeny embellishment of the truth—I'd found a recent letter from Mum that said her hip problem had flared up a bit lately.) 'As an only child I feel I have a duty to be reasonably at hand for her declining years. It may not even be that long. Maybe in a couple of years the time'll be right.'

I was quite astonished at the vehemence of her reaction. Gone was the sweet, charming angel I thought I'd known. Whilst it may be an exaggeration to say she'd been replaced by a snarling pit bull terrier, the fleeting image of such a growling cur did cross my mind as she berated me for reneging on my commitment to her, how I'd badly let her down, made her look an idiot before her friends and family, and how I was being so horribly self-ish and so on.

That last allegation really made me see red—to say that I was being selfish because I'd expressed a concern for the wellbeing of my own mother (even though I'd been just a wee bit economical with the truth), was taking things too far. Nevertheless, I kept my cool, because for one thing I'd achieved the result I'd intended, and for another, I'd been enlightened as to the true nature of this person I'd nearly been foolish enough to saddle myself with.

There was no point going into the café now; as the petulant filly stormed off, no doubt to slag me off to her folks, I took a deep breath and returned to my room. I no longer had any reason to hang around: I'd been in this particular time warp far longer than I'd have liked, and I just wanted to get back home—to my *real* home in the 21st century, to the warmth of my spacious living room and the even more spacious place my beloved Kate had for me in her heart.

Picking up the three letters I'd written, I almost vaulted down the stairs and scampered round to the back of the house to get my bike. I would have liked to use the Ariel, to get me home faster, but I was sure that wouldn't work. I just gave its fuel tank a loving pat and got the sturdy old Raleigh bike out for the journey. I sped off as fast as possible, slowing momentarily as I passed a pillar-box to thrust the letters in the slot while passing.

Passing through the city centre, I was trying hard to think my way back to my own time, but felt frustrated every time I saw a smart looking Morris Minor or a psychedelically patterned carrier bag. I'd had more than enough of the 'Swinging Sixties', thank you very much. Eventually, to my intense relief, as I was pedalling westward out of the city, I noticed the temperature dropping sharply and the light getting distinctly dimmer. Hooray! It was February again, in my 'own' century!

Just then, amid the rush-hour traffic slowly passing me, came a couple of youths in a souped-up Mondeo—you know, one of those with ridiculously ostentatious spoilers, fluorescent coloured lights on the bonnet and underneath, fog lights blazing and all the rest of it. The windows were wound down, and blaring from the interior came the unmistakable strains of "Lost In Your Love" by Tony Hadley[4]. I cringed; oh no, surely not! Then I'm afraid I just snapped.

'TURN THAT BLOODY RACKET DOWN!' I yelled—then immediately felt ashamed, and surprised at my own extreme reaction. I am generally very much averse to swearing, but on this occasion I'd been sorely provoked, and just couldn't help myself.

'SorrEEE, vicar!' one of the lads shouted back—and of course, the noise was turned up even louder. Fortunately the flow of traffic speeded up and the offending din faded into the sunset. I managed to calm down, and stopped at a conveniently situated flower shop to buy a big bunch of red roses. Discarding a few shillings and thre'p'ny bits still in my wallet, I used my credit card for the transaction.

Seldom have I sped up Clunmore Rise so fast, and soon my longing eyes were rewarded with the welcome sight of my home, wherein, I knew, was the object of my most tender desires. Wasting no time to rush inside, I found Kate sitting by a roaring fire in the living room, reading the newspaper. She looked up as I approached, greeting her with: 'Happy Valentine's Day, sweetie!'

'For me?' she exclaimed, in surprise rather than seeking confirmation that she was the intended recipient.

---

4. EMI

I peered deliberately round the room. 'Well, I can't see anyone else in here, so I guess they must be!' I joked.

'Oh darling', she replied, 'that's lovely—you don't usually do things like this!'

'Well, maybe I should do more often,' I responded.

She then looked slightly sideways at me and tentatively enquired, 'You haven't...er...you haven't been seeing someone else, have you?'

'Not since before I met you,' I replied, confidently. 'Cross my heart!'

'No, I'm sorry—silly of me. Of course you haven't.'

Glancing at the clock, I asked, 'Shall I dish out the dinner? I smelt it cooking as I came in.'

Kate agreed, and I carefully laid the dining table, served out the ratatouille Kate had cooked, poured a couple of glasses of our favourite sparkling white wine and turned on BBC Radio Roxbury's evening record request programme to provide some pleasant background music. We didn't actually say grace aloud, but I silently thanked heaven with all my heart for delivering me from a ghastly fate and bringing me safely back to where I should be, to my own time, my own home and my own loving, lovely wife. As we tucked in to a delicious meal, no-one spoke—except the Radio Roxbury presenter.

'And now we have a most unusual request—most unusual indeed. In fact, in all my years of broadcasting I've never come across anything like this before. It's from Bill Draper of Clunmore, for his darling wife Kate, and he would like me to play for her "their song", Dusty Springfield's "You Don't Have To Say You Love Me". Nothing unusual in that, you may think, but wait—this letter was sent in more than forty years ago! This letter has been carefully kept in our studios for all that time, waiting for this very moment! Yes, listeners, I can personally verify that the postmark on this dusty old envelope clearly dates it to July 1966! Most incredible! At that time Radio Roxbury didn't even exist as such—our studio was still being equipped, and we were only making test transmissions! How Bill Draper knew this programme would be on the air so far in advance, not to mention whether he and his beloved Kate would still both be around to enjoy it, I shall never know. One of life's great mysteries, I guess. Anyway, for you, Kate Draper, from your loving husband, here now is Dusty Springfield with "You Don't Have To Say You Love Me".'

Kate was amazed. 'How on earth did you manage to pull off a stunt like that? 1966? Why, we hadn't even met each other then!'

'Like the man said,' I replied, enigmatically, 'one of life's great mysteries!'

'Honestly,' she chuckled, 'you *are* a soppy old thing— why all these romantic gestures all of a sudden?'

My reply left her even more puzzled: 'Well, maybe just because I'd forgotten what a great thing I had until I thought I'd lost it!'

CHAPTER 13

How it all ended

Those last two excursions into the past had a profoundly disturbing effect on me. First, there were the events surrounding my 'phantom son', a phantom that haunted my thoughts and dreams for several months thereafter, and gave me many a sleepless night. As if that were not enough, the meeting with Harriet and how I'd become so infatuated with her that I could have destroyed my whole family really terrified me. It seemed clear to me now that no good purpose could be served by any further such trips, and as a result I firmly resolved never to travel back into the past again. I suppose in a way I did keep that resolution, though I could never have envisaged the strange turn of events that was to seal my resolve decisively.

People remarked on several occasions over the next few weeks and months that they'd seen a distinct change in me. I was, they felt, a little less outgoing, less adventurous, if you like, and more quiet and contemplative. This was hardly surprising in view of the inexplicable and mind-blowing experiences I'd been having of late. On some occasions I'd managed to change the course of history very much for the better. At other times, however,

I'd made things a good sight worse, but, thank God, I'd managed to get things back on course again. It really made me think hard about every decision I made, knowing that to choose one option rather than the other could radically (and perhaps irrevocably) alter the course of history forever after. I did try, though, not to let myself get too bogged down by the idea. I remembered how, back in my school days, the RE teacher had told us in one lesson that 'every action we do makes us either a little more, or a little less, like Christ'. OK, I understood the principle, and was able to apply it in some obvious practical situations, such as whether or not to join in the gossip about someone, or whether or not to ride my bike on the pavement. But then I was faced with the scenario of The Lamppost: what if I came face to face with one while walking along a street? Should I pass to the left of the obstacle, or to the right? Which course would make me more godly?

In the end I reached the radical conclusion that it didn't actually matter: the Good Lord was hardly likely to condemn me for choosing the 'wrong' direction in that case. And now, I eventually came to realize that I couldn't spend the rest of my life agonising over every little eventuality that arose: we were given common sense (and, one hoped, a degree of divine guidance), and for the vast majority of life's everyday decisions that was sufficient. For anything more demanding, the advice of one's spouse, friend, colleague, pastor, solicitor or whatever, could be sought.

So, I gradually began to adopt once more a moderately relaxed attitude to life, although I was constantly on my guard not to let my idle reminiscing of the past actually take me there. And, as the months passed, and started to turn into years, we as a couple began to progress to a newer level of, shall we say, maturity. We found ourselves just that little bit less energetic (although by no means ready for the scrapheap yet!). Although I was now working only three days a week, I still had quite a workload, and I felt the need to cut down on some of my other commitments, so as not to overburden myself. There'd be plenty of opportunity for my other interests when I'd retired completely.

As for Kate, she had long since retired; she did a bit of private tuition, and still managed to earn a few extra pennies from her small-scale costume dolls industry, although she'd had to cut back on that somewhat, as her vision was getting a bit blurred on and off, and she was finding it hard to work on the fine detail. I suggested once or twice that she ought to see an optician—it had been a few years since she'd last had her eyes tested—but she brushed the idea aside, saying it was nothing really, just a bit of tiredness. It was the same with the headaches, but being a determined soul (to put it politely!), and not one to complain about her health, she preferred to soldier on regardless, and in fact, she hadn't seen her GP for five or six years. Occasionally she'd feel sick, too, but she usually put it down to 'those prawns I ate yesterday' or 'the smell of sewage near the Bratsbys' house' where she'd gone to give their young daughter some private tuition.

I'd had some trouble with an abscess under a tooth, and the odd twinge of back trouble, but these ailments, with appropriate treatment, had sorted themselves out, and I was still pretty active, and had no difficulty in dashing about on my bike. We enjoyed seeing our daughters growing up into fine young ladies—Sally, the athletic one, had become a PE and fitness instructor at a health club in Berrington, and in the winter she would fly off to Switzerland, Norway and even Canada and work as a skiing instructor. That brought her in a tidy sum, which enabled her to live in some comfort, along with her American boyfriend Yancey, whom she'd met while skiing in Vermont. He was a sports photographer, and their two chosen professions went very well together. We'd hoped they would 'tie the knot' soon, but Sally always countered our hints with, 'Oh, he's just not the marrying kind!' Hazel, on the other hand, chose a career that was arguably less adventurous (but no less rewarding financially and in terms of job satisfaction). She'd become a graphic designer with a local publisher, and had bought herself a nice little flat in the desirable Holmgrove suburb of the city. She surprised us all one day when she brought home a somewhat unkempt-looking young man and announced they were engaged. Kirk was a jazz musician, with a suitably 'cool', 'laid-back' outlook on life. We were a tad bemused by his appearance at first, but once you got to know him, he was an extremely likeable guy. He was an absolute whiz on the tenor sax, but he was also pretty good on the vibes. I'd never been that keen on jazz myself (Kate was more into it, though), but after we'd been to a few of the concerts Kirk appeared in, I developed quite a taste for it, and we have several of his albums on CD.

My job had changed its emphasis somewhat, and I was now rather less tied to the workplace. The health authority had felt that a significant number of patients were missing out on certain aspects of care because they were relatively housebound, and hadn't the means to get themselves to the hospital for the diagnostic tests our department carried out. Many of these people, due to physical or psychological limitations, were unable, or unwilling, to use one of the volunteer drivers' cars, and to send an ambulance was deemed an uneconomic use of the Trust's resources. However, after some suggestions and discussions, it was decided that if they couldn't come to us, we should go to them. We had some highly portable items of equipment which could quite easily be taken to the persons in question and left with them after suitable instructions as to how to operate them. Alternatively the technician could connect up the equipment and set it running before leaving. A further visit was arranged for the following day to collect the equipment.

It was considered that I would be the best person to carry out these visits, as my hours and duties were more flexible than those of my colleagues, and besides, I had actually expressed a desire to do it. Most of the candidates for the home diagnosis tests lived in villages around the city, say four or five miles from base, so I was quite happy to cycle there—it was a good way to keep up my fitness level, and I received a more than adequate allowance for the use of my bike. Sometimes I'd be visiting someone in my own village of Clunmore, or a neighbouring village or hamlet, which meant I got home a little earlier than usual.

I've always been a real lover of the countryside—as my dad had been, in fact. Indeed, it was he who had instilled in me from an early age an appreciation of all things rural. On our Sunday afternoon walks after chapel he'd often stop and show me something I'd otherwise have missed, like the pattern of tiny coloured spots on the petals of a foxglove flower, or the little aquatic creatures to be found in the roadside ditches. He always used to say that, in contrast to the common saying, ditchwater is far from dull! He seemed to notice details that nobody else did, and some of that facility rubbed off onto me. For example, it seemed wonderful, on a damp, dewy morning, to see a beautifully formed, perfectly shaped spider's web adorned with sparkly droplets of dew. One winter's morning I was entranced by the effect of hoar frost that had built up on a chainlink fence around a tennis court near my home, and I dashed back to get my camera, which unfortunately I'd forgotten to bring. But in the brief interval that I did so, the pale rising sun had managed to melt the frost completely.

That, and other phenomena of nature, caused me to reflect how transient life can be—at this current instant of consciousness, we can look back on all our past experiences, and forward in anticipation of what may fill our lives in the coming years; we can look out in all directions to the wider world, and to some extent participate in the collective lives and experiences of mankind in general, and that for us is life, reality, our cosmos. And yet, in the vast, general scheme of things, we are so minute. As St James said, 'What is your life? You are a mist that appears for a little while and then vanishes.'[1] David, in one of his psalms, asks, 'Oh Lord, what is man that you care for him, the son of man, that you think of him? Man is like a breath, his days are like a fleeting shadow.'[2] In a rather more sombre vein, Thomas Hardy had one of his characters pen the following words in a suicide note: 'I am now about to enter on my normal condition. For people are almost always in their graves.

1. James 4:14.
2. Psalm 144:3, 4.

When we survey the long race of men, it is strange and still more strange to find that they are mainly dead men, who have scarcely ever been otherwise.'[3]

It was while I was cycling around the countryside on my errands that I had time to reflect on the strange experiences it had been my lot to undergo, and to try and see some purpose in it all. It convinced me that in our brief span of life on this earth we may have few opportunities to make any lasting impact on the world, least of all the universe, as a whole. And yet it did seem that, unless we are to descend into a sad state of purposelessness, we should make it our business to add something positive, however small our contribution may seem, to life in general. I had been extremely favoured and fortunate in having been given several extra bites of the cherry—I knew of no other person alive or dead who had ever been given the chance to go back in time and right a few wrongs (although I hadn't always made a good job of it, I had to admit). It did make me think, however, that we should use what fleeting opportunities we are given to prepare ourselves and others for whatever may lie ahead: old age…posterity…eternity?

I continued my travels in the locality for a year or two without any particularly noteworthy incidents (apart from the intriguing, and at times amusing, little sights and happenings that one comes across in the normal course of getting around). I was beginning to feel that, much as I enjoyed my work, the time was drawing inevitably closer when I should pack it in completely. It had been great to enjoy the company of my junior colleagues, and to join in the general conversation and

3. Desperate Remedies.

camaraderie of the workplace, but I had begun to develop contacts and friendships outside, and the attraction of full retirement was getting stronger all the time.

Kate and I had been making tentative plans to downsize our living space and move to a house or cottage that would be less of an effort to maintain—and a garden that, while still providing some outdoor leisure space, was considerably less like a sizeable tract of former jungle clamouring to revert to its original state. As we went about on our personal errands, we would often spot a nice little residence that we felt would suit us down to the ground, though usually it was firmly occupied and seemed likely to remain that way indefinitely. We had decided, however, that as soon as I retired, or was very close to doing so, we would make a concerted effort to find that certain little place. It was while I was collecting a piece of equipment from a disabled gentleman in the attractive little village of Mellingfield, about three miles to the south of Clunmore, that I was thinking how lovely it would be if we could find our dream cottage here. It was a relatively quiet, yet at the same time quite lively village, in that there was no shortage of activities going on regularly in the village hall, and at the primary school.

The school was fairly small, and relied on the revenue it gained from a good programme of evening classes and other meetings—you could learn conversational French, Italian and other languages there, be trained in karate or tae kwon do, and become a potential expert in creative writing, cookery and embroidery. These activities, as well as fulfilling the needs of the local inhabitants, attracted a fair number of folk from neighbouring villages. There was a thriving post office and general store, a lively and well-attended chapel, a quiet pub that served decent ale and cider, and a cricket team that was... well, frankly, rubbish! There was, however, a half-decent bus service— hourly at peak times and two-hourly at other times— linking Roxbury to the small but expanding market town of Rainswick, about 20 miles (30km, if you like) to the southwest, just beyond the strange, unfinished stone tower known as Hartford Folly.

We'd travelled through Mellingfield occasionally, and remarked what a pretty place it was—and virtually devoid of the sort of unsympathetic housing develop- ments that had disfigured so many other local communi- ties. It was therefore not surprising that, as I pedalled my leisurely way through its main street, admiring the fasci- nating variety of houses—ancient thatched cottages with leaning walls, a few half-timbered dwellings, sturdy 1940s ex-council houses, mellow stone cottages and the like—I should slip into thoughts of what might lie ahead for my spouse and me.

My mind drifted into a kind of warm, hazy reverie that pictured the two of us settling down in one of the houses in this little gem of a village. I tried to imagine how it would be when I didn't have to go to work at all: much as I enjoyed cycling here and there in the course of my profession, I felt it would be a real treat just to pedal off in whatever direction I pleased—to visit the lake up to the northwest, or explore the woodland areas further south, beyond East Pitchcombe. Or the two of us could drive to the garden centre on the Clunmore road, peruse the plants and products there, enjoy a lazy coffee and cake in the café there, and then come home to potter around in our small but well-kept garden.

In this dreamy mood, I was viewing the dwellings I was passing in a purposeful way, as though selecting the ones that, should they come up for sale, would be prime candidates for our future occupation. It was therefore quite a surprise, and one that brought me right back to reality, when I spotted, parked in the driveway of a neat little stone cottage, what was unmistakably *our* car. True, it looked a little more battered than it had seemed that morning (although I noticed it had a brand new exhaust), but the make, colour, and above all the regis-tration number, put it beyond doubt. I was quite puzzled: what errand had brought Kate here? Was she visiting one of her Dollybird friends, perhaps? Quite possibly—or some other missive related to her expanding range of activities, now that she was more or less retired. But that still didn't really explain the changed appearance of the car. I could understand the new exhaust—I'd fancied I'd heard a bit of a rattle from the rear of the car once or twice, though I hadn't thought it was too bad. It must have suddenly gone for a Burton, and Kate had popped into 'Exhausted Inc.' near Roxbury station to get it replaced. However, that didn't explain the dented near-side front wing (seemingly not a recent defect) or the missing trim in front of the driver's door.

A couple of other cars were parked in the road outside but I didn't take much notice of them. 'Well,' I thought, 'whatever Kate's doing here, I may as well pop in and say hello. Maybe she can explain about the car while we're at it!' So I quickly dismounted, leant my bike against the privet hedge and went to the door. I gave the antique knocker a couple of sharp taps and waited.

I got quite a shock when the door was opened by my daughter Sally. Hazel was there too, and they both seemed to be expecting me—almost relieved to see me, in fact.

'Oh, *there* you are, Dad!' cried Sally, 'we were just beginning to wonder where you'd got to.' Then, in a strangely condescending way, almost as if talking down to a child, she added, 'Been out for a little ride around, have you?'

'No!' I replied, with more than a hint of irritation in my voice. 'I'm actually at work, if you must know—I just happened to be passing when I saw…'

'Oh, Daddy, come on in, now. Never mind about work—you don't need to think about that any more!'

What on *earth* was she talking about? Of *course* I had to think about work! I had to get that monitor back to the hospital and download its data. I wasn't retired yet, for goodness' sake! 'Anyway, what are you both doing in this house? Whose is it? And where's Mum? The car's outside, so she must be…' My voice tailed off as I saw the girls exchange furtive glances.

'Look, why don't you sit down while we make you a nice cup of tea, Dad?' put in Hazel, and led me to an easy chair. 'Here's the paper, look—you've hardly glanced at it this morning.' She swiftly ushered her sister out into the kitchen and partly closed the door.

What the heck was going on? I wondered. Why were my daughters strutting around in someone else's house as if it were their own? Where was my wife, and why had the girls so quickly changed the subject when I'd mentioned her? I really had to get to the bottom of this mystery. I got up and moved stealthily to the door. Inside the kitchen I could hear them discussing me in hushed tones.

'He's obviously in denial, isn't he? I mean, that happens a lot, doesn't it, when a person's had a sudden shock, or a sad loss or something?'

'Yes, but it's a bit odd that it's happening now, so long after the event. I mean, he seemed to be taking it so well, didn't he? I thought he'd been really brave—I'd never have expected...'

'No, I'm not surprised—people often do suppress their grief when a loved one dies: they sort of push it down inside, but one day—often much later—something just sort of triggers it and it all comes rushing out again...either in floods of tears...or...or...depression...or denial. And the fact that it's a year to the day— well, I half expected *some*thing might happen. That's why I thought it'd be a good idea for us to call in today, just to sort of cheer him up and not let him get broody or anything.'

'Yeah...but he's in a bit of a state; I suppose the best we can...'

At this point their voices were drowned out by the sound of the kettle starting to come to the boil. I returned to my seat and began to fit the pieces of the puzzle together: no sign of Kate...a sad loss...a year to the day...the state of the car...

I looked around. Two large bunches of fresh flowers in vases...two 'Thinking of you' cards on the mantelpiece...bookshelves filled with *my* books. Then the penny dropped. I snatched up the paper and peered at the date—yes! Just as I'd figured—just as my thoughts had previously plunged me back into the past, this time they had propelled me into the *future!* The date on the newspaper showed that *three whole years* had slipped by in the time it had taken me to imagine myself retired and settled in this village! My first irrational instinct was to flee from this horrible situation—to get back to my own time. I was about to get up and slip quietly out of the door and get back on my bike...until a more rational thought came to the fore. Kate, my beloved, my life's companion, had died—a year ago. It seems I had borne it well, but still, the thought of spending my retirement on my own was by no means an appealing one. I had to find out what had killed her—and see if there was anything I could have done to save her from an untimely death.

This was definitely a time for thinking on my feet. The cue had come to put on a convincing act. I pretended to carry on reading the paper while working out my strategy. (There was no news worth reading anyway—another terrorist strike in Indonesia, the pensions crisis worse than ever, riots in Leicester—same old stuff.) As my daughters came back into the living room, bearing trays laden with cups of tea and fancy cakes, I addressed them with what I hoped would sound a sincere apology.

'Look, my loves,' I said, I'm *really* sorry, I realize I've been having one of my funny turns—a 'senior moment', if you like. I didn't want to trouble you before, but now that it's happened in your presence, I'd better come clean. They started about six months after Mum died. I just sort of go all forgetful for half an hour or so—sometimes longer, often much less. I don't fall down, or do anything stupid. I went to the post office the other day: posted off a parcel, bought a packet of stamps and got a couple of aerogrammes, but when I got home I couldn't remember a thing about it! Went back to check whether I'd actually taken the parcel there, and Bob the postmaster said I had, although he added that he thought I'd seemed 'a bit dreamy'. It's nothing to worry about, my dears—I've been seeing the doctor about it, and he reckons it's just a matter of getting my medication adjusted.'

I hoped I hadn't alarmed the girls too much, although I could see at once that they were quite concerned, to say the least. I was immediately subjected to an unusual degree of pampering, and advice on how to take things a bit more quietly. I had offers to help with this, that and the other thrust at me, some of which I pretended to accept, knowing (or at least hoping) I wouldn't need to take them up. But before I could do much more planning, there was some vital information I needed.

'Would you excuse me for a moment?' I asked, getting up and moving to what I hoped was the door to the study I'd always intended to have when I retired. I opened the door and found myself in a broom cupboard. Hastily inventing an excuse for my actions, I rummaged around with some items on a shelf and muttered: 'Oh, that's alright—I *did* put it away.' Quickly executing Plan B, I announced, 'I'm just going to the bathroom.'

'Can you manage all right?' asked Hazel, 'Do you want me to help you up the stairs?'

'I can manage perfectly well, thank you very much— I'm not *actually* an invalid, you know!' The note of irritation in my voice masked a mild sense of relief, because, of course, I was not at all sure where the bathroom was, but now I'd been given a useful clue. My aim was to have a snoop around the house in order to locate a particular filing cabinet. With the ladies out of the way downstairs, I first found the bathroom, rattled the toilet seat and noisily closed the door, while remaining outside on the landing. A quick check of the other rooms (facilitated by the doors being open) revealed a main bedroom, a smaller one with twin beds and…the study! It had originally been a small third bedroom, but, obviously, I had taken it over as my own personal den.

I did a quick visual sweep: numerous shelves stacked with books, files and, I'm ashamed to admit, quite a lot of junk; a desk with a computer (actually, a very nice ultra-modern one—I *was* in the future, after all); a decent-looking audio unit...and there, tucked away behind the door, was the filing cabinet. This was the one in which Kate and I had kept all our important documents—bills and receipts, guarantee forms, insurance documents and so on. It took me only seconds to locate the folder marked 'Certificates', and I whipped it out and opened it. The very first sheet of paper was what I sought—Kate's death certificate. I noted the date of my beloved's demise, but what I really wanted to know was the cause of death. And there it was—'Cerebral aneurysm'.

'Golly!' I thought, 'Poor love—a blood vessel bursting in her brain.' Then the penny dropped—of course! Those sudden headaches she'd been getting...the blurring of her vision...the nauseous attacks. All were classic symptoms of an aneurysm. How could I have missed what was so obvious now—with hindsight? I put away the dreaded document and replaced the folder. It briefly occurred to me to take the certificate with me, but then I dismissed the idea. Why should I want such a macabre souvenir of an event I was determined to prevent from happening? And anyway, after only a quick scan of the document its details had made such an impact on my mind that I knew they would be firmly etched in my memory indefinitely. In my haste to replace the folder, I clumsily dropped it, and several papers spilled onto the floor. I stuffed them back in the folder and put it away. I fancied I heard one of the girls saying something like: 'I hope Dad's all right up there', and although I had a perfect right to be rummaging around in my own study,

I somehow felt strangely guilty, as though I had a secret to hide. I dashed out onto the landing, and, noticing a small sheet of paper that had slid under the door, I grabbed it and stuck it in my pocket.

Nipping back into the bathroom, I availed myself of its facilities, flushed the toilet and trotted downstairs to my daughters. I was trying to think of a way to convince them I'd be OK if they were to be on their way so that I, in turn, could be on *my* way—back to my own time— when I heard voices at the back door (through the kitchen)—the babblings of a small child, and the unmistakable Transatlantic tones of Yancey, Sally's boyfriend.

'Come along, little fella,' I heard, and as the door was pushed open, in tottered a smiling, rosy-cheeked, fair-haired little lad. He paused for a moment, quickly took in his surroundings, and then made straight in my direction, enthusiastically calling, 'Ganga! Ganga!' as he toddled unsteadily towards me, his arms outstretched.

'Oh, hi Pop!' Yancey greeted me. (This set me wondering—he never used to call me that, but as I glanced at Sally and spotted her wedding ring, I realized that 'Not the marrying kind' had wed after all!) As the little lad reached me, I heard Yancey say, 'Thomas and I had a great time in the play park. He sure does love the swings!'

More vital information; but my greeting of 'Hello, Thomas' was met with a comment of, 'My, how formal all of a sudden! Whatever happened to "Tommy-boy"?' However, as I talked further to this little child, and interacted playfully with him, I felt a shiver run down my spine. This young lad—obviously my grandson—looked uncannily like a one-year-old version of myself, and, what's more, incredibly like a younger version of another boy I'd once met, whose photo I still carried in my wallet—a certain Master Timothy Draper!

As I considered this amazing—indeed, unsettling—likeness, I tossed their names around in my mind. Timothy; Thomas; Tim; Tom—the two were not a million miles apart in one sense. I hoisted the boy up onto my lap and ran my fingers through his silky platinum-blond hair. And for a while I felt I wanted to remain in this time-frame, and enjoy the delights of having a grandson—someone who, most strangely, appeared to have come along to fill the gap left by that earlier child. But before allowing my thoughts to wander further into the future, and picture myself kicking a football around the park with my grandson, I forced myself to get back on track with regard to the sad loss of my wife.

Much as I desperately wanted to get going right there and then, I felt it wasn't appropriate to make an excuse and just dash out of the door and leap onto my bike. I stayed there out of courtesy until the family group eventually made their departure, although, from an initial feeling of reluctance, I moved into one of positive enjoyment. I learned a lot of interesting things about my daughters and their lives—indeed, about life and the world in general. Hazel was still 'an item' with Kirk the jazzman, although at this particular time he was on a short tour in the Netherlands, and was unable to be with us. Hazel herself had landed a prestigious contract with a major publishing firm, and the couple had moved to a large edifice somewhat resembling a castle on Grants Hill, a posh area to the northwest of the city. They were still not actually married—that was planned for the following year—and had declared themselves not ready for parenthood 'just yet'. I shall enjoy watching all these developments pan out, I thought, as I waved them off and watched their cars disappear round the curve of the road.

Without a moment's hesitation, I said goodbye also to the nice little house I had come to live in, though with the expectation of seeing it again in 'real time', as it were. For some inexplicable reason, I felt it necessary to lock the place up before departing—almost as if to set the seal on my ownership of it. I swiftly mounted my bike and sped off, back into Roxbury and back to the same day in which I'd left it. My return to the department with the diagnostic equipment was barely commented on by my colleagues. I suppose I shouldn't have expected otherwise, but somehow the events I had just witnessed had heightened my expectation of further surprises. I was, in fact, highly relieved that I had been able to return to my own time, as I'd been getting an increasingly strong feeling that my powers of time transport were rapidly waning.

I got through the processing as quickly as possible, and left an hour earlier than usual. My colleagues didn't comment—since I was largely independent of them, they were used to my comings and goings at all hours of the day, and for all they knew, I was off on another health-related errand—which in fact is exactly what I was. I was eager to say something to Kate as soon as I went through the door, yet I felt I should bide my time and await a suitable opportune moment. I didn't want to go in with all guns blazing, so to speak. As it happened, I didn't have to wait long at all, as I found my loved one sitting on a stool in the kitchen with a rather bloody tea towel wrapped round her left hand.

'Oh my love, whatever's happened?' I asked, and received a fairly down-to-earth reply:

'Oh, it's nothing, really—I've just been a bit stupid. I cut myself with a kitchen knife as I was chopping some onions. I tried to put a plaster on it, but I couldn't seem to get the silly little bits of plastic off.'

'Here, let me see,' I said. It was, in fact, with some reluctance that the patient allowed me to treat her ailment. However, I removed the 'dressing', wiped away the excess blood and applied the plaster. 'It isn't like you to do this sort of thing,' I commented, 'you're usually so careful with kitchen things.' Then, following a thought that occurred to me, I enquired: 'Did you have one of your blurry vision episodes?'

She admitted she had, and I advised her strongly to see our GP and get something done about it. In her usual dismissive way, she brushed aside my admonition, and said that she 'might' make an appointment with the optician 'sometime'. I tried to tell her that wasn't good enough, but I could see that I was making no headway at all.

Deciding to take matters into my own hands, I called in at the medical centre next day on my way home and actually made an appointment on Kate's behalf, asking the receptionist if she would kindly ring her up on the morning to 'remind' her (I'd taken care to choose Wednesday afternoon, as I knew that was her time to relax and put her feet up after doing the weekly shopping at Sainsbury's). On the day, however, when I got home from work (and fortunately before I'd asked her about it), Kate told me she'd had a phone call from the surgery to say she was due to see Dr Squires in half an hour. She'd apparently said it must have been a mistake, but, on being assured it was a genuine booking, she'd rather crossly told the poor receptionist not to be silly (perhaps in somewhat stronger terms): she was perfectly well, had no need whatever to see a doctor, and would be obliged if she would cancel the appointment.

Whether Kate had guessed I was behind the booking she didn't say, but her slightly cooler-than-usual attitude made me suspect that she had. Over the next few days I wracked my brain for other ways to get my obstinate wife to be assessed by an expert. I realized I was going to have to resort to subterfuge to achieve my aim, so I made another appointment with the GP, but this time on my way to work I'd nonchalantly asked Kate to pick up a prescription for me. It would be ready at 3 (which I knew was just after her monthly appointment at the hair-dresser's), but I wouldn't be able to collect it, as I'd got to see someone in West Pitchcombe. I'd forewarned the receptionist of my wife's impending visit, and had asked her to ensure she was kept waiting so that Dr Squires would apprehend her and usher her into his room before she could protest.

Unfortunately, that little plan failed too. When I got home, Kate told me, 'Sorry, love—I didn't manage to collect that prescription for you. I was going to, but poor Mildred Bowman had a bit of a crisis, and was in a proper state on the phone. Her husband Robert (you know him, don't you? He's the one who started up his own licensed cab business)...anyway, he's in hospital— he had a heart attack yesterday. Fortunately it was only a small one, and they say they caught him in time, but it's really knocked her for six, and I just *had* to go round after my hair appointment. She'd spent the morning at his bedside but had had to come home for some essentials, and to sort out who'd be running the business and things. I went along to give her a hand and…'

I let her carry on talking, but the words were just passing me by. How typical of her, I thought—generous to a fault when it comes to dealing with other people's problems, especially where a health concern was involved, yet neglecting her own health. I'd tried to devise ways of getting her to attend to her own needs, but just couldn't seem to manage it. I was near to admitting defeat and simply letting nature take its course. But then another development occurred.

About a month later, one Wednesday afternoon, Kate received a phone call. 'Please come to the hospital at once; your husband's been taken ill—he appears to have had some kind of a seizure,' the voice on the line told her, and gave instructions as to go to the Neurology Department. She lost no time in jumping into the car and heading straight for the RRI.

She looked pale, worried and shocked on arrival at Neurology. But she received an even greater shock when, after sitting in the waiting room for five minutes, she was greeted by the neurologist, Dr Alan Griffiths, accompanied by an unusually healthy looking Richard Draper! I'd really hated pulling this stunt on her, but it was truly the only way I could think of to make Kate take her condition seriously. After she had picked herself up off the floor—very nearly literally—on seeing me, she let out a torrent of verbal abuse, which I shall spare the reader from having to endure. She then—*very* reluctantly— agreed to let Alan take a history and give her a neurological examination. I had of course had words with him beforehand, and he had totally concurred with my 'provisional diagnosis', even complimenting me on reading the signs so well and reaching a very logical conclusion. I naturally neglected to inform him that my diagnosis was based entirely on a death certificate yet to be written!

Normally a patient would have to be referred to a consultant by a GP, but Alan and I had known each other for many years, and my investigations had frequently assisted him in his work, so he was more than willing to accept the direct approach in this case. Not surprisingly, his detailed examination caused him to come to the same conclusion as my own, and he immediately ordered an MRI scan and an angiogram, to confirm the diagnosis. Although still somewhat mad at me for springing this surprise on her, Kate was actually quite grateful that I had gone to the trouble to do so, once Alan had managed to get home to her just how serious a condition she had.

The tests were, of course, positive, and treatment was organized promptly. The defect was dealt with by means of endovascular embolization. That's that clever procedure where they insert a tube into an artery in the groin and pass a catheter right up into the brain. They manoeuvre a metal coil into the bulging blood vessel and make the blood in it clot and seal it.

Kate was very soon back in circulation (to use an apt expression!), and was larger than life and ever more active, now that the headaches and other debilitating symptoms had ceased. She was even inclined to take more notice of me (well, just a bit) when I gave advice on medical matters. For once she'd been made to realize how important it is to check out any persistent health problems, and I think she'd come to appreciate that the borderline between good health and disability or death can sometimes be a very fine one.

So, here we are now—still together, thank the Lord. Three months after Kate's operation I finally retired completely. I felt I'd given the NHS more than its fair share of my time and effort, and my colleagues understood my wish to spend as much time as possible with my wife, especially after her cancelled appointment with death. They all thought she was very fortunate to have a husband who'd shown such insight into the possible cause of her symptoms, and determination to get something done about it. Of course, it hadn't been quite like that, but I couldn't tell them the true story—in fact, I haven't told anyone, not even Kate herself—only you, my hypothetical reader.

Soon after I retired, we put the house on the market and began the mammoth task of getting rid of umpteen years of accumulated junk. That was a far greater task than either of us could have imagined, but, thankfully, we were ably assisted by our daughters and potential sons-in-law. In some ways it was a huge wrench to part company from what had been our family home for so many years, but—time moves on, and we have to move with it (well, most of us, and nearly all of the time!).

We achieved our aim of settling down in the charming little village of Mellingfield, and our dream home is, not surprisingly, the neat little stone cottage with a privet hedge bordering the driveway that I had already visited. We'd done the usual round of looking at houses for sale in a number of locations all around Roxbury, but (somewhat to Kate's annoyance) I'd shown only a passing interest in any that were not in Mellingfield. When she'd enthused wildly about a wonderful kitchen, a sweet little garden, a spacious living room or a wonderful view from a bedroom, I'd irritated her greatly by muttering things like, 'Yeah, it's not bad' and moving swiftly to the next room. However, when at long last we came to visit *the* house (I could hardly contain my excitement when I'd seen the 'For Sale' sign as we'd driven by on our way back from another viewing), Kate was as enthusiastic as I was. We'd scarcely crossed the threshold before she'd got that strange inner feeling that this was it—our search was over. And even the vendors expressed the view that they felt sure we were just the right couple to care for the home they were leaving. I remarked with a chuckle that we were obviously destined to live here.

CHAPTER 14

Tale end

It's now a couple of weeks since I started to get these events down in detail from the brief notes I'd scribbled on various scrappy bits of paper, and even as I've been doing it, I've simply amazed myself at the incredible experiences I've had. As I remarked at the outset, it's been for my own benefit that I've put pen to paper (or rather, flesh to keyboard!), otherwise with the further passage of time I could well imagine that I'd dreamt it all. However, truth, as they say, is stranger than fiction, and I can't deny the reality of what's happened. At one point I really did begin to doubt that this had all actually taken place, and I seriously considered the possibility that it had somehow all been the product of an extremely over-active imagination. But then I checked in my wallet, and—sure enough— there was the photo I kept there of young Timothy, who'd been my son for just a few hours: a souvenir from the past.

Quite by chance the next day, I was taking a letter to the post office and put it in my jacket pocket, only to lose it through a hole in the bottom of the pocket. While fishing for it in the lining, I came across another piece of paper. This turned out to be the sheet of paper that had slid under the study door onto the landing when I'd dropped the folder containing Kate's death certificate, among other things. In my haste I'd stuffed it unread into that pocket and promptly forgotten about it. But on unfolding and examining it, I was astonished. You'd think that by now I'd have grown accustomed to surprises, but I certainly wasn't prepared for this—it was a copy (one of those smaller versions) of Thomas's birth certificate!

I gazed in wonder at this little document—I now had a souvenir from the *future*! I could see clearly the actual date when my grandson would be born! This, surely, could not be the product of a dream (unless I were still actually in one, I which case it was a pretty darn realistic one!). These two pieces of evidence (along with the other photos of Timothy, which I kept in a separate place) confirmed beyond any reasonable doubt that my experiences had been genuine. But at the same time this has stirred up a load of questions—mostly unanswered—in my somewhat bemused mind.

Probably the most obvious question was: Why? Why had all this taken place? Why had I, of all people, been allowed—privileged, even—to escape from the confines of the present, and to visit once again the past? For me, little old me, the unbending rules of time and space had seemingly been suspended: the expression 'past and gone' had lost its meaning. I had even been permitted to *change* the past—and the *future* as well! I've pondered on these and similar issues a great deal, and come to a few tentative conclusions. I don't pretend to know all the answers—very few of them, in fact—but, just for the record, this is what I believe my experiences have taught me.

First, almost without exception, we get only one stab at life (I was the exception, by the way). So it's vital we make the most of the opportunities we get. If, on our journey through this wonderful, mysterious, though often perplexing adventure called Life, we see an opportunity for fun or fulfilment, then grab it! If, for instance, you're trying to pluck up the nerve to make the first move with 'that special person', or if you're wavering over a good job offer or putting in a bid for your dream house, then I'd say: Go for it! A moment's hesitation could see the opportunity slip by forever. On the other hand, don't miss a chance to help somebody else. More than once while rushing to work I've passed some other poor cyclist wrestling with a chain that's come off its cogs, or someone who's looking lost; and, to my shame I've passed them by. Later, perhaps, I've regretted not stopping for a few seconds to help them out. My unwritten memo to myself is: Do it now, while you've got the chance. This moment will soon have passed, never to return.

My second conclusion is that, though we may try with all our might and wit to alter the course of events— whether to prevent something unpleasant coming, or to manoeuvre good fortune our way—some things are just 'meant to be' (or not, as the case may be). Such matters belong not within the control of mankind, but in the realm of (however you wish to call it) Chance, or Fate, or God (I prefer the latter).

And thirdly, since we are creatures of the Present, don't get hung up over the Past or the Future. The Past is a realm we have passed through and left behind. Our successes we can look back on with joy and satisfaction; for our failings we can seek forgiveness and make amends. The Future is largely unknown territory, and I've decided it's best left that way. Often we feel we'd like to gaze into some crystal ball and see what lies in store for us, but if we did, we might well get a nasty shock. As the wisest of teachers once said: 'Do not worry about tomorrow, for tomorrow will worry for itself. Each day has enough trouble of its own.'[1]

I'm truly thankful for my brief journey into the future, as it enabled me to give my dearest one a few precious extra years with me on this earth. That date in the future I've already visited is less than a year away now, and it's been fascinating to see events unfolding towards the position we'll be in as a family then—how we came to get this house, how Sally and Yancey's wedding went, how Hazel and Kirk moved to Grants Hill and so on. But beyond that day, the future will once more be uncharted territory, and I shall become just an ordinary person again. And you know what? That's just the way I like it!

Talking of Sally and Yancey, they were here earlier today. We hadn't seen them for a couple of months, as they'd been staying with Yancey's folks in the States. They came with some exciting news—Sally is expecting our first grandchild. She's just had a scan, which revealed that all's well—and it's a boy. I feigned surprise and delight, although of course this wasn't news to me.

'What are you going to call him?' I asked, nonchalantly.

---

1. Matthew 5: 34.

'I'm not sure, Dad,' Sally replied, 'we've been trying to think of names, but haven't come to any definite conclusions yet.'

'What about Thomas?' I suggested.

'Thomas...hmm...yes,' she replied, turning the thought over in her mind. 'Thomas. Yes—I like that!'

THE END

Printed in the United Kingdom
by Lightning Source UK Ltd.
130297UK00001B/1-15/P